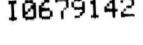

Changeling Press, LLC

**ChangelingPress.com**

**Wylde/Mars Duet**
*A Bones MC Romance*
**Marteeka Karland**

# Wylde/Mars Duet
*A Bones MC Romance*
**Marteeka Karland**

ISBN: 978-1-60521-897-7

Publisher:
Changeling Press LLC
315 N. Centre St.
Martinsburg, WV 25404
ChangelingPress.com

Printed in the U.S.A.

Editor: Jean Cooper
Cover Artist: Marteeka Karland

The individual stories in this anthology have been previously released in E-Book format.

# Table of Contents

# Wylde (Iron Tzars MC 9)
## *A Bones MC Romance*
### Marteeka Karland

Danica -- I've been attracted to the roguishly handsome biker from the very first time I saw him. Wylde's an incorrigible flirt. I know he acts like he's a player, but I've seen another side of him. Kids from all over the area flock to him because he's Wylde -- the guru of all things electronic. He has endless patience with the teens looking to learn his skill in video games, but he has none with adults. I love his twisted, sarcastic sense of humor, and that streak of protectiveness he shows on occasion. He's wicked smart and I love watching him use his intelligence and his wit. Plus, he's hotter than sin. So I flirt back.

Wylde -- I've got it bad. I come to the coffee shop just to be near Danica. The tiny barista has more heart than most people I've met. But she's the kind of woman who'll want forever, and that's not me. But when I realize the danger she and her sisters are in, I'll do whatever's necessary to keep them safe. Once Danica knows what I'm capable of, I know she'll run screaming into the night, and I'll never see her again.

# Chapter One

**Wylde**

"I'll take a double ristretto with iced vanilla double shot and organic chocolate brownie decaf, please."

The line behind me groaned.

One guy grumbled from behind me, "Some of us got places to be!"

"Yeah," someone else volunteered. "You shouldn't get something so complicated when the line's so long."

I just grinned, loving the disgruntled mutterings. Did my heart good. "It's amazing what you can wait for when you're, you know, *early*. My recommendation to people in a hurry is to start earlier. Then you're not in such a rush." I leaned in over the counter for a stage whisper at the woman getting ready to serve me. "Too much stress can lead to gas."

The young woman gave me a star struck smile, eating me up with her eyes and actually licking her lips. What can I say? I have that effect on women. Even if this one was a little young for my tastes.

"That was a... double... uh... and vanilla... decaf?" She graced me with a dreamy smile. The girl had no clue what she was doing, but I wasn't about to push her. Mainly because I saw the one person in the whole place who could make this situation better.

Danica James stepped behind the counter as she tied her apron around her slender waist. She rolled her eyes, giving me a look that said I was being a drama queen again. Instead of saying anything, she pulled out a big mug with the coffee shop's logo on it and filled it full of black coffee.

"Anything else, Wylde?"

I grinned as I paid for the cup and the coffee. "Nope. Thanks, Danica."

She raised an eyebrow, glancing at the tip jar pointedly. "Just put the tip in, Wylde. See how it feels."

Yeah, we had a thing going. And I always waited until she said it before I put in my tip. She always said it.

"What? Is that it?"

"Asshole."

Yeah, the groans behind me were amusing as shit.

"You're welcome." I threw up a hand and headed back to my table where I'd set up my laptop for the morning. I loved coming here. Not for the glacially slow Internet or the stimulating company that amused me so much. Hell, I didn't even come for the coffee, though it was the best in town. No. I came for Danica James.

The woman was sin and sex with a snarky attitude. She knew my drink as well as my moods and accommodated both. If I were the kind of man looking for a woman for my own, it would probably be Danica. Not only was she beautiful and sassy, but she was kind, as well. I'd seen her giving out the leftover pastries to a few homeless people who hung out a couple of blocks from Henry's Coffee Shop on multiple occasions. I'd also seen her paying for them out of her tips so her boss didn't get in a twist. I made sure to contribute as much as I could and not look like a creepy stalker. I also was pretty sure she knew what I was doing.

An hour later, I was banging away on a Discord channel I frequented, helping noobs learn to play Fortnite. The other barista approached me, a big smile on her face. She'd loosened a couple of buttons on her top so I had a good view of her cleavage. Which, I admit, was a pretty good view. But she wasn't my style. Mainly because she was star struck by my good looks, tattoos, and quite possibly my Titan GT77, but I didn't think so. She might surprise me, but didn't strike me as the computer geek type.

"Hey, Wylde." She smiled and set a large black coffee next to my empty mug. "Want me to freshen up your mug?"

I glanced at the cup she'd just set in front of me. "I think I'm good. I'll come to the bar if I need something." I smiled to take the sting out, but honestly, I could care less if she got offended. She wasn't stupid... exactly... she was just young and thought she could lead guys around by their dicks. I'd seen it a few times since she started. I'd also overheard her telling her girlfriends she could get me into bed with a crook of her finger. I had to chuckle at that.

Her smile faltered. "I was just being nice."

I sighed and looked up from the chat session I was in. Normally, I'd have my headphones on using voice chat, but it was crowded and I didn't want to disturb anyone. I could be a bastard, but I wasn't a complete asshole. Most of the time.

"Look, kid. I'm sure you're nice and all, but you ain't my type. Tell your friends I'm gay or something if you think it will help you save face. But I'm not interested. 'K?"

All right. So maybe I *was* a complete asshole. Wasn't the first time. Wouldn't be the last.

The girl stomped her foot. "You don't have to be so rude." Then she turned and flounced off.

"Making friends, I see."

Danica grinned at me from where she was wiping down a table while Little Miss Thang had moved back behind the bar. She glared furiously at me before going back to her phone.

I grinned at Danica. "I do my best."

She snorted. "Right. You do your best to piss as many people off as you can. Pretty sure you think they've made pissing people off an Olympic sport, and you're determined to win gold."

I barked out a laugh. Which got Little Miss Thang back to glaring at me. Only now, her anger spilled over to Danica. That wasn't happening. I met her gaze while I continued my conversation with Danica. The look I gave her was probably not very pleasant.

"Well, you know what they say. Better pissed off than pissed on. I mean, that's not really my thing, but I could do it. Honestly, though, she didn't take the hint so I had to go the not-so-subtle route."

"Just be careful of your coffee if Jordan serves it. Not saying she'd put laxative in it. Not *not* saying it either. Or maybe salt." She looked off, as if pondering which would be worse. "I think I'd prefer the laxative."

I sketched her a two-fingered salute and we both went about our business. It was one of many reasons I liked Danica. She knew when to leave a man alone, and she didn't throw herself at me either. Hell, I knew she wanted me. What woman wouldn't? But she never let on like she did. Which, I'll admit, was part of the draw. It was also the reason I didn't pursue her. Once the chase was over, I'd get bored and she'd get hurt. That was the last thing I wanted.

With a shrug, I turned my attention back to the chat. There were currently twenty-three people other than me. Questions flew around with some of the more seasoned players hanging out answering most of them. I was there to moderate and step in if things got heated. Mostly everyone behaved. Sometimes there were questions no one could answer and they'd turn to me. Looking at the string of chatter I'd missed while interacting with Jordan and Danica, I frowned. Looked like I needed to get them back on track.

**SoulHunter15**: *I can't believe they won't let me on the e-sports team. I'm better than half of em.*

**JustMadness**: *Bro that's sick. Gonna do something about it?*

**SoulHunter15**: *Nothing to do.*

**JustMadness**: *Merc a bunch a motherfuckers, bro. That'll teach em. lol*

OK, that wasn't going to work.

**Wylde**: *Soul, join me in a game. We'll walk through some things together then pop in. You ace the battle and they won't be able to keep you out.*

**SoulHunter15**: *You'd do that?*

**Wylde:** *I aim to please.*

I didn't, really, but this was my channel and I thought of all of them as kids. I knew some of them, and they were my age or older, but there were plenty of kids on here. Especially during the local e-sport season. Everyone was looking for an edge and I was happy to provide and support the gaming community. Violence, though necessary in my line of work with my club, was never condoned on my server.

It was with supreme irritation I DM'd with the bastard.

**Wylde**: *Madness, that's one. You don't get another.*

**JustMadness**: *Jesus, bro! Can't take a fucking joke?*

**Wylde**: *Keep it up. Just itchin' to ditch your ass.*

**JustMadness**: *Fuck you*

He left the server. I frowned. Looking into his profile gave me very little, so I started digging a little deeper. After thirty minutes, I knew I wasn't going to find anything from here. I needed my setup at the clubhouse, but I needed to square things with SoulHunter first. I opened another direct message.

**Wylde**: *Soul when do you want to start? Give me a day and time and I'll be there.*

**SoulHunter15**: *Don't matter. They ain't gonna let me in.*

**Wylde**: *We'll see. Day and time.*

**SoulHunter15**: *Maybe tomorrow?*

**Wylde**: *What time?*

**SoulHunter15**: *I get home at 3. How about 3 30?*

**Wylde**: *I'll be here. Looking forward to it. We'll do our best to get you in.*

I stared at the screen for a while, wondering if I'd gotten control of the situation. I seriously doubted it. Troublemakers like *JustMadness* didn't slink off into the night. They came back when they thought you weren't paying attention. Taking him down would take time, though. Right now, my focus needed to be on SoulHunter. If I could redirect the kid and give him something else to aim for, maybe I could avert whatever disaster Madness was trying to push the kid toward. And I had no doubt it was intentional.

I'd seen the name *JustMadness* around several times. Both on my server and others I frequented. Always, Madness was causing problems. Usually, it was stirring up an already ongoing argument or disagreement. But sometimes, like now, I found *JustMadness* planting dangerous ideas in the heads of users who seemed more than a little unstable. This instance didn't really seem like much, but I'd watched SoulHunter enough to know he was serious about gaming. I also happened to know he wasn't as good as he liked to think he was. Mostly because of users like Madness who knew he wasn't very good but liked to make fun of him behind his back.

Yeah. Not on my server. The only reason I let him stay on was because I could control and contain the damage. If I banned him outright, I might miss something important. Unlike some servers, I was able to heavily moderate mine. I'd written a program to help. It was amazing what AI could do if you knew how to use it. My software scanned everything being said or typed. If something seemed threatening or questionable, it notified me. As I used it, it learned. As it learned, it became more and more accurate until it had down the troublemakers to keep an eye on and new users it needed to learn.

In the meantime, I needed to find out where the kid was from and what school he went to and have a talk with the e-sports coach. Surely to God there was some place for the kid.

Needing to get back to my office where I could explore this situation more easily, I shut down my laptop and packed everything up. Glancing at the full cup of coffee Jordan had left hours earlier, I scowled. There were a few quirks I had. Taking a cup of coffee from just anyone was one of them. I didn't do it. I made my own or took it from Danica. Even Blaze didn't get to make my fucking coffee. Why was I OK with Danica making my coffee? No clue. Probably because she got me. She knew when to engage me in small talk and when to leave me the fuck alone. Very few people had that capability.

I glanced around the shop and found the woman in question. Danica was behind the counter waiting on a customer. As always, she had a smile and polite conversation if the customer welcomed it. This time, the young man she served was openly flirting with her. I wanted to growl my disapproval but held it in. Mostly.

There wasn't anyone in line and the guy kept Danica engaged even when she tried to go back to her work.

"I know a sweet little pizza place on the edge of town I'd love to show you. Tell me what time you get off and I'll pick you up."

"I appreciate the offer, Leo, but I don't go out on weekdays. My sisters have school, and I have to make sure they have their homework done."

"Surely you can find a sitter." This Leo wasn't taking no for an answer, but it wasn't any of my business. One thing I knew about Danica was that she could take care of herself.

"I probably could, but it's something I promised myself and my mother before she died. I don't go out during the week unless it's an emergency. Then I take the girls with me."

"Didn't you say they were your sisters?" Leo looked equal parts confused and irritated. He was good-looking. Athletic. I'd seen the guy around a couple of times. He was some kind of local sports hero in high school. Pretty sure he worked for his daddy now at some kind of family business, but I had no reason to find out. Until now.

"They are."

"Then why are you responsible for them?" The fucker sounded like a whiny little pussy. "Get someone else to take care of them so you can live your own life."

"They're my sisters, Leo. Not a responsibility. I could have passed them on to social services and visited them instead of becoming their guardian, but that wasn't what me or my mother wanted."

"Fine. What about this weekend? We'll go to a movie, then maybe to a nightclub. I have a friend who can get us into The Hudson."

She smiled but it didn't reach her eyes. "I appreciate the offer. I really do. But I'm not at a good place in my life to date anyone. I know you understand." Her tone was gentle and sounded truly regretful. While I was happy she'd turned him down, I didn't like the thought that she might be tempted to go out with him if she had fewer responsibilities. I thought that twit, Leo, was going to keep pushing, but he flashed her a smile.

"I get it. Some other time, perhaps. It's not been that long since your mother passed, right?"

"A few years," she said softly, lowering her eyes as if the grief were still close. "Five."

"You've grieved long enough. You'll be ready to move on with your life soon. When you do, I'll be there for you." The superior smirk he gave Danica made me want to bitch-slap the punk.

"I'm sure you will." She smiled up at him. "I really need to get back to work now. It was good talking to you." With that, she turned her back and began cleaning equipment behind the counter.

Leo scowled at her behind her back but didn't continue to try and engage her again. He picked up his coffee and headed out the door, dumping his untouched cup in the trash. If Danica really needed time before she dated anyone, Leo wasn't one to wait until she was ready. I was pretty sure Danica had no intention of going out with the dumbass anyway.

I dumped the now-cold cup of coffee I hadn't touched into the trash and brought the mug Danica had filled for me when I'd first arrived back to the counter. "Cup for the road, sweetie?"

She turned. There was a tired look on her face before she smiled brightly at me. Unlike the smile she'd give Leo, this one looked genuine. "Anything for you, Wylde." She refilled my cup. "Heading out early today? You usually stay until it's close to closing."

"Got some stuff I can't do on the laptop. Believe me, I'd much rather work here. The scenery is much more pleasant." I winked at her and she blushed.

"Perhaps you need to get some pictures for your office, then. Or maybe a potted plant."

"Plants are like pets. They require maintenance I don't have time to give. As to pictures? I'll do my best to find something suitable."

"Don't find anything too good. I'd miss seeing you here."

"Not to worry. You know I have to come see my best girl."

"Oh?" She tilted her head to the side quizzically. "I didn't think you thought that highly of Jordan." The woman in question had cut out early, as usual, leaving Danica to finish the day on her own.

"I don't." I picked up my coffee and gave her a small salute as I turned to leave, but not before I snapped a picture of her with my phone as she turned away.

# Chapter Two

**Danica**

I was tired. So fucking tired. Working two jobs sucked ass, but at least the second one was from home. I wasn't lying when I told Leo I couldn't go out with him. The girls were part of the reason, but mostly it was just that I had zero free time. Most nights I worked until midnight before I was done. Then I had to get the girls up and to school, or least to the bus. After that, it was back to the coffee shop. I worked five days a week, ten-hour days, because I needed the money. The owner liked the way I ran the place, so it worked out best for everyone.

The truth was, even if I had been free I'd have blown Leo off. I had exactly zero interest in the guy. Sure, he was good-looking, but he was a prick. A local football hero who had flunked out of college and fallen back on his family's money and pretended to be rich. I'd watched as one woman after another followed him around like a puppy dog as he cheated on her and treated her like shit. When he moved on, to a woman they all followed after him, begging him to take her back. I guess money does a lot for a woman's self-esteem. In the wrong direction.

Now, had it been Wylde...

The man was an enigma. He was so flippant about everything but when he was working, he was hyper-focused. Several times throughout his day, I'd come by and refill his coffee. Why not? He always tipped well, and I enjoyed his company. If I refilled his coffee for free once in a while, I doubted the shop would go under. He never noticed. Unless someone other than me brought him something. That, he wouldn't touch. Probably because I was the only one to actually refill his mug -- and he bought a new one every day. It was why I quit asking and just had it ready. He didn't seem to want a disposable cup, but wouldn't bring one of the dozens he already had.

He also pulled shit like he did today with Jordan, ordering some wild concoction no one could remember and he would never drink. If she'd actually managed to make it correctly, he'd just have said to give it to someone behind him and asked for something even more complicated. The man didn't want to ask for what he wanted. He was arrogant enough to want the people he interacted with daily to know what his needs were and meet them without him asking.

Yeah, he was a colossal prick. But he was *magnetic*. He was also sweet as he could be to me. The few times I'd left when he did, he'd always held the door for me and walked me to my car. It wasn't creepy or stalkery. It felt... protective?

Shrugging both men off, I finished cleaning up. At five I closed up. The last hour was spent preparing for the next morning. The girls rode the bus from school to the shop and did their homework while they waited.

Lemon and Apple were twins. At sixteen, they were outgoing and more than a little wild. Definitely wilder than I'd like, but I didn't really blame them.

"Ready to go?" I smiled as I prepped the last station for the morning. I always did it, even if I didn't open. It was easier on me when I did, and Jordan was never on time anyway.

Apple blew a bubble. "Sure."

"I need some shit for a school project." That was Lemon. Of course. She was the ringleader of the two, and pushed her boundaries enough to set my teeth on edge.

"Don't say shit," I said, fully aware she'd smirk at me because of my own use of the word, even if it was to correct her language.

Sure enough, she snickered. "Sure, Dani. I'll lay off the shit. Is 'fuck' OK?"

I sighed. "You're really pushing my patience."

"All you need to add is the 'young lady' part and you'd sound like an old woman." And of course, Apple had to add her two cents' worth.

"Living with the two of you is making me old. Come on. Where do you need to go?"

"Just Wal-Mart or something. It's pretty generic." Which meant it would likely be anything but, and she wanted to watch me run around like a chicken with my head cut off trying to find what she needed. They were little brats, but I loved them. They'd also had a rough time of it, losing their mother and being raised by their sister. Just like me, they'd never known their father. Our mom had been a good mother, but she'd had horrible taste in men. Or maybe she'd done it on purpose. She never confided in me, and it was too late now.

"Right. You got a list?"

She grinned, tapping her temple. "All up here."

"Yeah. That's not going to work. Done this too many times." I pointed at her phone. "Make a list and send it to me. We'll swing by a fast-food restaurant, then go in search of supplies. Deal?"

"Works for me." Lemon immediately ducked her head, her thumbs flying over her phone. They always had their noses in their phones, so it wasn't unusual.

Food was quick and light. We all ordered from the dollar menu. The girls might be brats, but they knew the score. Money was tight. They'd both tried to get jobs but I'd refused. School was their ticket out of here, and as long as I could keep food in their bellies and a roof over their heads, they weren't working. Besides, they were only sixteen. It was how I'd prevented them from starting jobs they'd both managed to score by lying about their age. I'd also confiscated the fake IDs they'd gotten their hands on. Didn't matter that it listed their ages as eighteen instead of twenty-one.

I studied the list Lemon had sent me. Yeah. Wal-Mart wouldn't have some of this stuff. Which meant heading to a specialty store with art or hobby supplies.

An hour later I was roaming up and down aisles looking for the few remaining things Lemon needed. Apple was helping, but had stopped to talk to a boy who looked like he was at least four or five years older than her. Maybe more. Closer to my age than hers. Which set my teeth on edge. I was about to call her back to me when Lemon snagged my attention.

I rounded a corner and ran into Jordan. "Hey! Watch where you're going, bitch!"

"Jordan?" I gasped at the anger in her voice and expression. "I didn't see you. It was an accident."

"Like hell! You've had it in for me since I started working at the shop. Now you're trying to kill me!" She wasn't subtle about voicing her anger. "You stay away from me, bitch!" She stabbed my chest with her finger before shoving past me.

"Fucker," Lemon muttered.

"I bet Deacon could take care of her." Apple's comment was as muttered as Lemon's. Both girls stared after Jordan angrily.

"Who's Deacon?"

"What?" Apple looked up at me, her eyes innocent.

"Deacon. Who's Deacon?"

She shrugged. "I have no idea what you're talking about."

"You said Deacon could take care of her." I narrowed my eyes at the girl, knowing I'd missed something.

She rolled her eyes. "I said someone should take care of her." She turned to her sister. "Right, Lemon?" Which didn't surprise me. They always had each other's back.

"Yep. Hey, Dani, I think I see what I'm looking for over here."

I sighed and followed the girl, knowing their game. She was trying to distract me. I let them get away with it because sometimes it was best to pick your battles. We moved down to the end of the aisle we were in.

"I think this will work." Lemon picked up some kind of glaze for the pottery she wanted to make for whatever art project she was working on. I didn't ask too many questions. I just bought what she told me she needed. It was the way we worked. They knew the score and only got what they absolutely needed, never going overboard when most kids would.

"Is that all? Is there anything else you need?" She looked back down the aisle in the direction of her sister and bit her lip. "Um..." That was when I realized Apple was at the very end of the aisle talking to a guy. Great. Just what I needed. My sixteen-year-old sister dating. Not happening.

I sighed, raising my voice. "Apple. Come here, please."

Apple rolled her eyes but said her goodbye and sauntered our way. Surprisingly, the young man looked at me and gave a respectful nod of acknowledgment. He was still too old for her, no matter how polite.

With a shake of my head, I gave Apple a warning look before addressing the man in question. "You know she's sixteen. Right?"

He narrowed his eyes. "No, ma'am. I didn't." Apple gasped and glanced over her shoulder. He nodded at Apple, a look of deep disapproval on his face. "You're in trouble, girl."

Apple shrugged. "Not like you can do anything about it."

"I can spread the word to my brothers. Good luck with you or your sister finding a date until you're eighteen." His look said that was a promise.

"I didn't do anything." Lemon raised her hands innocently. "So, I don't deserve that."

The guy raised an eyebrow. "Seem to remember you pushing me toward your sister. You're the one who told me she was nineteen."

With a shrug, Lemon turned back to the shelf she was looking at with the pottery glaze. "No worries. You're not the only fish in the sea."

"Nope. But me and my brothers are mean as shit. Any guy not your own age gets near you, they'll feel our wrath." He pointed at Apple. "Be seein' you in a few years, girl."

Apple gaped at him. I knew how she felt. He walked away and none of us seemed to know what to think.

"What the hell have you gotten into now, Apple?" I sighed.

"Trust me when I tell you, you do *not* want to know, Dani." Lemon pursed her lips and glanced at her sister knowingly.

"Shut up, Lemon!" Apple snapped.

"We'll talk about this when we get home," I said.

"Let's just get this stuff and get out of here."

We made our way to the checkout, chatting lightly with each other. I wanted with all my heart to ignore the fact that my baby sisters were not only interested in boys, but trying to hang out with men. There was no way that guy was still in his teens. Gave me hives just thinking about what could happen. And probably would happen if I didn't keep a closer eye on them. I just hated to smother them when they'd had such a rough life.

The girls were only eleven when our mother died. I'd barely been eighteen, but had dropped everything to become their guardian because there was no way I was going to leave my baby sisters to the tender mercy of foster care.

It was because I was preoccupied with the issue of Apple and her would-be boyfriend I missed the fact that two policemen were right in front of us until they didn't move to let us pass.

"Officers?" I smiled as I looked up at the two of them. They had hard features and looked at me with disapproval.

"We're going to need you to come with us, ma'am."

"Is there a problem?" My heart started pounding. I had no idea what was going on, but it had to be bad. We had no living relatives other than a great aunt, but she lived in California and we hadn't seen her in years. Surely if something had happened to her they wouldn't send the police to tell me. Was it the coffee shop? But why hunt me down?

"There is," the other one said. "Please come with us."

"What's this about?" I stepped in front of the girls who were looking belligerent at the officers. I got a bad feeling, but for the life of me I couldn't figure out why.

"It's better if we discuss this in private." The same officer spoke while the other one looked around as if making sure we were alone.

"I don't understand."

The silent officer snorted. The first one just sighed and shook his head.

"Of course, you don't. Please come with us." He held out his hand to usher us in the direction he wished for us to go. The officers led us to the back of the store to an office where he indicated we should sit. The store manager accompanied us after someone had called him to the back. Apple looked speculative while Lemon looked ready to take the officers apart with her bare hands.

"We've got rights," Lemon spat. "You have to tell us what's going on."

"Hush, Lemon. Not now."

"They can't just force us in here away from everyone. They have to read us our rights or something. Even then they'd take us to the police station. Not to the back room of a store!"

"Please, Lemon." I was becoming desperate. "What's going on, officer? Has something happened?"

"We were informed that you pocketed some items. Possibly to get high."

Apple and Lemon both gaped at the man. I knew how they felt.

"I beg your pardon?" It was all I could manage. I'd never been accused of stealing anything in my life, especially to get high. I didn't even drink alcohol. With two teenage girls to take care of, I didn't have time.

"Would you mind, please, emptying your purse?" the first officer asked politely, but it was obvious it wasn't a request. I knew I should wait, to get a lawyer or something, but I really had no reason. I hadn't taken anything.

While the girls sat quietly, I emptied out my purse. I only had a few things in it so I turned it upside down and dumped the contents on the desk in front of us. Out tumbled my wallet, a couple of tampons, my phone, a tube of Chapstick... and two bottles of metallic modeling paint.

The officer reached out and picked it up, looking it over. The store manager had a scanner with him and scanned the barcode on the tiny bottles.

"They usually go for metallic spray paint, but I suppose any metallic paint would do."

"What?"

He looked up at me in disgust. "Metallic paint. Apparently, it's better for getting high than some of the other colors."

"I didn't put that in my bag. We weren't looking at modeling paint. Lemon has a pottery assignment she's working on. The supplies we needed are in the shopping cart."

"Well, these are our paints. They have our barcodes. You dumped your purse out yourself. No one else touched it," the store manager snapped at me. He was right. I'd dumped it out myself.

"I didn't do this. And I don't get high. You can drug test me or whatever you need to do, but I didn't do this."

"I'm afraid you'll have to come with us." The officer took hold of my upper arm and urged me to stand. Then he started reading me my rights.

"What's happening, Dani?" Apple looked more fearful than her sister.

"This is horseshit!" Lemon spat. "You can't do

this! My sister didn't do anything!"

"How old are you girls?" the other officer asked. "You eighteen?"

"Yes." Lemon's voice was hard, authoritative.

"No." Apple spoke at the same time as her sister and immediately shrank back, a look of horror on her face as if she'd realized her words might cost them.

"Well?" The officer was losing patience.

Neither girl said anything else. Apple ducked her head while Lemon raised her chin in defiance.

With a sigh the officer keyed the radio mic clipped to his shoulder. "Dispatch, signal six CPS. Two minors at this arrest."

"What's happening?" I struggled as the other officer snapped handcuffs around my wrists behind my back. "Let me go!"

"Child protective services are on the way. They'll look after the kids until you're out on bail."

"NO!" Lemon stepped forward. One look from the officer stopped her. "We're not leaving Dani."

"Girls, just do what they say. It'll be all right."

"I'm calling Deacon," Apple said. "He'll know what to do." As she pulled out her phone and made the call, it struck me that I should probably tell her not to call the man who'd tried to get with my sixteen-year-old sister, but I was in shock.

"I-I don't know if that's a good idea, Apple." I was shaking. "I can't believe this is happening."

"Hey, lady," the officer handcuffing me said, irritated. "You do the crime, you gotta do the time.

"Deacon says he's on the way back. He said he'd take care of everything." Apple sounded a little more settled but still fearful.

My phone started ringing. Unknown number. Fucking spam callers. Now wasn't the time. When it stopped, Apple's phone chimed with a text. She read it, then looked back at me.

"Deacon says to answer your phone."

"Not happening," the officer said.

When it started ringing again, Lemon grabbed it and answered. "Hello." She looked at me steadily as she listened to whomever was on the other end. "At the hobby shop. They found two small bottles of paint in Dani's purse. They're arresting her." There was another pause. "They've called Social Services for me and Apple. We don't want to go with them." Another pause. "OK. I'll tell her." She ended the call. "That was Wylde. He said he'd be here in five minutes and that we could stay with him until he fixes this."

"Wylde?" His name came from my lips like a prayer. And maybe it was.

"Yeah. Said he knew you from the coffee shop."

"Oh, thank God!" I nearly sobbed in relief. If anyone could help me, it was Wylde. I looked at the officer in front of me. "The girls can go with him when he gets here. Wylde is my friend."

"Wylde? Funny name."

I frowned. "So? He can take my sisters. I'm their guardian. There's a paper in my wallet saying so. You can check with Social Services when they get here. It's all on record."

"That's up to them. But if you're their guardian and you say they can go with your friend, I don't see any reason why they couldn't."

Finally! The man was being reasonable. It was the one thing that might go right in this situation.

The officers ushered me outside and into the back of the patrol car where we waited. It wasn't even five minutes before a huge, dark blue Bronco pulled into the parking lot beside the cop car. There, larger than life, Wylde climbed out and stalked over to us. He looked angry as hell. Another man got out of the other side and walked over to the police. Wylde said nothing, but his gaze was focused squarely on me. It was the other man who spoke.

"I'm Wyatt Raven, Miss James's lawyer. What's the charge?"

"Shoplifting. She'll be booked in county. I'm sure they'll let you see her once she's been processed."

Mr. Raven gave the officer a long hard look. "I'll be accompanying Miss James." He looked to me. "Did they read you your rights?"

I nodded. "Yes, sir."

Wylde growled and took a step forward before catching himself. "You do everything Raven says, Danica. Don't say a word unless he says so. Understand?"

Again, I nodded, my gaze clinging to Wylde's. "Please take care of the girls, Wylde. I'll never ask you for anything else. Don't let them go with CPS."

"I've got them, honey. You do what Raven says, to the letter. He'll get you out, then bring you to me. We'll take care of everything."

"OK."

The cop shut the door while Mr. Raven climbed in the other side to sit beside me in the back seat.

"Take a few deep breaths, Danica. Everything will be all right."

I certainly hoped so. I couldn't afford to spend the night in jail. Not only did I need to help Lemon with her project, but I had to work in the morning. And yeah, I realized I had bigger problems, but I was in shock.

"Don't worry about any of that," Raven said. "I'll have you out in a couple of hours."

"Did I say that out loud?"

He smiled gently. "You did. It's OK. I'll take care of everything. We'll have you back with your sisters in no time."

I watched Wylde help the girls into the Bronco. He turned to look at me, giving me an encouraging nod. I had no idea how this situation happened or why Wylde had come so quickly or even how Apple happened to know someone who immediately sent Wylde to us, but I was grateful. If there was one thing I knew, it was that Wylde was a man of his word. He was also wicked intelligent.

Once we were out of sight, I let out a little shuddering sob before sucking it up and getting myself back under control. I couldn't break down. Now yet. Later. When I was back in my own home behind closed doors, I'd let it all out. Right now, I had to be strong. And I would. For myself. For my sisters. I'd get through this, and all would be well.

At least, I hoped so.

# Chapter Three

## Wylde

I paced restlessly in my office. I'd already sifted through the information from Danica's arrest. The nine-one-one call came from the store manager, who was acting on a tip from an anonymous source. The security footage had been erased, but I'd recovered it and found Little Miss Thang, Jordan, had been the one to take the paint vials from the shelf. Then she'd bumped into Danica, which was likely when she'd planted them in Danica's purse. I'd forwarded all this to Raven. He'd hotly growled that I'd breached chain of custody and gotten the information without a warrant and blah blah blah...

Bottom line was, he'd convinced the police Danica was innocent and they'd let her out. Raven was bringing her back to the clubhouse now. Which was the reason for my pacing. There was no way I was letting her go back to her house with the girls until I knew for certain she was safe. Jordan might not try anything else, but she'd just become my number one target. It would give me great pleasure to ruin her life. The only thing stopping me was Apple and Lemon. And who named their children Apple and Lemon anyway?

"Do the two of you ever shut up?" I was really about to pull my hair out. The girls had asked questions non-stop since the minute I'd shut the door to the cage I drove back to the clubhouse. Now we were in my office -- where I continued to pace -- and they were *still talking*!

They looked at each other, like they were communicating silently or some shit. It was unnerving. "Nope," they said in unison.

"Why did you come for our sister?" I was sure this one was Apple. She was the more reserved of the pair. Sweet, but slightly tart.

"Because none of your business." I smiled sweetly at them.

"You want to fuck her. Don't you?" And that was Lemon. Sour to the max.

"You need to watch your fuckin' language, girl."

She shrugged. "Soon as you watch yours, asshole." She had a bright smile on her face. I studied her for a long moment. To her credit, the girl didn't back down an inch, meeting my gaze as boldly as any old lady in our club.

I lifted an eyebrow. "You're gonna be a nightmare for me, aren't you." It wasn't a question.

"All depends on what you do to Danica." Instantly, her demeanor changed. They both did. Apple stepped up beside her sister, and they both gave me a hard stare that promised if I fucked with their sister they'd definitely put poison in my coffee. Or laxatives.

Probably the latter. Just so they could see me embarrass myself. Much more satisfying than killing me.

Instead of answering them, I avoided the question by asking one of my own. "Wanna tell me how you just happened to have Deacon's phone number to call him for help?"

Lemon raised her chin while Apple, bless her heart, ducked her head and took a small step behind her sister. "I thought you were the badass hacker of the club." Lemon gave me a superior smirk. "Don't you know?"

Oh no, she hadn't...

I narrowed my eyes at her. "Oh, believe me,

sugar, I will." And yeah, the sugar was a play on her name. Judging by the way her face darkened, she got it.

"If we hadn't, Dani'd be in jail right now. Then what would you have done?"

"Anything I had to, Lemon." And I meant it. She held my gaze with a hard one of her own. The girl was tough, I'd give her that.

"When you figure out how we had Deacon's number, come talk to me." Lemon glared at me. "I'd give you more, but this should be a piece of cake for you." With a glare, she snagged her sister's hand and stormed out of my office.

"Where are you going?" I called after them.

"You're the genius, asshole. Figure it out."

"Fuck." I scrubbed my hands through my hair. "I don't have fuckin' time for this."

As I watched the sisters walk from my office through the common room, I felt a smile tug at my lips before I squashed it. I absolutely would not be amused by these two.

"You both need to be turned over someone's knee!" I called out. Lemon just raised her hand in the air, middle finger standing prominently. My brothers hooted, so I gave 'em the middle finger.

"Don't worry. They'll get it." Deacon leaned against the wall next to my office. Big fucker had probably been standing there since I brought the girls back with me.

"You wanna explain yourself? Those two are way the fuck underage."

"I'm aware of that. *Now*." Deacon straightened. "Don't worry. Now that I know, I'll stay away." He met my gaze. "Still watchin' over 'em."

"Which one's yours? Because I know you *think*

one of 'em is." Which was something I'd be dissuading him of. Soon.

He shrugged, not rising to my bait. "Does it matter?"

"Yep." I crossed my arms over my chest. "Matters way the fuck up."

"Apple. I can't have her until she's eighteen and I won't go near her. But I'm gonna protect her with my life. That means I protect her sisters too, because Lemon won't hesitate to fuck a bitch up if they fuck with Apple or Danica. And if Lemon's hurt, Apple'd be hurt."

"Who the fuck names their kids Lemon and Apple?" I was cranky. I needed to get to Danica. The need rode me hard to protect her and I'd had to let Raven take over that role until the situation with her and that stupid shoplifting charge was cleared up, but it ate at me. And I had no idea why. I didn't get possessive over women. Why this one?

"That'd be Dani. She didn't want siblings. Her mother told her to name the twins to try to get her to bond with them. So, she thought up the most ridiculous names she could to get even with her mother. Turned out, her mother's plan worked. Dani would do anything in the world for those girls. Including giving up her future until she got them raised."

I snorted. "I doubt it stops there. She might as well be their mother. Seems you know them awfully fuckin' well."

Deacon gave me a level look. "Like I said. Apple's mine."

"That's something we're gonna have to have a talk with Sting about. How could you not know she was underage, you dumb shit? And what the fuck did you do with her?" I was angry, but mostly I was seeking a target for my anger. Deacon was a good man. There was no way he creeped after a sixteen-year-old on purpose.

"Talk all you want. Even she'll tell you I didn't do anything with her. I haven't even kissed her." He shook his head slightly. "Knew something was off, but I couldn't place what it was. She said she was nineteen. Lemon confirmed it and encouraged us to get together. Only thing I was waiting on was to meet and talk with Danica."

"Why?" If that bastard was thinking he'd make a move on Danica, I'd kill him right here.

"Like I said. Something felt off. I wanted to talk to their father first, but they said they didn't have a father. Only reason I knew about Danica was because I followed them to the coffee shop one day. Didn't see how they got to town, but I saw them walking. Each of them had a backpack slung over her shoulder. Curiosity got the better of me and I followed. When I asked Apple about it later, she got a panicked look on her face, but Lemon said they were enrolled at the community college."

"And you didn't press her then?" Anger was building inside me. I blamed Deacon for what I saw as taking advantage of a young woman, but I knew it was more than that.

"No. Of course not. I knew she'd tell me what was going on when she was ready, and I wasn't getting physical with her until I knew her story. I'm a lot of things, Wylde, but I'm not a moron. Or a creep. As I saw it, my job was to look after her until she came clean. It was Danica who clued me in to the fact they're only sixteen." He shook his head slightly as if beating himself up inside. "Felt like a dirty old man and I'm only twenty-six."

"How long have you known Apple?"

"Not long. Couple of weeks. Gave her my number the second time I met her."

I'd be checking that out soon as the bastard left my office. I needed to go after the pair, but figured I was the last person they wanted around them right now.

I scrubbed my hand over my face. "Fuck." Giving Deacon a hard look, I pointed my finger at his chest. "Keep an eye on them. But if you touch either of those girls, I'll beat you to a bloody fuckin' pulp."

He lifted his chin. "I'm not a pedophile, Wylde. And I'm a prospect with Iron Tzars." The man puffed out his chest in pride. "I know what we do. What we stand for. I'll earn my patch here, and it won't be by takin' advantage of a kid. Don't underestimate either of them, though. They're not typical teenagers."

"You'll still keep your distance." It was a threat and we both knew it.

"I will. Still makin' it known no one is to even look at Apple. I got two years to prove myself with Tzars before she's of age. That should give me time to solidify my position with the club and make a home for her." He moved toward me until we were almost nose to nose. "And if you hurt their sister, if you hurt Danica, I'll personally rip your arms from your body. Try workin' your computer magic with no fuckin' hands." Then he stalked after the girls.

"Go fuck yourself, Deacon!" I called after him. Like Lemon had, Deacon flipped me off without ever turning around. Then I shouted after him. "And I can use voice controls! And you're still a dumb shit!"

It took less than ten minutes for me to access the text messages between Apple and Deacon.

Surprisingly, there weren't many. Two or three exchanges each day. Always one in the morning when she got up and one in the evening before she went to bed. No funny business at all. She'd called him a couple of times, but the calls were less than five minutes. The last text had been thanking him for sending help.

**Deacon**: *I'll always come for you, Apple. You're still in trouble though.*

**Apple**: *I'm so sorry. I didn't get YOU in trouble, did I?*

**Deacon**: *Don't worry about me, honey. I've not done anything I'm ashamed to own up to.*

**Apple**: *Are you not going to talk to me anymore now?*

**Deacon**: *I can't promise I can. But I'll always be here for you. If you need me for any reason, you call or text. I'll have to talk to my president about this. Let him know what happened.*

**Apple**: *I'm sorry.*

**Deacon**: *Don't be, little one. Just promise to always tell me the whole truth from now on. Can you do that?*

**Apple**: *Yes. Just please don't go away.*

**Deacon**: *I'll always be around, honey. We'll work things out.*

OK, it didn't look like I was going to have to kill Deacon. At least, not right now. While I was at it, I checked Apple's messages. Which led me to Lemon's messages. With a frown, I skimmed over them. It looked like Lemon had purposefully pushed Apple and Deacon together because Apple was being bullied at school. That was something I'd have to look into.

Using a program I'd written, I hacked into both girls' phones and planted a bit of code to give me access to the phone's GPS, and made a clone of their devices. I could always track their movements as well as monitor any calls or text. And their browsing history. And to see if they were beating my level in Dice Dreams. If I felt bad about invading their privacy, I just reminded myself they were sixteen and already had eyes on the men in my club. This was as much to protect the Iron Tzars as it was to protect the girls.

Then I did the same to Danica's phone. That was for my own peace of mind, and I would *not* apologize for it. Better to ask forgiveness than permission in most cases. Besides, I was only going to use my powers for good.

By the time I'd finished, I saw Clutch pull up in the Explorer he'd taken to pick up Raven and Danica. The girls flew toward Danica as she climbed out of the front seat. She wrapped her arms around both of them. Time to get all three settled, because there was no way they were going back to Danica's house until I knew this bullshit with Jordan was finished. Which, by the way, I still had to dig into. There was lots of work for me to do tonight. Starting with that bitch Jordan.

I made my way to the parking lot and leaned against the Explorer. Raven was talking quietly with Danica, and she nodded several times before letting go of the girls and giving the large man a tight hug.

Yeah. Not happening.

"All right there, Romeo." I grabbed Raven's shoulder and pulled him away to wrap my arm around Danica's shoulder. Surprisingly, she melted into me. So, I tugged her closer. Then, to my alarm, she buried her face and bunched her fist in my shirt and *sobbed*.

I glanced up, my gaze finding Lemon's unerringly. She gave me a look that said I'd better not fuck this up or she'd carve out my liver. I gave her a slow nod and hugged Danica closer, kissing the top of her head.

"You're OK, pretty girl. Everything's OK."

"I d-don't know wh-what would have h-happened if you and Mr. Raven hadn't come to h-help us." Her slight body shook with her crying. I wanted to scoop her up and take her inside. To my room. To my bed. But that wasn't an option.

"Nothing happened because I will always be there for you. Me and my brothers." I let her cling for a while. Not because I needed her to, though. She needed to feel safe and to thank me and I was good with it.

"Thank you so much!" She finally pulled her face out of my shirt and looked over at Raven. "Thank you, Mr. Raven."

Raven nodded at her. Then that dickhead Deacon stepped onto the porch and leaned against a post. He was a distance away, but he'd come out to see the group.

"Deacon alerted us," Raven said. I wanted to punch him. Deacon didn't need to take any credit for this.

"Deacon's in enough trouble, Raven," I growled.

Raven shrugged. "Can't very well take him to task when he saved your girl there."

"She's not my girl," I said, even as I wrapped her tighter against me to prevent her from moving. "And Apple had his number because he was trying to *date* her! She's sixteen, for Christ's sake!"

Raven's gaze snapped to Deacon's. The big man didn't move or even flinch where he stood. Surprisingly, it was Apple who spoke up.

"He didn't know I was sixteen." She moved around Lemon who'd been shielding her from everyone. "He found out today when Dani told him. I'd texted him when we went to the hobby store, wanting to see him." She shifted her gaze to Deacon. "I'm really sorry. I just wanted to --"

"Hush, Apple." Lemon gripped her sister and yanked her back. I almost winced at the pressure she put on the other girl's arm. There would likely be bruises.

Immediately Deacon unfolded his arms and stormed from the porch. "That's enough, Lemon. Leave her be." He focused on Apple then, his tone softening. "What did you want, Apple?" Deacon didn't voice his question as such. It was a gentle demand. A command for her to tell him her problems.

Apple looked at Lemon who shook her head. Then Apple looked at the ground and stepped behind Lemon to rub her face on her sister's shoulder.

I sighed. "She's being bullied at school."

"Bastard," Lemon growled at the same time Danica gasped and turned around to face her sister.

"Bullied? Oh, Apple! Why didn't you tell me?" Danica moved from me to her sister and took her into her arms, hugging her tightly.

"Bullied." Deacon moved closer to our group. He placed a gentle hand on Apple's head. "Is that why you singled me out?"

She looked up at the big prospect, tears in her eyes and shook her head. "It was the excuse I gave myself to follow through with Lemon's idea for me to get you to be my boyfriend." Her voice was soft and meek. Tearful. "We kind of played you, but not really. Because I wanted you to be my boyfriend before that."

"Honey, you knew I couldn't." Deacon spoke gently to her, reaching out to brush a lock of hair off her cheek that had stuck because of her tears. "You're underage and it's illegal. I could get in big trouble."

"Not in Indiana."

"Apple…"

"Is that why you never kissed me?"

Danica let out a strangled squawk and Lemon rolled her eyes. "Please. You're giving me a fucking migraine, Dani."

"Language," Danica admonished but with no real heat.

Apple ducked her head again and Deacon curled a finger under her chin to raise her face back to his. "It is, honey. And why I never encouraged you to hold my hand or even to text me much. I knew something was up. I just didn't know what."

"Please don't hate me."

Deacon grinned softly at her. "Never, honey. You're my girl. You'll always be my girl."

"No, she won't," I snapped. "You're ten years older than she is!"

Deacon shrugged. "She don't want me when she turns eighteen, it'll be my loss. But she's gonna have that chance if she wants it."

Apple's eyes filled with tears again, and she looked like she wanted to run into Deacon's arms but was using every ounce of restraint she had. Finally, Deacon shook his head, muttering, "Bloody hell," under his breath and pulled the girl into his arms for a quick, tight hug.

It was only a few seconds, but when he pulled back he gripped her shoulders and leaned down to look into her eyes. "I'm always gonna be watchin' over you, Apple. You've got two years to live your life. After that, there'll be a reckonin'."

She nodded and swallowed. "I'm sorry, Deacon. I'll do whatever I have to, tell anyone who needs to hear everything I did. I'll even let them see my phone. You were so good to me, and I repaid you --" Tears spilled over and ran down her cheeks again.

"Nope. Not hearin' that, honey. I'm the adult here. I always knew that. Even if I thought you were older, I knew you weren't nearly as experienced in life as me."

"Enough of this," I snapped. "Let's get inside and get the girls something to eat. Then I'll take you to your room."

"We should really get home." Danica sighed, looking over the girls one last time. "My car is still in the parking lot at the hobby shop. I'll need to get it."

Clutch walked around the Explorer and waved her off. "Already taken care of," he said, pointing to the garage. "It was overdue for an oil change and a tune-up. Gotta say" -- Clutch scrubbed the back of his neck. --"for an '87 Tempo, car's in pretty good shape."

"It was my mother's," Danica said softly. "For some reason, she loved that car and took really good care of it. I'd planned on selling it after she died, then just never got around to it."

"No need to fix what ain't broken." Clutch grinned at her. "I'm takin' care of the maintenance on it. Filters and such. Checkin' the fluids and tires. Probably take me a couple of days 'cause there's shit in front of yours, so you might as well make yourself at home."

"But how am I gonna get to work? And the girls have school. We can't stay here."

"You let me worry about the logistics," I told her, glaring at Clutch. The big man just raised his hands and smirked at me. No way he was gonna be the hero here. "Besides, we need to figure out what happened tonight."

"I have no idea why Jordan did this," she muttered. "I've been nothing but nice to her."

"Who cares?" I shrugged off her worry, knowing she had no need because I was taking care of this. "What matters is that she never does this again."

"It was just a couple little bottles of paint," Lemon scoffed. "Why the fuck'd everyone make such a big fucking deal outta it?"

Danica sighed. "That's two f-bombs in one sentence, Lemon." The girl just smirked.

"It was the suggestion it might have been drugs," Raven said. "They used the arrest as an excuse to make sure the kids were away from a dangerous situation. It's why they called CPS in the first place."

"They didn't drug test me or anything."

"No." Raven smiled. "I threatened to sue the entire city if they did when Wylde got me the surveillance footage someone had erased." He raised an eyebrow at me. "Which I'm certain Wylde will look into."

"Damned straight." I took Danica's hand. "Come on. Food, then I'll get Iris to take you to your room."

I led them to the great room where supper was just being set out. Blaze and Walker's woman, Blossom, cooked the evening meal together while Walker hovered. The woman's puppy, Sparkle, sat in one corner watching intently, her eyes focused intently on Blossom as she set out food. When the dog let out a small whine, Blossom snagged a hotdog and knelt down in front of the puppy, who eagerly took the meat from her hand and ate. Blossom ruffled her ears before going back to the table.

Blaze let out a shrill whistle. "Feedin' time!"

Lemon rolled her eyes while Apple looked up at Deacon who winked at her. The girl gave him a faint smile before taking the plate Lemon offered her and filling it with a burger and chips.

Danica did the same, looking over her shoulder at me. I placed my hand at the small of her back to urge her forward to get a drink, then steered her to a table where the members with old ladies had taken seats. I noticed Deacon led Apple and Lemon there as well but didn't try to sit with them. Instead, he gave Apple's shoulder a squeeze before going to a table farther away with more of our brothers. None of the club girls were in the room. If I knew Sting's woman, Iris, she'd banned them while we had guests. Thank God.

As I watched the three eat and slowly allow the old ladies draw them into the conversation, I knew this was what I wanted for myself. I started to turn away and go sit with that bastard Deacon, then thought better of it. Instead, I dropped into a seat beside Danica and raised an eyebrow at Sting. The bastard smirked but nodded.

I'd just claimed Danica in front of my president and most of the officers. I was so fucked it wasn't even funny.

# Chapter Four

**Danica**

The room Iris led us to was more like a small apartment. There was a living room with a couch, TV, and a small eating table. No kitchen, but there were two areas in opposite corners of the room with privacy screens around them. On the other side of the screens were twin beds. One for each of the girls. Another room -- a smaller bedroom -- had two chests of drawers and one full-size bed. I had no doubt the girls would be moving their beds together. If they indicated they wanted to, I'd probably give them the bedroom. They'd slept together since they were babies, or at least in the same room. We'd discuss it.

"I appreciate you and the others putting us up for the night. It's not necessary, though. We'll be fine at our house."

Iris smiled gently at me. "Wylde wants to make sure all the loose ends are tied up before he'll feel good about you going back. Don't worry, though. That man is worse than a dog with a bone when he gets to looking into something. He'll make sure everything's good quickly. Wouldn't surprise me if he had it all worked out tonight and you can go home tomorrow."

"I have to work tomorrow. The girls have school. The guy from outside. Was his name Clutch?" When Iris nodded her head, I continued. "He said it'd take him a few days to work on my car."

"Don't worry. Sting will make sure one of the prospects is available to get you where you need to go. You and your girls."

I pursed my lips. "Didn't Deacon say he was a prospect?"

"Yes. He is. Don't worry. Sting will have a talk

with him. Besides, if you're not comfortable with him, you don't have to use him. Sting will probably assign someone else anyway."

"I take it he already knows about Deacon and Apple?"

"Not much in Iron Tzars Sting doesn't know about." She pulled me in for a hug. "You have my number. If you need anything, and I mean anything, you call or text. I want you to feel at home here."

"Why? 'Cause I gotta tell you, this all feels surreal."

Iris chuckled. "Yeah. The guys are like that. Just stick to the approved places and everything will be fine."

"What happens if I go wandering around on my own?"

"One of the guys will escort you back. They're big on secrecy, but since more and more of them have picked up women and children, they've taken more precautions. It's for our protection as well as theirs."

"So you're separate from the club? That sounds a little too secretive for me."

Iris cocked her head, thinking about whatever she was going to say next. "Not exactly. The old ladies aren't technically part of the club, but our husbands don't keep secrets from us. If they feel like there's a need to, they tell us there's something going on they can't discuss. But that's never happened. Sting is my man. He's also the president of this club." She smiled. "I choose to involve myself, and he trusts me enough to include me. I don't have an official say in what goes on with club business, but he listens to my opinion in private and takes that into account."

"Why take me and the girls in tonight? I'm sure it's fine at home."

"Because Wylde wishes it. He's an asshole, but a lovable asshole." She grinned. "He's also an invaluable member of this club. If he wants you here, you're here."

"That's why Clutch took apart my car. Isn't it?"

"Likely."

"Wylde's idea? Is there really anything wrong with my car? Because I am pretty good about keeping up on the maintenance."

"Now you're beginning to see how sneaky these guys are." Iris's mirth spilled over to me, and I couldn't help but grin. "Get your girls settled. Tomorrow they can ride to school with the kids here. Monica and Daisy will love to meet them. Only..." She trailed off, looking speculative. "Might want to keep a close eye on Daisy and Lemon. Daisy cleans under her nails with a big bowie knife in the common room while she stares at a prospect. If Lemon gets in on that, they're all fucked."

I couldn't help myself. I burst out laughing and promptly started choking on the water I'd been sipping from. Iris offered me a tissue while rubbing my back gently. When I got myself under control, Iris squeezed my arm gently. "It'll be all right. I promise."

When she left, I sighed as I closed the door. What a day.

The girls were at the table working on Lemon's project together. They often helped each other with homework. Apple looked up as I turned toward them.

"Everything OK?"

"Yes. Iris said one of the prospects will take you to school with the other kids in the compound tomorrow."

Apple's face lit up and she sat up straighter. "Deacon?"

I frowned. "Likely not. And you know why." I hated seeing her duck her head in disappointment, but this had to be done. "You could get him in big trouble, Apple."

"But I'm sixteen. That's legal in Indiana!"

"You're still a minor. Deacon's not. It might be legal for him to be with you, but he's part of a club, Apple. I don't pretend to know what goes on here, but I've heard rumors. While I have no doubt they're good people, what if the rules of his club say you both have to be eighteen before he can have anything to do with you? Wylde mentioned more than once they'd have to talk to Sting about that situation. What if you've gotten him in trouble because you lied to him?"

"I'm sorry. But Dani... I really like him." God, I hated that lost longing in her eyes.

"I'm sure you do, honey. Seems he likes you too. But until you're eighteen, you need to leave him alone. Promise me."

She sighed, looking so crestfallen I felt bad, even though I knew it was for her own good. "I promise, Dani."

"It's only because I love you, Apple." I brushed a finger down her cheek. "Even if I did give you a horrible name."

Lemon snorted. "Not as horrible as mine."

I raised an eyebrow at her, my lips twitching to keep from grinning. "Well, it fit. From the day you were born you were a bit... tart."

She smirked. "Yep. Don't expect that to change anytime soon. And Dani? Wylde better not hurt you."

I gave her a quizzical look. "What do you mean?" My heart sped up and I felt my body dampen in sweat. There was no way Lemon could know I had a secret crush on the guy. That would be too humiliating.

"All this." She waved her hand around the room. "He came when Apple called Deacon. He brought Raven to help you. He got Clutch to kidnap your car. He set us up here. That man wants you."

"Lemon!" That girl was going to give me an ulcer. "Wylde is my friend. He comes to the coffee shop."

"Why do you think he comes to the coffee shop? You haven't seen his computer setup. Me and Apple have. Trust me when I say he doesn't need to go to a stinking coffee shop for Internet access. He's there for the company."

"Maybe he likes the coffee."

"Coffee? Danica. He can get coffee anywhere. He's there for you." Lemon didn't back down an inch.

"I'm sure you're mistaken. That man has women all over him."

She waved her hand in the air, dismissing my comment. "Whatever. I'm just saying. I trust Deacon with Apple more than I trust Wylde with you. Why? Because Deacon has proven he likes Apple for more than a one-time fuck. Wylde hasn't done the same with you."

"My God, Lemon! Can you please tone it down?"

She shrugged. "Just saying."

I was about to scold Lemon more when there was a knock at the door. "We'll talk about this later."

"Won't change my mind," Lemon muttered.

Grinding my teeth, I went to the door. When I opened it, there was Wylde. There was a scowl on his face as he looked past me to the girls sitting at the table. Apple had her head down, working studiously, but Lemon glared openly at him. He returned the glare.

"We need to talk."

- 46 -

"Of course." I backed out of the doorway to let him inside, but he shook his head.

"In my office."

"I'm coming too," Lemon said, standing so suddenly she almost knocked her chair over.

"No," Wylde snapped. His voice was so authoritative, even Lemon responded. The girl sat back down in her chair abruptly, as if he'd shoved her back. "This is between me and Danica. The two of you need to concentrate on getting your schoolwork done."

"Wylde," I said, putting my hand on his arm.

He looked down at me and his expression softened. He sighed and looked back at Lemon. "Please."

"We have a right to know what's going on too."

"Lemon, stay with me." Apple looked from her sister to me and Wylde.

Lemon scowled at us but subsided. "Fine. But I want to know everything when you get back, Dani."

"She always this bossy?" Wylde ignored Lemon and spoke directly to me.

"Yes," Lemon said before I could answer. "She's always this bossy. Why don't you ask her if you want to know something about her?"

"Because she's a little brat and I don't like talking to her? That good enough reason?" Wylde still looked at me.

I rolled my eyes. "You're as bad as she is." I stepped out into the hall and pulled Wylde along with me as I closed the door. As I did, I saw him purse his lips. The gleam in his eyes said he was trying not to smile. "You're goading her on purpose? Why would you do that?"

He shrugged. "It's fun. What better reason?" His grin was positively wicked. "Come on." Wylde snagged my hand and tugged me down the hall back to his office.

Once inside, he ushered me to a couch and sat beside me. He opened his mouth to say something, but Sting, Iris, and Deacon entered shortly thereafter.

"Don't you believe in knocking?" Wylde scowled. He wasn't looking at Sting, but Deacon.

The big man said nothing, but Iris sighed. "Really, Wylde. The door was open."

"Ain't talkin' to you, Iris. You're welcome anytime you want." He nodded to Deacon. "Him, on the other hand…"

"Good God, Wylde," Sting snarled. "Can't you lay off trying to rub people the wrong way for just a little bit? You're not going to ruffle Deacon."

Instantly, Wylde's demeanor changed. He grinned broadly and put his arm around my shoulders. "Whatever you say, boss man."

Sting shook his head, sitting on the other couch in the office and tugging Iris to sit in his lap. Deacon sat on the other end from them and waited silently.

"Give me the rundown," Sting said. "What happened and how is it being handled?"

"Apparently, the owner of the hobby shop Danica brought her sisters to is a relative of Jordan. The footage was erased from a computer at the store minutes before the police were called."

"Nice. Who called the police?"

"Came from a phone in the store's name. I hacked into the nine-one-one system, and there was no call placed for shoplifting at or around a reasonable time. Turns out, those two officers were friends of the store owner. There was a call placed by a phone registered to the store to one of the officers' personal cell."

"So they didn't go through the normal channels to call this in." Sting played with his beard next to his lower lip.

"Nope."

Raven appeared in the doorway looking much different than he had when I'd seen him before. Now, he was in a tight white T-shirt and jeans with motorcycle boots. Before, his dark brown hair had been pulled back and tied at his neck. Now, it was wild and hanging past his shoulders. He still had the neat stubble, but it added to the messy look. Also, I noticed tattoos just peeking out from under his shirt.

"Which was another reason I was able to get Dani out as soon as I did. They knew they fucked up. I have a feeling they'll have to answer for it tomorrow."

"Yeah." Wylde grinned. "Especially since I sent the whole incident to the local media." He blew a bubble like he didn't have a care in the world.

I looked up at him. "I can't keep up with your moods or figure out what you're really feeling."

He winked at me. "Have to keep you on your toes, darlin'."

That wink was followed by a panty-melting grin. Like this, Wylde was positively irresistible. That breakaway lock on his forehead covered one eye and seemed to taunt me, wanting me to brush it aside. The man's charisma was off the fucking charts. This wasn't something new to me. I'd known it since the first time I'd met him in the coffee shop. That roguish look was hot enough to scorch. With him sitting so close to me, his arm securely around me, the heat from his body seeped into me and filled me with… him. Looking up into his eyes now only made me long for something I knew I could never have.

My breath caught, and I had to look away. I

lowered my head while the conversation around us continued.

"Good. So that problem's taken care of for now."

"Yep." Again, Wylde popped a bubble.

"And tomorrow?" Sting raised an eyebrow as he glanced over to Deacon, who'd been silent through the whole exchange.

"I'll take all the kids to school. Including Apple and Lemon."

"No fuckin' way," Wylde snarled. Instantly he was up, pacing the length of his office. "You said you'd stay away from Apple, Deacon. That's decidedly *not* staying away from her."

"I've given Sting my word to keep it professional, Wylde. I want the right to watch over Apple like she was my own."

"She's not yours to protect."

Deacon leveled him a look. "She will be."

"Boys, rein it in." Iris sounded every bit like she was in control of the situation. I envied the confidence she showed. There might be only two of them -- not counting her husband -- but Iris took charge like it was nothing. She fully expected everyone to listen to her.

"You're arguing with each other when neither one of you will make this decision." Iris met my gaze with a kind one of her own. "Deacon's requested this, but you don't have to agree to it."

"And have Apple hate me?" I sighed. "Honestly, I'm not naive enough to think that, just because I tell her not to do something, even if it's for her own good, that she won't find a way to do it." I looked at Deacon. "So, I'm going to trust you." I glanced over at Sting. "You're his president."

"I am."

"You know everything that happened?"

"That Deacon and Apple have been talking for a few weeks and that she's sixteen? Yes. I also know you had no knowledge of the budding relationship."

"I know that technically, in Indiana she's of legal age." My gaze shifted back to Deacon. "But I'd prefer it if you waited to explore anything with her until she turns eighteen. Especially since you're a lot older than she is."

The man nodded at me respectfully. "I wouldn't have it any other way, ma'am. I'm ten years older and, though she's mature for her age, my life experiences far surpass hers. I'll protect her with my life and watch over her and her sister, but I've got to cement my place in Iron Tzars and have a way to provide for her that you'll approve of."

That startled me. "What?"

He shrugged. "This is an MC. You have to know there are some things we do that you wouldn't like."

"I suppose. Hadn't really thought about it. Perhaps I should."

Sting smiled. "Deacon is a good man, Danica. He wouldn't be a prospect with us if he wasn't. Once he becomes a fully patched member, he and I will sit down and talk about this future. If that future includes Apple, she'll be included too."

"I don't understand. Sounds way more serious than I'm ready for." I gave a nervous chuckle, trying to lighten the mood when I was getting a little spooked.

"Our club skirts the law on occasion, but we have legitimate businesses as well. If Apple decides she wants to let Deacon take her on, there will be things to discuss. We fully expect mates to talk to each other and take that into account." Sting gave his wife a squeeze and dropped a kiss on her cheek. "But that's a couple years or more away. Deacon requested to be the one to take them to and from school, along with the other kids. I wanted you comfortable with the arrangement."

"And if I'm not?"

"Then Clutch will continue to do it."

I looked from Deacon to Sting, then finally settled on Iris. Maybe it was because she was a woman and close to my own age, but I trusted her more than I trusted just about anyone here. Except maybe for Wylde.

"If my sister were in Apple's position, I'd trust Deacon with her life, Dani. He's a man of his word. All the men here are. If they're not, they don't get into Iron Tzars."

"All right." I swallowed. "Did you know she was being bullied at school?"

"Not before today. Thinkin' just my presence when I take her to school will help. If not, we'll reevaluate in a week or so. She knows she's got backup now."

"I still don't like it that she didn't tell me."

Iris moved from Sting's lap to sit on the couch beside me. "Dani, you're taking care of two teenage girls. You're their guardian. Right?"

"Yeah. So I should have known."

She shook her head. "How many jobs do you work?"

"Two. One at the coffee shop, one from home."

"Really? How many hours a week do you pull?"

"Um…"

"More than fifty?"

"Not much more than that." I have no idea why I thought I needed to underplay how much I worked. These people couldn't judge me.

"How about you try again, darlin'." Wylde spoke next to my ear, and I jumped.

"Fine. I work at least sixty hours a week. More when I can."

"To provide for the girls and keep a roof over their heads and food in their bellies?" Iris raised a questioning eyebrow at me.

"They're my sisters." I lifted my chin. "I love them and will do whatever it takes to provide for them."

"As you should," Iris continued. "But did you ever stop to think that maybe they were trying to work this out themselves? To take care of you?"

I gasped and tears threatened. "I'm the adult," I whispered.

"And there's nothing saying you can't need a little help from time to time," Sting said. "Wylde? I assume you're looking into the bullying?"

"Yep. Started working on that the second I found out. It's being taken care of. The parents don't nip it in the bud, I will."

"I'm not sure I like the sound of that." Knowing Wylde, there was no telling what he'd do if he had to be the one taking care of it. "Why not let me talk to the parents or the school, and you don't have to be bothered with it."

"No bother." He grinned. "I enjoy taking care of bullies." Again, he popped a bubble.

"Good. You'll let me know if you need to take further action, Wylde. They may be bullies, but we're still talkin' about kids here."

"Mostly." I caught the muttered word and snapped my head in his direction. He gave me an innocent look. Sting didn't appear to hear, but I got a sick feeling in the pit of my stomach. He cleared his throat. "Understood, prez."

"I'll keep an eye out too," Deacon said softly. He

left the room and it was just the four of us left.

"I'm so sorry about this," I said. "But I'm grateful you were all there to help me and keep the girls out of foster care. Even for a night."

"You're welcome, Dani," Iris said with a smile. She gripped my hand then stood. "I'll see you tomorrow. Is Wylde taking you to work?"

"Yep." Wylde didn't give me a chance to answer. And of course, he had a big grin on his face as he chewed his gum. He blew a bubble before snagging a tissue and getting rid of the gum.

"Good." She squeezed my hand once more. "Good night." Iris and Sting left together.

"Night," I said, waving. "You're taking me to work?"

"Oh, yeah. You think I'm going to leave you there alone with that bitch, Jordan?"

"She's harmless. Though, I confess I have no idea why she did this."

"She did it because she's jealous," Wylde said.

"Jealous?"

"Yeah, pretty girl." He grinned. "She thinks we've got something goin' on."

I blinked. "But we don't."

"Not yet." He winked at me, and I almost had to fan myself. He had boyish good looks with his wild hair and erratic temperament, but there was an underlying... something... about him that made me shiver.

"Not yet?"

He shook his head. "Nope. But there will be."

Before I realized what he was going to do, Wylde leaned in and brushed a kiss over my mouth. I stiffened before shuddering as pleasure coursed through me. When I whimpered, he grunted and licked the seam of my lips. One hand went to my jaw while the other gripped my hair at the back of my head. He held me still for his kiss and I found myself accepting it greedily.

My whole body felt like it was going to go up in flames. All from a simple kiss. I'd fantasized about Wylde before. Who wouldn't? He was boyishly handsome with a lean, hard body. He wasn't overly muscular, but the veins and muscles of his arms and chest played lovingly under the T-shirts he wore. Myriad tattoos spread over any skin he had exposed except for his face. His fingers, his hands, even up the side of his neck. Now the man, the reality, was kissing me more passionately than I'd ever been kissed in my life.

When he ended the kiss, he rubbed my nose with his and smiled at me. My gaze was unfocused, and all I could really see was Wylde.

"We can have some fun together if you want. It's by no means a requirement, but I think you're as fascinated by me as I am by you."

My mouth watered for more of his taste, but was this really a good idea? "I'm not sure I'm ready for a man like you, Wylde."

He chuckled. "Honey, no one's ready for a man like me. I promise I'll take you on a ride you'll never forget. Doesn't have to be anything heavy. Just mutual pleasure and enjoying each other's company."

Had he dumped ice water on me I'm not sure I'd have been more shocked. I hadn't expected anything from him, for him to return my attraction, but to dismiss what I felt as mere lust wasn't something I was ready to concede. I genuinely *liked* Wylde. Had from the very first. I'd known he was a player, but hadn't considered he'd want to play with me.

"I'm sorry, Wylde. I'll admit I'm attracted to you, but I'm not into one-night stands."

"Nothing wrong with one-night stands, but I never said this was a one-time thing. I think we can enjoy ourselves for a long time."

"I'm not sure I understand what you're getting at." I was wary of him now. I stood and moved across the room near the door in case I needed to make a run for it. I knew he wouldn't hurt me. Not physically. But the beating my heart was currently taking certainly qualified as a beating in my book. Might be my own fault for building him up in my mind to be my ideal man, but it still hurt.

"We can pleasure each other. Whenever we like. As much as we like. No strings attached."

"So, fuck buddies?"

He grinned. "Now you're getting it."

Ouch.

"As appealing as that sounds, I'm gonna have to pass." He froze, as if that wasn't the answer he was expecting from me. "I've got two teenagers to look after, Wylde. One of them is very interested in a member of your club who is ten years older than she is. To make matters worse, he returns that attraction. How can I set an example for her if I'm engaging in casual hookups myself?"

"No one said she has to know about this."

"Trust me. Kids have a way of finding out." I shook my head. "I'm sorry. If this means you no longer want to help us, I'll get someone to take me home until Clutch has my car ready for me to drive. I'll have to make payments or something, but he'll get this money back."

"No one said I no longer wanted to help you, Dani. I'll do that no matter what." He shrugged. "I just thought you might need some adult companionship, and I want you."

"I'm sorry." I ducked my head, then headed out the door back to the room with the girls. This was gonna suck. Big time. Wylde might want me, but I wasn't in the position for casual sex. No matter how much I wanted to experience more of his kisses. And find out what it felt like to have him kiss me again. All over my body.

Yeah. I was fucked.

## Chapter Five

**Wylde**

I was fucked.

And yeah, I was an asshole. I knew the second I pitched my proposal to Danica it was a mistake. Truth was, I was trying to cover for myself. My reaction to her was not at all what I expected. I had intended to lean in to kiss her and let that be it, but noooo... I had to go all out.

I could -- and did -- have any woman I wanted. It hadn't always been like that. I was a computer geek in school when it wasn't cool to be a computer geek. Since finding a home with the Iron Tzars, I'd imitated the look and attitude of many of my brothers. Combine that with my own quirky personality, and it worked.

I became more athletic, building muscle and becoming capable of handling myself in any situation that got thrown at me. I was smart as shit and not only was I the motherfucking tech guy, I was a badass motherfucking tech guy. It got me what I'd always wanted. Recognition. Appreciation. That got me women.

Then I met Danica.

I didn't want to have a relationship with her. I didn't *do* relationships. I saw passion and a thrill for living that I had in myself, and wanted to explore that with her. I knew, if I was patient, I could have a fucking good time with her. But I realized right away she wasn't that kind of woman. If she gave herself to a man, she'd expect it to be for love. I wasn't capable of that.

As I watched her go out the door and through the common room, I had a moment to regret what I'd said to her. My chest ached, but I knew it was only that

I regretted hurting her. She was a sweet woman with a good head on her shoulders and a heart the size of Texas. She deserved a man who loved her. Who worshiped her. Unfortunately, that man wasn't me.

I shook myself. Enough of this. I gave her my pitch. She rejected me, and I didn't blame her. Yeah, my pride took a hit. I hadn't been turned down by a woman for sex in a very long time. But I'd survive. I'd find another woman who enflamed me like Danica did and enjoy the hell out of myself until it was time to move on. Besides, if she knew what it meant to be an old lady to a member of the Iron Tzars, she'd thank me. Dani didn't deserve less than being a man's old lady and I refused to bring a woman into this life. This club.

Fuck it. I had work to do. Starting with taking care of the bullies at Apple's school. Then I'd move on to Jordan.

Turned out, phone calls to the parents of the kids in question with screenshots of their social media posts were enough. At least for all but one. The one woman who held out, not believing her daughter had done anything to Apple and, if she had, Apple had deserved it, received a healthy dose of what her daughter had been dishing out to Apple. I'd basically posted copies of what her daughter had posted about Apple to the mother's social media and tagged her church and top hundred friends, along with a recording of our phone call. If that didn't work -- which judging by the replies she was getting, and the phone call I got at midnight from the woman in question, it was getting the desired effect -- I'd do something more drastic. Like post pics of her and her other daughter's husband getting it on in her bedroom. 'Cause, you know. Motherfucking tech guy.

Jordan was going to require something more. It

was after midnight, but I wanted to make a point with this. The app I used on all the club's phones prevented anyone but a top-level hacker from tracing where it had come from. And by top level, I mean on the level of Giovanni Romano at Argent Tech and myself. Possibly Data and Zora or Suzie at Bones, but I wouldn't give them more than a thirty percent chance of decrypting it. OK, so maybe I'd give Suzie a slightly higher percentage on that, but only because I knew she'd hacked into Giovanni's system on more than one occasion.

Sitting back in my chair, I punched in the girl's number on my phone and put it to my ear, waiting to see if she'd answer a call from an unknown number after midnight.

"Hello?" The sleepy voice on the phone at one time might have aroused me. Now, it just filled me with rage. It was a shock, really. Sure, I was angry at the woman, but she was sleeping soundly when, as far as she knew, Danica was in jail and Apple and Lemon were in foster care until Danica was released.

"I traced every single event of today's shenanigans back to you, Jordan. You planted the paint in Dani's purse. It was your relative who owned the store and erased the security tapes. Your relative's friends who were called to play bad cop, worse cop."

There was a pause before the rustling of bedding as she either rolled over or sat up. "Who is this?"

"Not someone you ever want to fuck with."

"Well, Someone I Don't Want to Fuck With, I have no idea what you're talking about. If you call me again, I'll take my phone to the police and have them find you."

I chuckled. "Good luck with that, Jordan. In fact, I encourage it. Once the whole story comes out, I imagine it will be you and your cohorts in jail overnight. Maybe the cops lose their jobs. My advice to you? Leave Danica and her sisters alone. You do that, we'll all be golden."

"Fuck you," she muttered before ending the call.

Yeah, I didn't believe that would be enough, but it was the first step. Also, the cops would definitely be losing their jobs given all the illegal shit I found on them both. They were dirty to the max, not only taking bribes, but at least one of them was using phony charges to coerce women into sex in exchange for not taking them to jail. And yeah, the dumb shits weren't smart enough to turn off their body cams before some of the encounters. It had been erased, but, again, I was the motherfucking tech guy.

That information was sent to the chief with a note saying if he didn't do something about the two, the same information would be passed to the media with further information showing he was aware of everything and allowed it to happen.

Another phone call to the hobby store manager, telling him I knew he'd set Danica up for false arrest and possible rape by dirty cops, and he'd promised to leave town if I kept quiet. I'd told him I'd keep quiet if the police chief did the right thing and arrested his friends. Unfortunately, I wasn't sure if the investigators would be so forgiving. He'd made his bed; he could lie in it.

Satisfied I'd done all I could for now, I powered up my gaming gear to get on Fortnite. I was hoping to catch SoulHunter15 on. Sure enough, I found him.

I found the server and game the kid was on and slipped into his game. I'd long ago used a hack to be able to watch without anyone knowing I was there. Sure enough, the kid couldn't play for shit. At least not where he was in the game presently. This was going to take some noobie teaching and a shit ton of patience I wasn't sure I had. Not because I didn't like introducing noobs to the game, but I hated trying to help someone who thought they knew more than they did. It was counterproductive and a waste of time since they never took anything I said to heart.

Later. I'd deal with him later. We weren't supposed to meet up until three thirty tomorrow. I'd figure something out by then.

* * *

The ride with Danica to the coffee shop was strained. She barely looked at me, her face tense. She was polite and thanked me when we left the clubhouse and when I dropped her off, but there was a distance between us that had never been there before. I didn't like it.

I waited outside instead of going in. It wasn't my usual time. I liked to wait until there were a bunch of people before going in to make my orders. The more people, the more outrageous the order. Just because I could.

Danica always got there at five in the morning. Her help got there at six unless it was Jordan, who never got there before eight. For a busy coffee shop, having only one person there to run things had to hurt business. Dani never seemed to struggle to handle the crowd, but it took all her concentration. The last thing she needed today was me to distract her.

Once the customers started rolling in, I left. I'd brought her in the Bronco, and I hated driving any kind of vehicle other than my bike. If I was going to babysit today, I was doing it with my bike on hand. Not a damned cage.

The ride to the clubhouse didn't take long. One

of the prospects, Breaker, had my bike out and ready when I rolled into the clubhouse. He'd make sure the Bronco was full of gas, then park it.

I straddled my bike, breathing out a contented sigh before starting it and taking off. I needed a ride. Since Danica was safely at work and Deacon was keeping watch at the school, I decided I'd take a couple hours to unwind. I needed a break. Just for a couple of hours.

A couple of hours turned into most of the day. By the time I got back to the coffee shop, it was after two in the afternoon. That was usually a downtime for Danica, but it looked like the place was hopping.

I slipped in, taking my usual place next to the window where I could keep an eye on my bike and Danica all at the same time. If she noticed, she didn't acknowledge me. To be fair, there were at least five people at the counter and she was waiting on all of them at the same time. Jordan -- or anyone else -- was nowhere in sight.

"That's one caramel macchiato for you, a chai latte with oat milk and brown sugar here, a caramel joe for you, a strawberry refresher with coconut milk, and an iced Ristretto ten shot with breve, five pumps of vanilla, seven pumps of caramel, four Splenda, poured. Not shaken." She grinned as she served the last asshole with his cup. Bastard. I shoulda thought of that one.

Once all of them had paid, she took a breath before wiping down the already spotless bar. Surprisingly, she stepped away with a new mug of fresh coffee and headed my way. She sat the mug on the table and started to walk away, but I snagged her wrist.

"Sit."

She blew one coffee-colored curl out of her face.

"I'm not a dog, Wylde."

I sighed. "Please, Dani." I nodded to the chair across from me. "I'm sorry about last night."

She shrugged. "You want what you want. I'm honestly flattered, given all the women you have after you." The flirty smile she flashed me looked a bit strained but was no less lovely. The woman really was appealing on a whole other level.

"I'm not the type of man to want forever, honey. Doesn't mean I don't care about you; just means I can't give you what you deserve."

"It's OK, Wylde. Really." She stood and laid a hand on my shoulder and squeezed, smiling at me before she headed back to the bar.

As I watched her work, I found I wanted to be the man to give her what she deserved. I wanted to be *that man*. But I simply... wasn't. I had too much going on. Too many responsibilities. Not to mention my club. To bring her into my world meant she had to be mine. Always.

There was no leaving the Iron Tzars for any reason other than death. Expulsion meant death. It's how this club had worked since its inception in the nineteen forties. I couldn't change that, *wouldn't* change it. Iron Tzars did work no one else could or would do, and it was usually a permanent solution. For that reason, what happened in the club, stayed in the club. We'd never risk a disgruntled member leaving and ratting us out. It would bring down every chapter all over the world. And the Iron Tzars were many.

While I waited for her shift to end, I logged on to the server where I was supposed to meet SoulHunter15. I got on at three, anticipating he'd be there at three-thirty like he said. By five, he still hadn't shown up. The shop was closed, and Danica was cleaning up. I'd searched the other servers the kid frequented and found only one mention of him. That son of a bitch *JustMadness* had called him to DM when he got on. I could see where Hunter had logged on, but the DM had either been removed or hadn't happened.

That was something else I needed to get a handle on. I had a bad feeling about Hunter, though I wasn't sure if it was for himself or for others around him. Either way, I'd reached out to him. That made him my responsibility. Next thing I needed to do was find out who he was and see if there was going to be any damage to contain.

"I'm done, Wylde." Danica stood at my table, her backpack slung over one shoulder while she picked at the strap.

"Good." I shut down my gear and packed everything up. I still had my bike but I'd brought a helmet for her, not intending to ever drive a fucking cage again. The thought made me break out in hives.

I strapped my gear to the back and handed Dani the helmet. "Climb on the back. Your feet go on the pegs. Watch the pipes when you get off because they'll be hot."

"I'm not sure this is a good idea, Wylde. Maybe you could get someone to bring my car. The girls and I need to get home anyway."

"Get on, Dani." My tone was a little gruffer than I'd intended, but I was not having one of my brothers bring her back to the clubhouse. I knew Clutch wasn't done with her ride yet and, Goddamnit, I wasn't ready for her to leave!

With a sigh, she did as I instructed. Once she had her helmet on and was securely behind me, I grabbed her wrists and brought them around my waist. "Hang on tight."

When I took off, she squeezed her arms around my middle tighter, looking over my shoulder as we rode. For some reason, I wanted to take her on a good, long ride. I wanted her to experience something that gave me the most peace I'd ever had in my life. Other than, perhaps, being in her presence.

And where the fuck did that thought come from? And why did her arms wrapped around me feel so fucking good? Didn't matter. I was driving for a while because I fucking wanted to.

She held onto me while we rode, her hands sometimes bunching in my shirt, sometimes gripping my belly and chest over top of my shirt. When we stopped at traffic lights, I placed a hand over top of hers and felt her trembling. Neither of us spoke and I didn't hurry. It was over an hour later when we rolled into the compound.

I didn't take her to the front like I should have. Instead, I pulled my bike around to the garage and pulled into my normal spot. No one was around. The area was lit only by the scant sunlight coming in through the door.

I shut down the bike and sat there, trying to gather my thoughts. What the hell was I doing?

"Wylde?" Danica's soft voice was like a gentle caress over my senses. The woman had bewitched me. Pure and simple.

She handed me her helmet and started to climb off the back. I snagged her hand to help her...

Then pulled her to me, picking her up and setting her on my lap. Somehow, she managed to straddle my legs as my arms settled around her and pulled her to me.

"What are you doing?" Her voice was a mere

whisper of sound. I could feel her breath brush my lips.

"I'm going to kiss you, Danica. Tell me now if that's not what you want."

"This isn't a good idea."

"Not the question. Do you want me to kiss you?"

She hesitated, nibbling her bottom lip as she struggled to form a reply. It was really all the confirmation I needed. Threading my fingers through her hair, I pulled Danica to me, meeting my mouth with hers.

I felt like my whole world tilted. Just like before, nothing I'd ever experienced could compare to the feel of her lips sliding against mine. Dani's whimpers were the sweetest music. Her skin like the finest silk beneath my touch.

Her thighs tightened fractionally around my hips, and she wiggled against me. My cock was a steel pole mashed against her sex. I grunted when she slid up my length, my hands sliding to her ass to make her move like that again. And, God, the woman could move!

The more I kissed and stroked her, the more Danica fell under my spell, the more her lithe little body seemed determined to drive me out of my mind. Already I was near coming in my jeans. That hadn't happened in my entire life! I wasn't certain I'd ever wanted a woman more than I wanted Danica James at that moment. Through it all, there was only one thought running through my head.

"Mine…" I growled out the possessive, meaning it with everything in me. I pulled her to me even tighter, needing to crawl inside her skin. I needed inside her with my entire being. Needed to feel her silken pussy wrapping around me, milking me as she came. I needed my seed inside her, taking root so that she'd be mine forever.

"Ride me, Danica. Grind against my cock. Make yourself come."

"Wylde! Oh God!"

"That's it! Yes! Do it!"

Danica threw back her head and screamed, her hips snapping as she rode out her pleasure. My cock ached like a motherfucker, but I absolutely would not come in my pants.

I lifted her to the handlebars of my bike and snagged the button and zip of her jeans, jerking them off her hips along with her panties. Surprisingly, she wiggled out of them, helping me as much as she could, balanced as she was. Thank God, her jeans legs were wide enough to slip over her feet because I didn't think I could wait long enough to pull her sneakers off.

There she was, her legs spread, bare pussy glistening in the setting sun peeking into the garage. Not tasting her was simply not an option. Looping an arm around her thighs to hold her, I dove for her, fastening my mouth over her pussy and devouring her. Like a starving man at a banquet, I ate Danica's sweet little cunt until she was screaming and wriggling beneath my mouth. Her clit was a swollen, protruding nub under my tongue, throbbing with each stroke as I took her higher and higher.

Had my cock ever been harder? Had the need to be inside a woman ever been greater? I thrust my fingers inside her wet heat, finding that spot inside her that set her off again.

The second Danica screamed, I unfastened my jeans, freeing my cock. The relief was immense, finally released from the confining fabric. I grunted even as I tried to keep from coming.

"Get on me, woman. Get on my cock!"

"I can't..." She shook her head even as she reached for me. Her hand circled my shaft and she pumped it up and down. Her legs were still spread, my fingers inside her. Danica took in a shuddering breath, one tear streaking from the corner of her eye. "Wylde!"

"Your move, baby. Take me or not."

With a cry, Danica scooted back across my lap, her pussy kissing the head of my dick. Then, with a shuddering breath, she sank down on me. Tears overflowed her lovely eyes as she threw her head back and moved to take me deeper until she was flush against me, her clit hitting my lower abdomen as she situated herself.

God! The feel of her tight and hot around me! My cock throbbed and ached, likely spilling precum inside her.

"Hot little thing, ain't you." My voice was a husky growl. I pulled her closer, finding my mouth with hers as I urged her to move on me. It wouldn't take much. I was so fucking close to coming! "Fuckin' hot little thing!"

"Wylde! Oh, God!"

Danica came with a startled scream. She raised her head to meet my gaze, shock and tears making her eyes glisten. I held her gaze as I let myself go. Hot seed exploded from my cock into her greedy pussy. The more I came, the more she milked me, wanting all I had to give her.

I pulled her to me once again to kiss her. Tenderly this time. Praising her for the gift she'd given me. And I recognized it for the gift it was. This wasn't a woman to fuck just anyone. In fact, hadn't she told me much the same thing just a couple of hours ago?

That memory brought me crash landing back to earth. Danica hadn't wanted casual sex. And I wasn't offering anything more.

Carefully, I extracted myself from her. That was when I noticed the streak of blood on my cock. And her thighs.

"Danica. Honey." I met her gaze with a startled one of my own. She stared at me, wide-eyed, her lips trembling and tears streaking down her cheeks. "Did I hurt you?"

She shook her head, but I knew she was lying. The evidence was all over my cock.

"Come on. Let's get you dressed and go back to the clubhouse." It wasn't adequate in the least, but it was all I had. Of all the things, I never thought Danica was a virgin. Not at her age. It made sense, though. If she'd been taking care of twin teenagers by herself, she wouldn't have had much of an opportunity for sex.

Danica scrambled for her clothing, shrugging into them while I fastened my jeans. I tried to pull her back into my arms. Needed to. To reassure her. But really, what was there to say? I couldn't take her on as my old lady, and she would never accept anything less.

The second she was dressed, Danica hurried out of the garage and ran straight for the clubhouse. She never looked back at me once. What the hell? That wouldn't do at fucking all.

I stalked toward the porch that led to the common room where I fully expected to find Danica. Brick met me at the door.

"What'd you do to her, Wylde?" Brick looked after Danica as she fled. I watched her round the corner without slowing. When he faced me, he frowned. "She was crying. What the fuck?"

"We went on a ride." I scrubbed a hand over my

face. "I thought she'd enjoy it. Didn't say she was afraid or anything."

"Well, you did something. Best you figure it out, or Iris might have your balls. She really likes Dani, and her girls like Apple and Lemon."

"Yeah." I rested my hand on the back of my neck. "I know what I did."

"Well?" Brick snapped at me, fully expecting an answer.

"That's between me and Danica." I grinned up at him. "None of your business, big guy."

"Not good enough. What did you do, Wylde?"

I shrugged. "We had sex. I gave her the choice and she chose to fuck me. Satisfied?"

"Not in the least. It had to be something more."

With a lift of my chin, I stubbornly refused to tell him. It might have been a little childish, but really. It wasn't his business. Or anyone else's but mine and Danica's. Finally, I sighed, not meeting Brick's gaze but stomping toward him up the stairs. "Women," I muttered.

"Yeah?" Brick snagged my arm as I tried to pass him. "Maybe it's not women, Wylde. Maybe it's you."

"Look, Brick. I really like Danica. She's a sweet, hardworking girl. But I can't be what she needs. I know that and accept it. I thought we could have some fun together but should have realized that wasn't something she could accept. I fucked up."

"What did you actually say to her? That you wanted to fuck her and nothing else?"

I winced. "Well, when you say it like that, it sounds worse than it was."

"Fuck." Brick scowled at me. "Then you went and fucked her." Then his gaze narrowed and his fist shot out, grabbing me by the throat. "Did you force her into that situation? If you did, I'll kill you right here, Wylde."

"I didn't. I kissed and played with her, but the choice was hers. She's the one who made that move. She'll tell you that if you ask her." I was telling the truth, but in my heart, I knew it was so much bullshit. I knew she needed more than I could give her, but I'd taken what I wanted anyway. She might have been the one to slide herself down on my cock, but once it was all over, she knew she'd given herself to a man who'd never feel for her what she did for him.

"You're the one who brought her here. You warned everyone off her. You same as claimed her in front of Sting and the rest of the club! We were waiting for you to make an appointment with Ace for her tatt, for fuck's sake!"

"What? Hell, no! You know I've never been serious about a woman." I shot Brick my most impressive cocky grin. Difficult given the man was literally squeezing the life out of me. "I'm not a man to settle down. You know that."

Finally, Brick let me go with a hard shove. "Yeah? Did Dani know that? 'Cause I'm bettin' she didn't."

"She'll get over it. She'll also see I'm right. There's no way a woman like her would be happy with a man like me." Get over it? Right. I'd taken her virginity on my bike. I doubted that was something she'd get over. I doubted it was something I'd get over.

"Never thought Serelda would be happy with a man like me either."

"Come on, Brick! All you have to do is have one five-minute conversation with the woman to know I'm not for her. I like her. I really do. But I'm not willing to bring her into this life. I could never keep her happy and we'd both be fucked."

I finished my rant just as Danica came into the room with her sisters. They had the few things they'd brought with them or they'd been given by the old ladies. She had her gaze firmly fixed on Brick. The girls? Well. If looks could kill…

"I'm terribly sorry to bother you, Brick, but could you see if Clutch has my car ready? I know he said it might be a couple of days, but I really need to get the girls home. Besides, I've got a second job I do from home I need to catch up on."

"I'll see what's going on, Dani. If he's not done, I'll personally take the three of you home and see you get to school and work." He glanced at me while continuing to speak to Dani. "You can count on everyone here to make sure you've got what you need."

"I don't need that. I just need to get us all home and our lives back to normal."

"I understand." He motioned for the girls to precede him out the door, but not before giving me an angry snarl.

"Fucker," I muttered as I headed back to my office.

This was really for the best. I knew it. Obviously, Dani knew it. Apple and Lemon would be better off too. Once they all thought about it a day or two, they'd see I was right.

# Chapter Six

**Danica**

That had really happened. I'd had sex. With Wylde. Knowing he wasn't offering anything other than a few pleasurable moments, I'd still given myself to him willingly. I'd been the one to fuck him. He'd taken what I'd offered. *On his bike*! It hadn't even been in a bed! There was nothing about love or even mutual respect. It was all about lust. He'd told me as much at the coffee shop. I'd told him I couldn't do that, then I'd promptly gone against my own declaration.

How was I ever going to be able to look Apple in the eyes after this? It was bad enough I had to face Lemon, but I'd forbidden Apple from seeing the man she wanted romantically and I'd been unable to follow my own instructions.

Brick drove us to our modest house. It was a two-bedroom, one-bath. Not exactly great for three women in the house, but it was what it was. It had been my mother's and had come to me when she died. When the girls were old enough, it would be theirs too.

"I know Wylde was an ass, Dani, but the three of you are welcome to stay at the clubhouse. You don't have to leave because of him."

"I appreciate it, but we'll be fine. It's not like there's anything hanging over us." I smiled at him, trying to hold in the remaining emotion. I'd let out some of it but had to get myself under control for the girls. They knew something was wrong, of course, but I didn't tell them what. "Thank you for all your help. Please thank everyone else for us. I'll pay Clutch for the work he did on my car. I'll just need a total and a couple of months."

"Honey, don't worry about that. He's helping

you because he wants to. I'll send Clutch for you to get to work tomorrow. Deacon will come with the other kids for Apple and Lemon."

"I'd appreciate it."

Brick squeezed my shoulder. "You have Iris's number?"

"I do."

"Use it. I can't stress that enough."

"Thank you. I will."

We got out of the vehicle and walked to the house. Apple wrapped her arms around my waist as we walked. Lemon unlocked the door, glancing back at Brick. She threw up a hand at him before we all went inside. Brick stayed there until we had the door shut.

"Get ready for bed. You have school tomorrow." I didn't need to tell them that. The girls might be sassy and brats, but they were never malicious toward me. Any attitude they showed was all a deflection. I knew it and accepted it. I was much the same way when I wanted to be.

"Dani?" Apple wrapped her arms around me. "You OK?"

"Yeah, baby. I'm fine." I really wasn't.

"Bullshit," Lemon barked. "What did Wylde do to you?"

"Nothing, Lemon. He didn't do anything. It was all me. Everything was on me."

She snorted. "Not buying it."

"Let's just go to bed and start the day fresh tomorrow. OK?"

The girls did as I asked, Lemon gave me a fierce look while Apple looked worried. Those were my girls. Lemon was the protector. Apple the nurturer. They would both make fierce adults, women I'd be proud to stand beside.

The girls shared a room, and I had my mother's old room. Once the door was shut and locked, I took a blanket to drape over my shoulders and my pillow to cry into, sank into a corner behind a chest of drawers, and cried until I'd exhausted myself.

\* \* \*

## Danica

The next day, good as his word, Brick picked me up at four-thirty for my shift to start at five. Deacon would pick the girls up at seven so they could get breakfast before school, but Apple always made them breakfast. Likely, the little imp would make breakfast for everyone in the school carpool. That's who she was. And she'd still be trying to impress Deacon.

Once at the coffee shop, I went about my morning, readying for the day. Surprisingly, Jordan showed up when she was supposed to at seven with a smile on her face. She worked hard which was, again, uncharacteristic. I wasn't about to question my good fortune, though. And I didn't mention what had happened a few days before.

Wylde didn't show. While I was grateful to not have to deal with the drama, I couldn't help but miss him. Which was *so* not good for me.

"If you want to go on home, I can close up." Jordan grinned as she looked up from her phone. She'd done her fair share of work today, but she was still attached to her phone. I didn't mind, and I got it. Apple and Lemon were much the same. Weren't most people?

"I appreciate it, Jordan, but I'll stay. It was one of the things I promised Henry when I took the job as manager. I'd always open and close."

She shrugged. "Suit yourself." She picked up her

stuff -- including what was in the tip jar -- and left with a wave. I shook my head with a sigh. For someone who was willing to let me go home, she sure booked out of there in a hurry. And her actually working today was probably her excuse for picking up all the tips instead of dividing it out like we usually did.

The last hour was busier than usual. I could have used Jordan's help, but as always, I managed. As the last customer left, Henry Dorson walked in. The owner of the shop greeted me happily. He was in his sixties. This shop was his retirement project. It had been something he'd wanted to do before he retired. To make his living with it. He came in and worked from time to time now, but mostly, he left it to me. It made him money and I took care of the day-to-day running, so all he had to do was write the checks.

"You're here by yourself? I thought we always had two people from seven to five?"

"We do. Jordan had some stuff to do so I let her leave early. It's fine, though. Only got busy this last hour and I kept up."

"I know you did," he sighed. "You always do. But part of being a manager means you need to keep your people where they're supposed to be. You always cover for her, but we both know Jordan draws a check. She doesn't actually work."

I sighed and shook my head. "She tries. Sometimes."

He snorted. "It's the sometimes part that pisses me off. We need to talk, Dani. On the clock, of course."

"Is this about what happened the other day? Because it was all taken care of."

"Look, Jordan's parents are big in this town. They're making a ruckus. They say you lied or whatever and ruined their relative's and friends' lives.

The two cops involved are on administrative leave pending an investigation. The hobby shop manager has left town." He reached out and took my laced fingers into one of his. "I'm not telling you this because I'm firing you. On the contrary, I'll probably give you a raise if you stay through this." He grinned. "I just wanted you to know, because I'm sure they're going to make life uncomfortable for you for a while. This shop goes under without you, Dani. I'm well aware of who makes this place successful." He smiled gently. "I'll make sure I'm around more for the next couple of weeks. It'll help keep the fuss down."

"I'm so sorry about this. I never thought anything would blow back on you."

"From what I'm hearing, none of it was your fault. Jordan's parents are the only ones involved who don't believe that." He stood. "You're a good girl, Dani. Know that I'm solidly in your corner."

"Thanks, Mr. Dorson. I appreciate the support."

"Always. I think of you as one of my own kids, Dani. So does Mai. She sends her love."

I couldn't help myself. With everything that had happened with Wylde and how raw my emotions still were, a couple of tears slipped from my eyes.

"Now, now, sweet girl." Henry pulled me into his arms and gave me a big hug. He and his wife were never shy with affection. "None of that. A girl as beautiful as you are should never cry." He pulled back and looked down into my upturned face, a frown looking back at me. "If it's this situation with Jordan, don't worry about it. If there's something else, tell me and I'll fix it."

"I'm afraid that's my fault."

The voice came from the open door. Wylde stood there, in snug-fitting jeans and a tight, white T-shirt, showing off the tattoos on his arms as well as his muscles. He was mostly lean, but he was extremely fit. Veins roped his arms, and his shoulders and chest tested the material of the cotton he wore. He was simply to God *mouthwatering*.

I groaned. "Not now, Wylde."

"I've seen you here before," Henry said, moving away from me to extend his hand to Wylde. "Henry Dorson."

"Wylde." He took Henry's hand in a firm grip, nodding at the older man. "I'm around here often."

"Well, as you can see" -- Henry pointed to the closed sign he'd obviously turned over when he came in. --"we're closed."

"I'm aware. Came for Danica."

Mr. Dorson looked back at me with a raised eyebrow. "Is he the reason you're upset or is it only the situation with Jordan?"

"You know about that, huh?" Wylde narrowed his gaze at Mr. Dorson.

"Everyone in town knows. Her parents are livid."

"You takin' it out on Danica?"

Now it was Mr. Dorson's turn to narrow his eyes at Wylde. In fact, the older man stepped between me and Wylde, putting his shoulders back and standing up to him. "Dani is like family to me and my wife. Not only do we know exactly why this place is as successful as it is, we consider her another one of our children. I told her if she'd stay here through all this, I'd be giving her a much-deserved raise."

"And Jordan?"

He shrugged. "That's up to Danica. She's the manager. She can let her go or not. I'll support either decision."

That seemed to satisfy Wylde. He gave a crisp nod, then flashed a brilliant smile. "Well, that's settled. Jordan's gone and it's time to go home, Dani."

I sighed. "Wylde, I simply don't have the energy to spar with you tonight. Brick is supposed to either bring my car or send someone to pick me up who's not you."

"I volunteered."

"Then un-volunteer!" I snapped. "I'll call an Uber before I'll go anywhere with you."

"No need for that." Henry put an arm around my shoulders and guided me toward the door. "I'll take you home. We can stop and get the girls something to eat on the way so you don't have to cook."

"You know Apple will have supper ready. She always does." I grinned up at the older man. "If you give her a hug, she might pack up something for you and Mai."

"I'd never turn down anything that young woman cooks. It's a miracle what she can do in the kitchen. If she wants to earn some extra cash, tell her the offer is still open for her to make muffins for the shop. All the proceeds will go to her."

"I'll remind her." I tried my best to ignore Wylde, and I was pretty sure Henry was doing it on purpose. But when Wylde didn't want to be ignored, it was pretty hard to do.

Henry tried to move us past Wylde, but he snagged my hand and tugged me in his direction. "I'll take her home. We have some things to discuss."

"I'm sorry, young man. If she wanted to go with you, she would have." Henry gently extracted my hand from Wylde's. "If you'll excuse us."

"Well, I ain't excusin' ya." This was a side of

Wylde I hadn't seen before. I'd see him annoyed. I'd seen him amused when he wanted people to think he was angry. I'd even seen him intense and hyper focused. I'd never seen him truly angry. He was angry as shit now.

"Look, Wylde," Henry said. "I knew Warlock. I don't know anything about your club other than you're not bad guys, and you protect the people in Evansville. Right now, you're making yourself into the very thing Warlock fought against. Accept the fact Dani doesn't want to go with you. I have no idea what's going on and don't want to know. But you need to back the fuck off."

OK. That wasn't like Henry at all. The man never used bad language and he was never an overly aggressive person. As evidenced by the soft handling of the Jordan situation. It was why he would most definitely be at the shop as often as he needed to be in order to keep me safe and comfortable.

Wylde took another aggressive step toward me. Henry moved with him, still in front of me.

"You're not gonna win this one, old man."

"That's where you're wrong. *Young man.*"

"I think we all need to take a step back," I said, pushing past Wylde and taking Henry's arm. The older man had the same hard look as Wylde. Both men looked as badass as they came. Which surprised the fuck out of me. Henry never seemed like that kind of person. He was always so passive and congenial. "Henry will take me home. I'll talk to you… uh… later, Wylde." Which would translate to never. My heart couldn't take it and I wasn't putting myself through a conversation with him.

Wylde growled, but backed off. If reluctantly. I wasn't taking the reprieve for granted. I hurried along with Henry, who helped me into his truck, shutting the door with an admonishment for me to fasten my seat belt. If the situation had been different, I would have smiled. The man really was like a surrogate father. If I'd known my father, I'd have wanted him to be just like Henry.

Henry drove me to my house where Lemon sat on the top step on the porch. She stood when Henry pulled into the driveway. Right behind him, Wylde pulled his motorcycle to the curb and stopped.

"Fuck me," I whispered.

"You want me to call the police?"

"No. I don't think that'd be the wisest decision given the present circumstances. Wylde's not going to hurt me. He's a lot of things but he's not that big of a bastard."

"You don't want him here, honey, he doesn't stay. It's that simple."

I had to smile, though it was probably a weary grin. I was fucking tired and emotionally drained. "With Wylde, nothing is ever simple."

"I've got a forty-five in the glove box that says otherwise."

"No, Henry. I'll be fine. If nothing else, Lemon will protect me. Between the two of them, my money is on Lemon every single time."

That got a bark of laughter out of Henry. "You make a good point. I'm still going to walk you to your door. Stay inside and I'll come around. That way you've got a buffer as long as you want one."

I shouldn't have let him do it, but I took the coward's way out. Henry opened the door on my side and helped me down from the big truck. Wylde stood next to us not saying a word. Henry kept himself between me and Wylde, his arm around my shoulders as he escorted me to the door. Lemon took it from there.

"Heard you had a rough time with Asshole over there." She jerked her head in Wylde's direction. "I can kick his ass if you want me to."

"How'd you know about that?"

She shrugged. "Word gets around."

"It's fine, Lemon. Go on inside."

"You go with her, Dani," Henry said. "Pretty sure Wylde was just leaving."

"Not leavin' till I talk to Dani."

"I think everything that needed to be said was said." I didn't look at Wylde. Couldn't. If I did, I'd lose what little composure I had. I'd thought the time away from him would lessen the impact, but I was pretty sure even years away would bring this same aching need in my heart I felt now.

"Five minutes, Dani. That's all I'm asking."

I wanted to give in. God knew I wanted to. My heart wouldn't hold up under the strain if I did. Instead, I shook my head before opening the door and urging Lemon inside.

"No, Wylde."

Then I met Henry's gaze. He nodded for me to go on inside.

"Lock your door, honey," he said as he turned to face Wylde. "I'll see he leaves."

Again, like a coward, I did what Henry said and shut and locked the door. I couldn't help but peek out the peephole and watch as Henry confronted Wylde. I could hear them arguing. Wylde insisting he was going to talk to me before he left. Henry telling Wylde I didn't want to talk to him.

I was seeing a side of both men I'd never seen before. Henry had always seemed mild and quiet.

Even-tempered to the extreme. Now, I was seeing a strong, alpha male determined to get his way against an equally strong alpha male. And I wasn't entirely sure Wylde would win that fight.

For Wylde's part, he looked half crazed. His hair was all over the place where he kept running his hands through it. He argued with Henry for several minutes before finally throwing his hands up in the air and stalking back to his bike.

*That fucking bike.*

I doubt I'd ever be able to look at another motorcycle without remembering what I'd done with Wylde on his. He might have done it so many times it didn't mean a thing to him, but that had been my first time. I'd done it willingly. I couldn't say I regretted it. At least not all of it. I'd never known such pleasure existed. But giving myself to him when I'd expressly told him I couldn't do casual sex shamed me beyond measure. Wylde had proven to me I could, indeed, do casual sex. With him. Now, I just needed to convince my heart. And that wasn't happening.

"I'll kill him for you if you want, Dani." Lemon laid her hand on my shoulder and squeezed.

"No, honey. It's as much my fault as his. He's just trying to make himself feel better and I'm not ready to let him yet."

"You better never be ready." Lemon pulled me away from the door and to the kitchen table where Apple had made me a plate of whatever she'd made for dinner. I was too distracted to figure it out just now. "What'd he do?"

"Nothing, Lemon. We just had a falling out is all."

"Bullshit."

I sighed. "Lemon…"

"No, Dani! He doesn't get to hurt you. Not for any reason or in any way."

I reached over and took the younger woman's hand. And she was a woman. They both were. "I'm so proud of you, Lemon." I looked over at Apple. "You too, honey. You're both going to be fierce wives and mothers. I'm proud to have had even a small part in raising you."

"We love you, Dani," Apple whispered. "We just want you to be happy."

"I will be. *I am*." I brushed a tear from my eye. "I am."

As we ate, the girls told me about their day. Apple hadn't been bothered by her bullies, and Lemon had punched a boy in the balls when he'd grabbed her ass. He hadn't wanted anyone to know he'd had his balls beaten by a girl and Lemon hadn't wanted to get suspended, so neither of them had turned the other in. I figured that wasn't the end of the story, but was willing to let it go because I was fucking tired.

After supper, I tried to help Apple clean up, but Lemon had insisted I go to bed and she'd help her sister. Normally I'd laugh and send Lemon on her way. The girl hated anything domestic. This time, though, I just wanted a cool shower and bed. I'd start a new day tomorrow. Maybe I could start to put all this shit with Wylde behind me.

And maybe pigs could fly.

# Chapter Seven

## Wylde

I ground my teeth in frustration. I couldn't even find peace on my fucking bike! Every time I even looked at my Harley, I could see Danica laid out over the handlebars, her legs spread for me to eat her sweet pussy. I wanted to bash that old bastard, Henry, but that wouldn't have gotten me anywhere. Besides, I wasn't too proud to admit there was something in the old man's eyes that gave me pause. He wasn't just an old man. He was a warrior, plain and simple. I might go up against him, but not without a little recon first. I might be an asshole, but I wasn't a dumb shit.

I sat down the street from Danica's house on my Harley. Christ! I could still smell her! Feel her silky skin! Danica was the woman who was destined to haunt me until I died.

This was crazy! I could have any woman I wanted. I didn't have to sit here and mope over one who wouldn't talk to me. Maybe I needed to cleanse my palate, so to speak. Lord knew there were a horde of club whores who'd fuck me willingly. All I had to do was crook my finger.

Yep. That's what I'd do. Fuck this shit.

I started my bike, revving it a couple of times. Not to get Danica's attention or anything. I just felt like making some fucking noise. Maybe I'd take a ride before I went back to the clubhouse. Maybe that would settle this pain in my chest.

After a couple of hours, I rolled back into the compound, exhausted, the pain inside me growing with each passing minute Danica refused to talk to me. And yeah, I'd called her and texted her. After the first couple of each, she'd turned her phone off. Which frustrated me to no end. I could still track her and the girls. Unless she'd taken off without a phone -- which she'd never do unless both girls were with her and their phones were on and at their house -- she was still home. So no worries there.

Fuck this fucking shit.

Again.

I parked my bike in front of the clubhouse. Normally, I'd never leave it out, but I just didn't feel like putting it up. Either a prospect would see it out and put it up or it would still be here when I got ready to leave.

Stomping up the stairs, I snarled at anyone who got close to me. I also got more than a few glares from my brothers. Yeah. Wasn't dealing with that. I knew I'd fucked up. Literally. I even got why Danica didn't want to talk to me. What I didn't get was why I couldn't charm her into talking to me even though she didn't want to, and why it fucking mattered to me that she wouldn't fucking talk to me. This was what I wanted! She wasn't the woman for me. She was way too fucking sweet and wonderful to be part of Iron Tzars, and that was what she'd be signing up for. To say nothing of Apple and Lemon. OK, so Lemon would fit right in, but that wasn't the point. The point was I wasn't a one-woman man. I wasn't looking for an old lady.

Swearing inventively and creatively, I powered up my gaming gear. Maybe if I killed things online, I'd blow off some steam. Yes. That would help.

I was deep into a battle when Deacon burst through the door to my *locked* office. One big, booted foot landed heavily on the floor where he'd kicked it open.

I jerked off my headphones. "What the fuck,

man? Knock next time!"

"Did. You didn't fuckin' hear. Get your shit and come with me."

"What shit do I need to get?"

Deacon stalked in and grabbed me by my shirt. "Now, you fucker!"

I stumbled after him, swearing at him the whole way. Once outside, Deacon shoved me into the back seat of that fucking Bronco. The second Deacon climbed in the front seat, Clutch stomped on the gas and we took the fuck *off*.

"What the fuck? Why are we taking off outta here like our hair's on fire?"

Deacon didn't turn away or answer me. Clutch filled me in.

"There was a raid on Danica's home."

"What? A raid? What the fuck does that mean?" I got a sick feeling in my stomach. That band continually squeezing around my chest, tightening even more.

"It means," Deacon continued, "the police got a call from someone claiming to be Apple, saying she and Lemon were being held hostage in the house by Danica. Apparently, Apple told the dispatcher Dani had stabbed Lemon and had a gun, threatening to kill the girls, then herself. She stressed that her sister had snapped or something. That this wasn't in her character. But Lemon needed medical attention or she'd die and Apple was afraid Danica would kill both of them."

I thought I was going to puke. "Why the fuck did you bring me here, Deacon?" My voice was barely above a whisper. This couldn't be happening. "I'll make it worse." If I'd pushed Danica to this, I'd never forgive myself. Sting wouldn't have to cull me from the Tzars. If this was my fault, I'd take myself out.

"Because, you dumb shit, Apple called *me*. It wasn't her who made the fuckin' phone call."

"You better start makin' sense, motherfucker," I snarled. My head was spinning. Was this my fault? Had Danica snapped because I'd pushed her too far? But that didn't make sense. Danica would harm herself before she harmed those girls. And if she harmed herself, the girls would definitely be harmed. So there was no way to work this out in my head.

Then something occurred to me.

"Wait a minute. Are you saying they got swatted?"

"What's that?" Clutch asked glancing at me in the rearview mirror.

"Someone calls the police claiming to be someone else. Convinces them there is imminent danger if they don't intervene. Then the police go in like a SWAT team, expecting heavy, dangerous resistance. It's a prank, but anyone calling in something like this is expecting someone to get hurt." Or killed, but I couldn't say that. Not now. It just... stuck in my throat.

"Then, it's looking like that's exactly what happened," Clutch muttered.

"Apple said the cops burst in with assault rifles. Lemon, of course, attacked the second they burst through the door. It's a thousand wonders she didn't get shot instead of backhanded like she did."

"Is she OK?"

Clutch shrugged. "Fixin' to find out."

"Where's Stitches? If they're hurt, he needs to be here." My heart was pounding. Why would anyone swat Danica or the girls? This made no fucking sense.

"He's on the way. Was at the hospital in the middle of a shift."

Deacon had yet to speak, but I could feel the anger and fear rolling off the man. He was really gone on Apple. I could see sweat trickling down his temple and the pulse at his neck beat like mad.

My chest felt like someone was sitting on it. My pulse raced. Sweat beaded my brow and upper lip.

"What about Dani? Was she hurt?"

Neither man spoke.

My world dropped. I couldn't breathe. I was totally going to puke. Thankfully we pulled up outside Danica's house and I shoved open the door to the vehicle and stumbled out.

Police cars were all over the place. Lights flashed. Cops milled about, some in tactical gear. Ambulances with red flashing lights mingled with the blue from the cops turning the place into something out of an urban warzone. I thought I saw Raven giving some dumbass hell, but all that was on the peripheral. I had to find Danica. *Right fucking now.*

"Danica!" I bellowed her name as I charged toward the house. A cop stepped in front of me, but I shoved him away. Two more took his place and the fight was on.

I'm not sure what happened after that. I know I got hit more than once. Then I got tazed. At one point, someone waved an ammonia capsule under my nose, and I started fighting again. Then Stitches smacked me across the face.

"Snap out of it!"

"Christ, Stitches." Was that Henry? What the fuck was he doing here? "Now's not the time for fuckin' movie lines."

"Look. It had to be done. I left the hospital in the middle of my shift. Second doc in the ER was understanding, and it wasn't too much for him to handle for an hour or so, but I could still get fired. If I am, I might as well have some fun out of this before I get my fuckin' license pulled for abandonment."

"The man's worried about Danica, Stitches. Leave him be."

"Oh, yeah? Worried, huh? I heard what he did. The whole fuckin' club knows. According to him, he doesn't feel anything for her but a healthy dose of lust. If that's the case, he's acting fuckin' crazy and needed his head smacked."

I sat up, my head pounding, my muscles aching. "Motherfucker." I stumbled to my feet and turned back to the house.

"You under control now?" Stitches asked, stepping in my line of sight to the house. "'Cause if you're not, you need to go back to the fuckin' cage and calm the fuck down."

"Where's Dani?"

"She's in the house with Lemon."

About that time, a feminine voice filled the air around us.

"Deacon!" Apple flew from the house straight into the big man's arms, sobbing uncontrollably.

"I've got you, honey. You're safe."

"They broke in a-and started yelling!" she cried, shivering against Deacon as she told him what happened. "I d-didn't c-call the p-police for help, D-Deacon. I s-swear I d-didn't!"

"I know, baby. This ain't your fault."

"Will Dani be OK?"

"Stitches will take care of her. She and Lemon are in good hands."

"They sh-shot her, Deacon!"

That was all I could take. I rushed on to the house, following Stitches as he entered. Lemon sat on the couch with an ice pack on her face and a killing glare for one of the police officers.

"You better pray I have to go to the hospital, motherfucker," she said through gritted teeth. "If they release me here, I'm comin' after you."

"Threatening people isn't helping, Lemon," Henry replied to her calmly. "Let me take care of this."

"Where's Dani?" I snapped as I stepped around Henry to look at Lemon.

"In her bedroom. They shot her." She turned her glare back to the police officer she'd been giving hell.

"We thought she was ready to kill you and your sister," the officer tried to explain.

"And when I told you she wasn't?"

"I wasn't sure if you were her or one of the hostages. All I knew was there was an adult terrorizing two girls. Then your sister came at me."

"Well, who wouldn't?" Lemon replied. "She thought someone was breaking in, trying to hurt us! She was defending us and you fuckin' *shot her*!" The longer she spoke, the louder Lemon got. Finally, she threw the ice pack she'd been holding to her swollen face at the officer with a frustrated screech.

Henry met my gaze. "Danica's going to be OK. Scared to death, but OK. Go take care of her. I'll try to keep Lemon from killing anyone." It sounded like it was a real possibility.

I nodded and turned to go deeper into the small house. It wasn't hard to find Dani. There were EMTs and police near her room. I could hear Stitches talking to her and Dani's voice answering him. She sounded in pain and stressed.

When I entered her room, her fearful gaze landed on me. Her breathing quickened and seconds later, she dissolved into tears.

"Wylde," she breathed, tears streaming down her cheeks.

"Where you hit?" My throat was tight and I barely got the words out.

"My arm. It's not bad."

"She'll be OK. Gonna get her to the hospital for an X-ray and some antibiotics. Probably'll need a few stitches too." He still probed her arm, dabbing it with some gauze.

"Why ain't the EMTs in here doin' this shit?" I pointed to Dani's arm while Stitches continued to clean and dress it.

"I put them and the cops out. They were stressing her more. Figured I could do as good a job as they could." He gave me a wry look. "I *am* a doctor, you know." He went back to work. "Bullet passed through her arm. As long as her bone wasn't hit, she'll get to go home in a few hours."

"Not home," I snapped. "Back to the fuckin' clubhouse. You and the girls."

To my complete and utter shock, Danica didn't argue with me. Just nodded her head. "OK."

"Apple is with Deacon," I told her. "Lemon is giving some cop out there hell while Henry's trying to keep her contained. If Stitches says Lemon can go, I'll have Clutch and Deacon take them back to their room at the clubhouse. My brothers will watch over them."

She nodded. "Thank you, Wylde. I'm sorry we're a bother."

"Honey, this ain't your fault. But I swear to you, I'll find out who did this."

Sitting there on her bed, Dani looked so fucking small and scared. I wanted to kill someone for this, but I wasn't sure who needed to die. Yet.

"All right, Danica," Stitches said when he'd

finished bandaging her arm. "Let's get you to the hospital. I'll take care of this, then you can join your sisters."

"I need to see them before I go."

"Not a problem, sweetheart." I gave Stitches a sharp look. He had no business getting that familiar with her. "I'm sure there's no getting either of them to leave until they've seen you anyway." He smiled. "Come on. I'll help you."

"Like hell." I shouldered Stitches out of the way and scooped Danica up in my arms. Finally. *Finally.* The band around my chest eased. Slightly. Seeing the blood on her shirt and how pale her face was still hurt, but I could breathe. Mostly.

I carried her back through the house until we found her sisters in the living room. Apple started crying again. Even Lemon's lower lip trembled before she cleared her throat and scowled at Danica.

"You scared the fuck outta me, Dani. Don't fucking do it again."

Surprisingly, Danica smiled. "I'll try my best, Lemon."

Apple gripped Danica's hand as she continued to cry. "I d-didn't d-do it, D-Dani. I s-swear!"

"Honey, I know you didn't. No one thinks you did."

"Who would do such a horrible thing?" Apple sobbed.

"I'll find out, Apple," I said fiercely. "I swear it."

She looked up at me, then at her sister. Lemon nodded and that seemed to satisfy Apple. "I believe you."

"You better find that son of a bitch before I do." Lemon was going to be a handful for someone.

"I'll find him."

Lemon nodded at me, then stood. Henry helped her out of the house while Deacon took Apple. The girls got into the back of the Bronco while Deacon got back in the front. Clutch was still in the driver's seat. He started the SUV and took off.

Stitches opened the door to his vehicle and I slid in the back and situated Danica on my lap. I held on to her tightly, trying my best to be careful of her arm. She was stiff, but still clung to me, not meeting my gaze.

"Hey, baby. Look at me." She shook her head, but I gently took her chin in my hand and tilted her head up to me. "I've got you. You're gonna be OK."

Tears flowed over her cheeks, and she shook her head. "No, Wylde. I don't think I will."

I hugged her closer, kissing her forehead. "Yes, you will. I won't have it any other way."

"Why are you here?" Her question was so soft I almost didn't hear her. But I did. And I wasn't sure I had the answer for her. Mainly because I wasn't sure myself.

When I opened my mouth to tell her that, something else entirely came out. "Because I think I love you, Dani." I shook my head, wanting to take it back, but the strangest thing happened. That fucking band around my chest… disappeared. Relief flowed over me, consumed me, and I knew it was the fucking truth.

"What?" Now, she met my gaze with bright, wide eyes. "What did you say?"

"He said he loved you." Stitches, the asshole, sounded entirely too pleased with himself. "Because, like a fuckin' dumbass, he's been trying to deny it since he first stepped foot in that fuckin' coffee shop. Now. Would you please put him out of his misery and tell him you love him too? If you don't, let me know. I'll take you on."

If I'd been able to, I'd have punched Stitches in the taint. But I was in the back seat with Danica in my lap, and he was in the front seat driving.

"Asshole," I bit out.

"We all have one, Wylde. You just happen to be everyone's asshole."

# Chapter Eight

**Danica**

The visit to the hospital was a flurry of activity. Stitches had pushed everything through in a big Goddamned hurry, and I couldn't say I wasn't grateful.

My arm wasn't broken. The bullet had somehow gone through the side of my arm through the muscle but had missed the bone. Still hurt like a mother, but not as bad as it could have. Stitches cleaned and sutured what needed closing, then rebandaged it. He also insisted on IV antibiotics as well as sending me home with some oral pills. The man was thorough and careful. The whole while he worked on me, Stitches berated Wylde like a naughty child for treating me the way he had. For the first time since I'd met Wylde, the man had absolutely nothing to say for himself.

Once we got back to the clubhouse, Wylde carried me to the room the girls and I had shared before. Iris and several of the other old ladies were with Apple and Lemon, as well as Deacon.

I wiggled, a hint for Wylde to put me down. When he didn't, I patted his chest. "Please, Wylde. Set me down."

He growled, obviously not liking the idea, but did it anyway. Once on my feet, I went to my sisters. Both of them let me hug them. Apple clung to me like she was still terrified. The poor thing probably was. Hell, I was still shaken. Even Lemon, my tough girl, hugged me back fiercely.

Assured they were physically OK, I turned to Deacon, who was sitting on the couch beside Apple.

"Thank you, Deacon. Apple told me she called you, and you were there almost instantly."

"Woulda been there sooner if I hadn't had to drag his dumb ass out of his office. Fucker was playin' a fuckin' game. Had to kick the fuckin' door in." Deacon glared at Wylde like this was all somehow his fault. I tried to ignore the pang I had in my heart that after our confrontation he'd calmly gone back to his club to play video games. He'd said he loved me, but did he really mean it? Or was it just the heat of the moment?

Deacon squeezed Apple's shoulder before standing. When he did, I stepped into his embrace and hugged him as fiercely as I'd hugged my sisters.

"Thank you so much for being there for Apple. I don't know what would have happened if you hadn't been."

"I'll always be there for her. I'll look after all of you, though I'm pretty sure Lemon could do that on her own." When I pulled back, he had a huge grin on his face. "Girl's hell on wheels. Gonna make a fine old lady to some poor bastard."

"Like fuck," Lemon muttered. "I might find me an old *man*, but I ain't no one's old anything. And I damned sure ain't no fuckin' lady."

That sent the women into peals of laughter. Odette, the newest member of the group, actually wiped tears from her eyes, she was laughing so hard.

"Lord help me." I couldn't help but grin. "Though she has a point. Maybe that's the stance I'll take too." Lifting my chin, I looked back at Wylde, who had leaned against the wall with his arms crossed over his chest, a strange, bewildered look on his face. His gaze never wavered from mine.

"Double-dog dare you." Lemon rolled her eyes as she scowled at Wylde. "Though, I'm pretty sure you could do much fuckin' better. Man's a fuckin' asshole, and I'm pretty sure I fuckin' hate him."

I took a deep, long-suffering breath. "Are you trying to see just how many times you can use the word 'fuck' in a sentence before I reach my breaking point?"

The girl shrugged. "Dunno. Maybe. It's my favorite word."

"Why don't you get some rest, Danica?" Deacon patted my uninjured arm gently. "I'll watch over the girls."

Wylde snorted. "Yeah. Watch over 'em. Especially Apple. Right?" The innuendo was clear, and I sucked in a breath. Not because of the implication Deacon would do something improper, but because of the look Wylde's words put on Deacon's face. This wasn't going to end well.

I probably should have at least tried to stop Deacon, but I wasn't really ready to forgive Wylde yet. The man had hurt me more than anyone in my entire life.

Deacon moved past me, his strides quickening with each step he took. The impact of his fist against Wylde's face echoed through the small room with what seemed like a deafening crack. Wylde grunted, stumbling but not going down. Surprisingly, he didn't retaliate, which was surprising.

"Open that fuckin' mouth again." Deacon's face was a mask of rage. Wylde lifted his chin but didn't say anything. "Done fuckin' with you, Wylde. One more wisecrack and we're gonna have it out. Even if I am just a prospect in this club. I got no problem takin' you to task over these women."

Lemon tossed Wylde the ice pack she'd been holding to her cheek. "Looks like you might need this more than me, big guy. Now why don't you get the fuck out?"

"I deserved that," Wylde said with a nod to Deacon. "Stay with the girls. Keep them safe."

Deacon cocked his head like he didn't understand what was going on. Then Wylde turned his attention to me and held out his hand.

"Come with me, Dani."

I shook my head even as I took his hand. The second my hand touched his, Wylde closed his fingers around it, lacing his fingers through mine. I could see the emotion in his eyes, the need shining there. Which wasn't a new thing. Wylde made no secret he wanted me. But there was something else there. Something... vulnerable. He was clinging to my hand like it was his lifeline.

Knowing it was a losing battle, I finally nodded my head, going with him when he led me from the room. I'd never seen Wylde so subdued. It was like he was a completely different person. Well, except for goading Deacon. But I got the feeling that had been a measured attack. One thing I'd noticed about Wylde but had dismissed until that very moment was how he never did anything without a reason. Even when he ordered outrageous drinks at the shop to make it difficult on everyone, it was to get my attention, something I hadn't thought about until this very moment. There was a method to his madness, as it were. I also thought there was an underlying reason he was the way he was.

He opened the door to another room and led me inside, never letting go of my hand. Once the door was shut, he scrubbed a hand over his face and looked around the small room. It wasn't dirty, but was really messy. Kind of like Wylde.

"Sorry. The place is a mess."

"It's fine." I was at a loss as to what to do as Wylde went around the small room picking up clothes and chip bags. And pizza boxes. And empty cups of what was probably coffee. Oh. and there was more than one pair of underwear laying around, thankfully masculine and not another woman's. I might have had to kill him over that.

I ducked my head to hide my smile. It was just so... *normal*! It wasn't like I thought the man would have some sort of basement command center or anything, but a normal apartment-like room wasn't what I expected. OK, so maybe I *had* expected that. But for him to be concerned about any mess in his private space didn't seem like Wylde either.

"Wanna sit?" He indicated the big leather couch in front of a massive TV on the wall. They were the only two things in the living area other than a coffee table running the length of the couch.

"Sure." I was nervous, not knowing what to expect. But this quiet, almost introspective Wylde wasn't it.

We sat in silence for a long time. Wylde wouldn't look at me. He jogged his leg and stared at the blank TV.

When I couldn't stand the silence any longer, I reached over and placed my hand on his knee, stilling his leg. That brought his gaze firmly to mine. The intensity there made my breath catch.

"I'm sorry, Dani. Not for making love to you. I'll never be sorry for that. For forcing you out of your comfort zone when I knew what your expectations were before you had sex with me. I was the experienced one in that encounter, and I pushed you further than you were willing to go, and I did it on fucking purpose."

"It's OK."

"No, baby. It's not. It makes me the worst kind of bastard and, more importantly, it forced you into leaving the protection of my club and straight into the arms of a psychopath."

"You couldn't have known this was going to happen." Much as I was wary of where this was going, I couldn't let him take the blame for the attack on me and the girls.

"Maybe not, but I might have found out what was being planned once I continued digging in something I've been working on for a few days. But that's not the point. You guys were safe. Here. In the compound. By hurting you the way I did, I same as forced you out."

I shook my head. "Still not buying it, Wylde. I get what you're saying, but it's not something you had any control over if you didn't know this was going to happen. Did you know?" I raised an eyebrow at him.

He sighed. "No, baby. I didn't know. I've been looking into a couple users on my Fortnite server. One I believe is a disgruntled teen somewhere. The other is a troublemaker, trying to cause chaos and using that kid to do it."

"You think that had something to do with what happened to me and the girls?"

"I don't know, baby. I just have a weird feeling. And I never ignore those feelings."

"What can I do to help?"

"Nothing. I'll figure it out. That's actually the easy part." He reached for my hand and laced his fingers through mine. The gesture was so tender it made tears form in my eyes.

"What's the hard part?" I didn't try to stem the flow of tears. It was just too much trouble. Wylde reached out and caught one as it dripped down my cheek.

"Fixing my fuck-up with you."

I stared at him for long, long moments, not sure what to say but needing to voice my one burning question. Finally, I cleared my throat and pushed forward.

"Did you mean it when you said you loved me?" I couldn't hold his gaze, not wanting to see the regret I was afraid would be there. It surprised me when he cupped my cheek in his big palm and urged me to look at him. What I saw there was fierce. Unbending. Undeniable.

"Yes, Danica. I meant every Goddamned motherfuckin' word. I fuckin' love you more than anything in this Goddamned world."

"I thought you weren't looking to settle down. Does that mean you love me but you don't want me in your life?"

"No. It means I have to have you in my life, Dani. I have to be in yours. I've never loved another soul in my entire life."

That startled me. "What?"

"You heard me. As emotionally unavailable as I've always accused Cyrus of being, I'm worse."

"Is that why you snark at people? To make them hate you sometimes?"

He shrugged. "Maybe. It's easier to keep people at a distance so I don't have to form attachments. Because I honestly don't know what to do with this shit I feel for you. And can't imagine feeling it for anyone else. Things like tonight are why."

"Because, if you love someone, you risk getting hurt when they're taken away from you."

"Or when they leave."

I sucked in a breath. "Who left you, Wylde?"

"Everyone who's ever been in my life. My mom. Foster parents. Friends."

"They died?"

"Some of them. My mom just split. Never knew my dad. The sisters at the Catholic home for boys where I lived after that said I was too much trouble and turned me over to the state. Foster parents came and went. Same reason as the sisters kicked me out. When I went to the military there were guys I thought of as friends, but most of them either died or moved on with their lives. Everyone but Cyrus. That's where I met him."

"But you ended up here. With Iron Tzars."

"I did." He lifted his chin. "Because of Cyrus. They've all stuck by me like no one ever has, but sometimes even they want to cut me loose."

"I think you're wrong, Wylde. One thing I've learned from watching everyone and talking with the women here is that this is a family. You may get mad at family, may hate some of the things they do, but you never give up on them." I shook my head. "No one here would ever give up on you."

He snorted, giving me a wry look. "Don't bet your sweet ass on it."

"I absolutely would."

"You saw Deacon attack me. Ain't sayin' I didn't deserve it, but he'd have happily continued if he thought he could have gotten away with it."

"And who would have stopped him?" I glared at Wylde. "You certainly weren't going to. You didn't lift a finger to defend yourself. Or even prevent him from hitting you and I know you could have."

"Told you. I deserved everything he dished out and more."

"Uh-huh. You baited him. You wanted the exact reaction from him you got."

The widening of his eyes said he didn't expect me to notice that. Then they were veiled once more.

"You know, Deacon's got plans on claiming Apple for his own. He'll wait until she's eighteen, but only because he feels like she should be eighteen. If he felt like sixteen was old enough to take him on, he'd do it now."

"Deacon's a good man. I can see that with the way he is with Apple and Lemon. And the respect he showed me."

"He's been texting her for a little while now. I hacked his and Apple's phones. You know. To see what he was saying to her. And to make sure he wasn't talkin' to another woman while he was talkin' with Apple."

"Wylde! That's a huge invasion of her privacy! And Deacon's!"

"Also put a tracking app on her and Lemon's phone." He met my gaze with a cocky grin. It was the first time I'd seen a glimpse of the Wylde I knew. "Put one on yours too."

"Good Lord." I threw up my hands in exasperation, but the smile tugging at my lips wouldn't be denied. "Why would you do that?"

"To keep track of you guys, of course. The girls were having trouble at school. You had a crazy bitch after you. Seemed prudent."

"Why not just ask permission to do something like that?"

"You might have refused. And I'd have done it anyway. I just saved myself time and aggravation."

"You're sounding more like you now." I laid a palm against his cheek, giving him a little smile.

"Feeling better?"

He shook his head, swallowing once. "I could have lost you."

"You didn't. You came for us."

"Not soon enough. I waited outside your house for a couple hours. Then rode a couple more. If I'd stayed --"

"You might have gotten shot. Or worse."

"You *were* shot!" he barked, shooting to his feet, keeping his back to me. "You were fucking shot, Danica!"

"I was. But Stitches fixed me up and I'm fine."

Wylde whirled around, facing me again. He looked like his namesake. His hair was a mess, his eyes were wide like a madman.

"I could have fucking *lost* you!"

That was all the warning I got before he pulled me up from the couch and lifted me into his arms. My breast mashed against his chest. Automatically, I wrapped my legs around his waist. My breath caught just before Wylde grasped my hair at the back of my head and pulled me to him for a desperate kiss.

Everything he'd told me about his upbringing, how he hadn't had a stable home life or anyone in his childhood he could count on came crashing down around me. The instant our lips met, I knew this was something no one ever saw in Wylde. Fear. Wylde was afraid. Of losing me? Maybe he really did love me. At least, as much as he was capable of love.

I'd figure it out later. Right now, all I really understood was that he needed me. This man, who pretended not to need anyone, needed *me*. I'd give him everything he needed and be thankful he'd set his sights on me.

Wylde wasn't gentle. His kiss bruised my lips.

His arms wrapped around me so tight I could barely breathe. It was even better than when he'd fucked me on his bike. I could taste his need and was certain he could taste mine. Because, God knew, I was fucking ravenous for him.

Somehow, we ended up in the bedroom. Wylde planted a knee and lay down with me on his bed, covering my body with his bigger one. He never broke our kiss, thrusting his tongue as he ground his cock between my legs. I welcomed the contact, more turned on than I'd thought possible. I met his tongue thrust for thrust while I ground my pussy against his dick.

"Gonna fuck you, Danica. Gonna fuck you till I find oblivion." His words were gruff. Fierce. I knew I was about to get the fuck of my life.

Wylde grabbed my shirt and yanked, ripping it down the front. Then he shoved my bra over my breasts before squeezing and kneading one with his palm. His big body shivered over me, and he gave a defeated groan.

"What you fuckin' do to me, woman!"

He found my nipple with his mouth and took it between his teeth. I cried out when he bit down, but the pain was the sweetest, darkest pleasure. His name exploded from my lips as I arched my chest to him, letting him take what he wanted. And he didn't stop there.

Wylde made his way from one breast to the other. He tugged at my shorts, pulling them down my hips along with my panties. Tossing them to the floor, he shoved my legs apart before making his way down my belly, nipping and licking and sucking all the way to my sex. Once there, he devoured me. Growling between my legs, he covered my pussy with his mouth. He snarled, thrusting his tongue deep, rubbing my clit with his upper lip, the hair of his beard a delicious abrasion.

I had no hope of keeping up with him. Wylde took me over the edge and I screamed over and over as one orgasm tripped into another. Still, he didn't let up. By the time he finally crawled his way back up my body, I was a mindless, thrashing mass of nerves.

"Wylde! Fuck!" I clawed at his back, needing him closer, needing to stop him so I could regroup and get a hold of myself. But the need, the stark desire and raw emotion in Wylde's face told me he needed this. Needed me.

He fumbled with his jeans to unfasten them, setting his cock free to thump gently against my belly. Like I'd done when we were on his bike, I reached between us to grasp his cock. Looking up into his savage, untamed beauty, I guided him inside me. Then we both lost our Goddamned minds.

The first time we'd had sex, I'd been so afraid of losing myself along with my virginity I hadn't fully committed to the moment. Once I'd orgasmed, reality had crashed down on me like a falling mountain. Now, I surrendered to him. Letting him take me wherever he needed to go.

Wylde surged inside me, fucking me with a savage abandon. Hooking one of my legs over his arm, he changed his angle just enough to trip me into another, surprise orgasm. This time, when I screamed, Wylde did too. His bellow filled the room as his cum filled my pussy. As he held himself deep inside me, I felt his dick pulse with each spurt of cum.

When he was spent, Wylde collapsed over me. His breathing was as heavy as mine. Sweat coated my body. A sweet lethargy stole over me as Wylde clung to me as tightly as I clung to him. He was still fully dressed where I was naked. Well, except for my panties hooked around one ankle where he hadn't managed to get them off completely.

He rolled us to one side, stroking a lock of my hair off my face where my damp brow held it. As he looked into my eyes, I saw a kind of anguish on his face. He continued to stroke my cheek as tears spilled from his eyes.

"Wylde?"

"Did I hurt you, Dani?" He spoke softly, still stroking my cheek, seemingly oblivious of his own tears.

"Of course not." I wiped the moisture from his face. "You could never hurt me."

"I can't lose you, Dani. I can't."

"You won't." I gave him what I hoped was a reassuring smile. "You'll never lose me. I'm yours."

Then he rolled me to my back and put his head on my breasts. With his arms wrapped securely around me, I tangled my hands in Wylde's silky hair, taking comfort in the sensation.

With a contented, exhausted sigh, I closed my eyes and let sleep take me.

# Chapter Nine

**Danica**

The next week was an exercise in patience. Because we still didn't know who'd called in the swatting incident, I'd taken time off from the coffee shop. Wylde rarely left his office. When he did, he snarled at everyone in the immediate vicinity for not bringing him coffee. So I started making sure he had fresh coffee every couple of hours, three or four meals a day, and plenty of snacks and soda. As far as I could tell, once I started leaving provisions on a table just outside his office, he didn't come out. For any reason. By the middle of the second week, I was becoming alarmed.

"What's going on?"

Bellarose, Atlas's wife, gave me a soft smile. "This is apparently what he does when he's hunting."

Odette shrugged her delicate shoulders. She was Cyrus's woman, and Cyrus was Wylde's closest and best friend. From what I'd learned over the last week, Cyrus had as many issues as Wylde had with emotions but because he had a mild form of Asperger's Syndrome instead of emotional childhood trauma. Though, I was becoming aware that more than one of the men and women in this close-knit group had had rough lives. "Cyrus says it's how he works. He gets hyper-focused." She smiled. "If you're worried he doesn't want you here, don't be. Cyrus says you're good for him. That you understand what he needs and provide it without him or anyone else having to ask."

"Do you know what he's working on? I assume it's something for the club. I don't mean to intrude, but I've barely seen him for over a week. When I do, he's a completely different person than the Wylde I've seen before."

"It wasn't for the club to begin with. Wasn't more than a project for him." The big man approaching us was as large as the others, but had a slightly more civilized look about him. Sort of. "Once his woman and her sisters got caught up in this mess, it became the club's business."

"I don't understand." I had the thought I should be afraid of this guy because he looked so intense, but it was hard to fear him when he looked down at the woman next to him with such love and affection in his gaze.

"Wylde thinks what happened to you might be linked to a couple of gamers he's been engaging with. The harder he digs, the more roadblocks he's come up against. Which makes him more all the more suspicious." He smiled at me. "I'm Roman. You've already meant Winter." He indicated the woman at his side.

"Yes. I've met Serelda too."

"If there's a way to figure out who did this, Wylde will get it done." Winter smiled.

"I know. I'm just worried about him. He barely comes out, and when he does he snaps at everyone."

Instantly, Rose's face hardened. "He being mean to you?"

"Me? No! Not at all. I just don't see him much. I try to keep him fed and coffeed, but he must be, as you say, hyper focused on this."

"He is." Cyrus came up behind Odette and put his arms around her, pressing a kiss to her cheek. "It's his way. He gets cranky and locks himself in his office. I like that you started taking him food." He gave me a small grin that didn't quite reach his eyes. It was nothing like the smile he gave Odette. It was oddly sweet, because I could see the same looks from Wylde. Apparently, the two men were more alike than either wanted to admit. "Let's the rest of us keep out of his way."

As if on cue, there was a frustrated roar followed by a loud crash from Wylde's office. Roman gave a long-suffering sigh while Cyrus snorted.

"Speaking of which," Bella said, taking my arm. "Maybe we should get him some more coffee. Or, you know, leave it at the entrance to the dragon's lair." Her lips twitched, but I could also see she was at least half serious. Probably trying to protect me. It seemed like everyone here tried to take care of both me and the girls.

"Mother fuck!" Wylde roared from his office.

"Nope." I surprised myself with that. "You guys go on and clear a path. The man's been holed up in that office for over a week. It's time he came out and took a break."

"Not sure that's a wise idea, little sister," Roman said with a worried look. "He's pretty intense when he's on the hunt."

"Don't care. This isn't healthy and he needs a break. Even if it's only for an hour." I put my hand on the doorknob to turn it. Locked. I looked up at Roman with a raised brow. "Well?"

"Don't look at me," he chuckled, backing away a couple of steps with his hands raised. "I ain't goin' in there."

"Are you scared of him?"

Roman barked a laugh. "Might be. If I am, ain't no one here who'd fault me. Wylde's a real prickly pear when he's deep on a hunt."

For some reason, Bella paled. She gave me a forced, watery smile. "I'm sorry, Dani. I need... uh... I need to go…" She turned to leave. Atlas, her husband, rounded the corner and met her gaze. The big man stopped in his tracks before looking around the group, searching for the threat.

"It's all right, Atlas." Winter wrapped her arm around Rose. "Memories are not kind at the moment."

Atlas nodded as Winter helped Rose to her husband. He picked her up and practically surrounded her small body with his fierce embrace. Then Bella wrapped her arms and legs around him and Atlas carried her away from the group.

"Did I do something wrong?" I'd never forgive myself if I'd unintentionally hurt Bella. She was so sweet but fierce. Apple reminded me a lot of Bella. She was so sweet and kind to everyone, yet there was a protective streak inside her reserved for her inner-most circle. I was all too aware that included me now.

"No, Dani." Roman's features were strained, as if he too were remembering something unpleasant. "It wasn't you. It's the situation. The last time Wylde was this focused on hunting his prey, the compound was attacked and Bella lost the baby she was carrying."

"Oh, God," I whispered, covering my mouth with my hand. "Is the club in that kind of danger now?"

Roman shook his head. "No. Wylde thinks everything is aimed at you and the girls."

"But if we're here, wouldn't that put you all in danger too?"

"Absolutely not. From what Wylde says, even if this guy commits or incites violence, it's not going to be something like what happened last time. It will be something like what happened at your house. No matter what, though, we've learned and adapted since the last attack. No one will get close to us like that again." If anyone else but one of the men in this club had made that statement, I'd have chalked it up to wishful thinking. But not here. I could see on the faces of everyone here -- including the women -- they meant business.

Another thump from behind the door to Wylde's office, followed by another enraged yell, and I'd decided enough was enough. Putting my shoulders back I met Roman's gaze with a steely one of my own.

"Open it. Then clear us a path from here to his apartment."

Roman studied me for a long moment. I was afraid he might refuse my order -- and it was nothing but an order. Then he gave a slow nod. "You heard the lady. Make a hole." He pulled out a key and unlocked the door before stepping back himself.

I waited until everyone was gone before taking a deep breath and opening the door. The smell hit me first. Was that Indian food? Stale coffee and dirty sock smell was next. Followed by onions. The trash was mostly contained to one corner of the room, though that was rapidly filling. And Wylde? The man looked like a maniac. His hair was on end, his face a mask of rage. Dark circles under eyes that were red-rimmed, probably where he'd been rubbing them, told the story of how hard he'd been working and how focused he was.

"Wylde, please come with me." I held out my hand.

"I can't, Dani. I have --"

"It can wait."

"NO!" He roared at me before closing his eyes and taking a breath. I couldn't help but jump. "I have to find this fucker before he does something else! I *cannot* lose you, Dani!"

"You won't, Wylde." I kept my voice calm but firm. I didn't want him to get his back up, but I needed him to know I meant business. "You've been at it for a week and a half. How much have you slept?"

"Catnaps here and there. Mostly I just rested my eyes a few minutes at a time." He was making an obvious effort to calm himself, but his eyes were restlessly moving over the eight or nine monitors on his desk and mounted on the walls in front of his desk. *This* was more like the basement command center I'd expected him to have.

"That's what I thought." I looked pointedly at my hand still stretched out to him. "Please, Wylde."

"Dani --"

"I'm not taking no for an answer. Now, please." It was the voice I generally used with the girls when I wanted them to do what I said without argument. Generally, for them to go to bed when they were engrossed in a movie, or a game, or anything other than the fact they needed to be in the bed to rest for school the next day.

Surprisingly, it worked on cranky, sleep-deprived bikers too. Wylde stood and took my hand. Not without a bit of grumbling, but I called it a win.

"Is everything important you need on your desk?"

He stopped and narrowed his gaze at me. "Why."

"Because when we come back in here next time, I'd like to be able to breathe. The trash needs removed, and I don't want someone mistaking something you need for trash."

"No one goes in my command center."

I nearly smiled at him but knew that would put his back up and he'd buck me. Instead, I kept my tone and my features firm and even. "This is happening, Wylde. The room is going to be cleaned. The floor vacuumed. No one will touch anything on your desk. What about the couch? Is there anything there that you'll need later?"

He stared at me a moment as if weighing how far how he could push. I could all but see him formulating and discarding ways to get around me. Finally, he sighed before walking to the couch and picking up two stacks of notebooks and printouts. He picked up a plastic tote and dumped out the contents in the corner with the other trash and put the stack in the tote along with a couple of other stacks. The tote was now full to overflowing, but he had everything he needed on or under his desk in less than five minutes.

"There. That's it."

"Good. Come with me."

Surprisingly, Sting stood outside the door to the office well out of the way, but making a presence. I laced Wylde's fingers through my own before stepping through the door into the hallway.

"Sting, could you please ask someone to clean Wylde's office while we're gone? Everything he needs is on or under his desk. Don't let them touch that. Everything else needs picked up and taken to the trash." I smiled up at him, trying not to sound too much like I was giving orders in the middle of a biker club. And to the president, no less. "I'm not trying to order you around or anything, but I'm asking. I need to stay with Wylde to make sure he takes care of himself for a couple of hours."

"Not a problem, Dani. I'll have the prospects get on it. We'll have it cleaned and… uh… aired out when you get back." Yeah. The smell wasn't pleasant.

"We appreciate it."

"*You* appreciate it," Wylde grumbled. "I don't need a break. And I don't need my office cleaned. Don't want no one fuckin' around with my shit."

"Honey, not only do you need your office cleaned, if you don't take a shower in the next ten minutes I'm not going to be able to stand to be near you." I gave him my best exasperated look, frowning as fiercely as I could. "And if you don't get at least a couple hours sleep, you're not going to make any more progress and you'll end up breaking something important."

"An hour." He stuck his chin up, looking for all the world like a grumpy toddler. While I'm sure I wasn't the only one making that comparison, I was pretty sure Wylde wouldn't appreciate me stating it.

"Whoever this is isn't going anywhere, Wylde. You'll be better able to find him if you're fresh. You've not had a break since you brought us back here." When he opened his mouth to argue, I plowed on. "You've got to rest. Take a shower. Have a decent meal. Sleep for a few hours. When you get up, maybe you can look at the problem from a different angle and get the answers you need." When he opened his mouth again, I put my hand over his mouth. "Do you love me?"

He jerked back, pulling my hand from his mouth gently. "Of course, I do, Dani. You know I do."

"Yes. You do. And since I know you love me, I know you'll do this for me." I tugged him after me down the hall. To my shock, he only muttered his discontent, but followed me without further argument.

Once in his rooms, I led him to the bathroom where I started the shower. Wylde stood there, watching me like a wary animal wanting what I offered but afraid I'd hurt him. While the water heated I turned back to him, meeting his gaze steadily. Instead of reaching for him to take off his clothes, however, I stripped off my own clothes. That seemed to prompt him to do the same.

When we were both naked, I stepped into the shower and ducked my head under the spray. Wylde stepped in behind me. Thankfully, the shower was plenty big enough for both of us, so I reached for him and pulled him under the water with me. He groaned as the hot water fell over him, resting his head on my shoulder.

"I've got to find this fucker, Dani. I can't let him go."

"I'm not asking you to let him go. You're going to find him. It sounded like you've hit a wall." I shrugged. "Both figuratively and literally. If I'm going to do my part to save the clubhouse from you tearing it down around everyone's ears, you've got to be able to see through this. The only way to do that is to get you rested and comfortable. It starts with getting you clean. After that, we'll lay down together and take a nap. When you wake, maybe you can see what you're missing."

"Fine. But you're not leaving me until I go back to my office. That's the only way I do this."

"Never said I was going anywhere, Wylde. And I intend to be with you when you go back to your office, too. Because I'm not letting you get in this shape again."

He lifted his head and gave me that cocky grin I loved seeing on his face. "You're a regular little general, aren't you?"

"When I have to be." I smiled up at him. Then I proceeded to wash him from head to toe.

Wylde soaked up my touch like he was starving for me. I knew I needed him. This was different from the other times we'd made love. While the lust was still there, the urgency was tempered. As I washed him, I ran my hands over his body in worshipful caresses. I traced myriad tattoos over his muscular chest and arms. One snaked around his hip down his powerful thigh. I washed his hair, combing my fingers through the silky strands with loving care. When I was finished, his cock was standing proudly from the thick next of curls between his legs.

"Dani…"

I smiled up at him. "You need me."

"I'll always need you."

"Take what you need, Wylde. Make love to me."

He did. Wylde turned me to face the wall, urging one leg up so my foot rested on the bench. Then he wrapped his arms around me and entered me from behind.

I sucked in a startled breath, then leaned my head back on his shoulder while he surged into me with slow, lazy strokes. Wylde kissed my neck and shoulder, all the while his cock moved inside me.

When he began to move faster, his breaths coming in short pants and grunts, one hand slid down my belly to find my clit. When he did, I shuddered, gasping out as the orgasm overtook me. My pussy squeezed his cock which triggered his own orgasm and his seed exploded inside me hot and wet. Wylde shuddered around me, groaning in a long release. Both of us were panting, the sounds of our breathing echoing off the walls.

"Thank you," he whispered in my ear.

I smiled. "You're welcome."

Wylde washed my pussy tenderly before turning off the water. He stepped out and snagged a couple of towels before drying me thoroughly. I helped him dry off before he lifted me in his arms and carried me to bed.

I crawled in. Wylde climbed in beside me. It was like he couldn't stand for our skin to not touch. He groaned as he turned onto his side, pulling me against his hard body, my back to his front. Then he wrapped his arms tightly around me before settling himself. The second he stilled, he started snoring softly. He'd been going at it for over a week. Exhaustion had finally done him in.

I had to smile. I had no idea who he was hunting or what problems he was having in finding the guy, but I knew beyond a shadow of a doubt he would. He'd find the motherfucker who'd hurt me and my sisters and he'd make the bastard pay. My job from here on out was to make sure I took care of him so he could take care of all of us.

## Chapter Ten

**Wylde**

I gasped as I sat straight up in the bed. I had no idea how long I'd slept, but I was wide a-fucking-wake now.

"Wylde?" Danica was still beside me. Just as she'd promised.

"It's all right, honey," I said, leaning down to kiss her. "I have to get back to my office. I know what to do."

She stretched and smiled up at me. "Good. Next time, don't fight me." I shot her a cocky grin over my shoulder as I stood. When I bent over to snag the clean clothes someone had put on the chair beside my bed, she slapped my ass.

"What the shit?" I chuckled. I couldn't help it. I knew what I had to do, and I was about to catch this guy. Today.

"That's for giving everyone shit. Now, play nice. I'll get dressed and meet you in your office with breakfast."

I leaned in and kissed her once more. "I love you, Dani." I straightened and hurried to the door. "You're the best!"

"I love you too," she called after me.

When I entered my office, I did a double take. Everything was clean. The only sign of the last week and a half was the clutter on my desk, and even that wasn't as bad as it normally was. It didn't reek of curry or onions or sweaty gym socks any longer, and all the pizza boxes, chip bags, and Red Bull cans were gone from the corner. Even the coffeepot Danica had set up outside my office was now inside the office in that same corner. The scent of freshly brewing coffee hit me like a shot of adrenaline. Snagging a cup, I inhaled deeply of the wonderful aroma.

I was ready to do this. More than ready.

I sat, flexing my fingers as I took a breath to center myself. Then I got to work.

Two hours later, I was grinding my teeth. Not in frustration. In anger. Thank God it was Sunday. If not, I might not have enough time to stop a disaster from happening.

"I'll be back, love." I tried to speak calmly as I snagged my phone and a gun from my desk drawer but wasn't sure I'd pulled it off.

"What's going on?" Dani had been reading a book on the couch in front of my desk. True to her word, she hadn't left my side even once since she'd brought my breakfast. God, I loved this woman!

"I've got to get the others ready. What time is it?"

"Just after ten. What is it, Wylde?"

"I tracked the two users on my server I had the bad feelings about. My instinct was right. This is all related." I checked my weapon, making sure the clip was full but didn't chamber a round -- I wasn't ready for that yet -- then holstered it before snagging one more handgun and doing the same. "I'll be back. We've got to plan this thoroughly or there could be problems."

"I'm coming with you, Wylde." She stood and I pulled her to me with one arm, giving her forehead a hard kiss before snagging her hand and hurrying to find Sting. I sent a mass-alert text, calling for the officers to assemble in church. It was a security measure I'd been working on improving since the attack on us a couple of months ago that had injured some of our women. Especially Bella. I had found the problem too late to prevent it, but I'd upgraded our alert system substantially in the days and weeks after.

I met Sting and Brick in the hall as they answered the summons. Neither man looked annoyed I'd done this, which, considering it was Sunday and they always tried to take that day as what we'd started calling family day, surprised me. Also, I was surprised the others weren't right behind them.

"Where's everyone else?"

"On the way. Clutch said to start without him if we had to, but he was on the way."

"Start without him?" My anger spiked. "I wouldn't have sent out an alert just 'cause I fuckin' felt like it!"

Sting's brows knit together. "Take it easy, Wylde. He was under a car when the alert went off. He's just taking time to scrub the worst of the grease from his hands. And shrug off his coveralls."

"What the fuck is he doing that deep in grease on a fuckin' Sunday?" This was insane! "I've got critical information, and we need to act today before the school opens on Monday!" I opened the door to Church, continuing to rant and mutter. "Thank fuck it's so early in the morning. Might be able to stop this guy before he can get to the school and plant more guns in case he runs out of ammo."

"Wylde?"

"If we let the cops and school officials know today, they can make plans and have a working solution in place."

"Wylde."

"I might have used nefarious means to get the info I did, but if they can prove they'd have discovered the evidence eventually, without my help, they might be able to use it in court anyway."

"Wylde!" Sting grabbed my arm, spinning me

around.

"What?"

"Today's Wednesday. Not Sunday."

I stared at him, not sure I heard him correctly. "Wednesday." This was not computing. "It's Sunday. It has to be Sunday!" My heart pounded and suddenly the room wasn't big enough or had enough air. My lungs seized and a panic threatened to overwhelm me. "No fuckin' way! NO! It's fuckin' Sunday! It has to be!"

"Wylde, tell us what's going on." Sting's grip on my arm tightened.

"Wylde?" Dani stepped between me and Sting, placing one palm on my chest, the other on my cheek, urging me to look down into her upturned face. "Talk to me. We can't fix whatever this is unless you tell us what's going on."

I swallowed, taking a breath before nodding once, then facing my president and vice president. "I told you about JustMadness and SoulHunter15."

"Yes. Continue." Brick was all business. Looking at his hard features helped settle me. These were my brothers. They always took me seriously and never dismissed me even though I was sometimes erratic and all the time an asshole.

"Madness has talked Hunter into taking revenge on --" I abruptly cut off, remembering Dani was all too near. She couldn't hear this. "Dani, I need you to go back to my office and stay there."

"Wylde, I --"

"Now, Dani! Please." There was urgency in my voice as I took her face in my hands and leaned down to be able to look her in the eyes without either of us missing something in the other's face we needed to see. I was certain she saw my panic. I definitely saw her worry. "I promise I'll tell you everything as soon as I can. But right now, I need you to do two things for me. First, go to my office and shut the door. Then I want you to text the girls. See if they'll answer you." I smiled, but I wasn't sure it was all that reassuring. "Please. I really need this."

She searched my features for a long moment before nodding her assent. "OK. I'll go. Whatever you're doing, be careful." She kissed me for a lingering moment before doing what I asked. Once I was certain she was out of earshot, I filled my brothers in even as I activated an all-hands alert for the rest of the club.

"Madness has talked Hunter into taking revenge on Dani for rejecting him and taking up with me. He's going to Harrison High School to find Apple and Lemon, but he's also indicated he'll get revenge on everyone in the school for not giving him the respect he feels he deserves."

"Do we know who we're lookin' for?" Sting pulled his weapon and checked the clip same as I had before heading back to the main part of the clubhouse. The all-hands alert had locked down the club girls and families to their rooms while letting everyone else know they needed to be armed and ready to ride in five minutes. Even now I could hear bikes roaring into the parking area in front of the clubhouse.

"His name is Leo Winston. Graduated a couple of years ago with a football scholarship, then promptly flunked out of college. He blames the university as well as his high school teachers for not preparing him to do better."

"Where does Dani come into play?" Brick asked.

"He's been hittin' on her at the coffee shop. Asked her out a few times. She's always been nice but has steadfastly refused to go out with him. Apparently, he learned she'd taken up with me. Which is where

Madness comes in. She's been planting seeds for him along the way. Why is anyone's guess. Even before me and Dani were a thing. Apparently, he's finally snapped. The chat I found between them today happened about an hour ago. She pushed Leo into going ahead with this. Even calling him a pussy for not defending himself. He's supposed to go to the school, shoot it up until he finds and kills Apple and Lemon, then he's comin' here. For me."

"She?"

"Yeah. *JustMadness* is Jordan. She works with Dani at the coffee shop."

"And Dani? What's he plannin' to do with Dani?" Brick looked ready to do murder. I didn't blame him.

I shook my head. "His punishment for her is to leave her alive to deal with losing everyone she loves."

Sting's face was a hard mask of rage. "Not on my fuckin' watch."

Sting stormed through the clubhouse, through the common room, to the parking lot. Like the seasoned, hardened warriors I knew the Tzars to be, every single man was accounted for.

"This is sensitive, boys," Sting called, his voice ringing. "Got a threat to Harrison, where all our older kids are, then the club. Gonna need five of you to come with me to the school. The rest of you stay here and lock down the compound. No one gets in or out. I don't care who or what the situation is, you get permission from me or Roman before you even think about approaching the gate to let someone in. The person we're watchin' out for is a young man a couple years older than the kids he's attacking. Wylde has sent his picture to your phones. Study it." He repeated himself. "No one gets in without express permission from me or Roman." There was a collective grunt of understanding as the men hurried off to secure their stations and prepare the compound for attack.

As I was calling nine-one-one, I heard Dani calling my name frantically. I turned and she was running as hard as she could across the parking lot to the upper end where we'd gathered.

"Wylde! *Wylde!*"

I headed in her direction and was aware Sting and Brick had done the same. "Dani, what's wrong?" That sick feeling in the pit of my stomach started churning again. I could see it in her eyes before she ever voiced it. "It's started," I muttered. Dani's wide, frightened eyes told me all I needed to know. "It's started!" I yelled. "We need to go now!"

"Apple says the classrooms are all locked down, but Lemon was late to class and is out in the hall somewhere. I can't get her to answer her phone, Wylde!"

I turned and sprinted to my bike, started it up, and left the compound like a hellhound. So help me, God, if even one hair on either of those girls' heads were harmed, I'd kill that motherfucker with my bare fucking hands in front of God and everybody, and damn the consequences.

We arrived at the school before emergency crews or police. Which was another thing I was pissed about. They were pretty fuckin' quick to get to Danica's house when they had, yet no one was here yet. Not a rational thought, but one I'd be bringing up later. After they got here to clean up the fucking mess I was about to create.

"Stop, Wylde!" Sting called -- but fuck that shit.

I stormed to the back entrance to the school. As suspected, it was locked. So I shot the latch several times until it gave with one solid kick. I switched to a full clip before entering fully, needing the maximum amount of ammo available to me without reloading. When I killed this fucker, I was gonna kill him to death.

Making my way slowly into the school, I could hear the *pop pop pop* of automatic fire. Screams filled the air as the subtle pops of the assault rifle was replaced by a loud *BOOM* of a large caliber handgun. Unless I was mistaken, that was a three-fifty-seven Magnum. If the guy hit someone with that, it didn't really matter where it struck. Someone was either dead or missing a limb.

I came to the first room, just a few meters away from the exit. I tapped on the door before opening it. There were a few whimpers and the teacher had a baseball bat in her hand, ready to attack, but I placed my finger to my lips.

"The way to the back door exit is clear," I said. "Take your class and head out. Don't make a sound and whatever you do, do not stop running or look back. There'll be men outside to get you to cover and the police are on the way." Then something occurred to me. "Do you have a resource officer I need to watch out for?"

She nodded her head. "Three, but I think... We think they were the first ones..." Her voice broke, but she clamped her lips together to keep from showing how frightened and grief-stricken she was. She took a breath then added. "There's three ROTC teachers also. They've been trained as well."

"Good. Get your students to safety."

The teacher nodded and urged the students out. One large boy seemed to take over from there, putting another boy in charge of leading the class out and he brought up the rear. When his teacher tried to stay behind to help the other kids deeper in the school, he gently took the bat from her hands.

"Please, Mrs. Bradley. You know you can't fight a gunman with a bat." He was kind and spoke softly but insistently.

That seemed to be all the woman needed because she nodded in agreement. "I know. You're right, Obie." Tears streamed down her face. "But everyone else needs help too."

"I know," the young man said as he urged her out of the class to follow the others. "But that guy's better equipped to handle this than we are." He met my gaze, and I knew that kid wanted in this fight with everything in him. Much as I wanted to give him his shot at vengeance, I couldn't.

"What's your full name, Obie?"

"Obadiah Mason."

"I'll find you later. We'll talk." Obie nodded once, then followed the rest of his class to the outside.

I continued on, listening for the gunfire to judge where the shooter was. Each room I passed, I gave instructions on how to get out. Some I sent back the way I'd come, but as I got closer to the gunfire, I started sending them out the window.

It wasn't long before Blaze and Cyrus joined me. I couldn't deny I was glad to see the big men.

"What took you so long?"

Blaze shrugged. "Had to make sure all the kids you sent out got to safety."

"Police?" I asked, needing to know they were on the way and why there seemed to be a delay.

"On the way. There was a scheduled shutdown of their communications system for an upgrade. At the same time, there was a cell outage all over the southern half of the city. Seems like a coordinated attack to me."

"Wondered why Dani hadn't let me know if she'd reached Lemon."

"If I ever tell you sat phones are overkill again, remind me of this."

"Blaze and I will take over from here, Wylde." Cyrus clapped me on the shoulder. "Orders from Sting. You're to find Apple and Lemon and get them to safety, then stand down."

"Like fuck. This fucker's mine."

"Out of the question," Blaze snapped. "You have your orders. Follow them or I'll forcibly remove you, and that would waste time we could use to fix this."

He had me there. "Fucker," I muttered, but I knew I'd follow Sting's instructions.

The next classroom we liberated had Apple flying into my arms. She sobbed into my shoulder to muffle the sound, shaking uncontrollably.

"Where's Deacon?" She asked the question in a whisper, but I heard her.

"Not sure, honey. I'm sure he's not far."

"He's not." The man in question had a Ruger in one hand and a rifle slung over his other shoulder. Apple immediately let me go and jumped into the big man's arms, wrapping her legs around his waist and her arms around his neck. Her slender body shook with her sobs, but she didn't make a sound other than to whisper.

"I can't find Lemon. She's out there somewhere in danger."

"She's tough, honey," Deacon responded quietly. "I'd worry more about that fucker than I would about her." I knew Deacon meant it, but also that he was still worried about Lemon. We all were.

"The important thing now is that you're safe,

Apple," I said before my gaze landed on Deacon. "You keep her that way. Hear?"

Deacon gave a short nod. "I will. I'll get her to the others, then come help you search for Lemon."

"You'll do what Sting says," I snapped, not wanting the other man hurt. I tried to tell myself that, if he were hurt or killed, it would devastate Apple which would, in turn, upset Danica, but I had the uncomfortable thought it might upset me too. Which I absolutely would not acknowledge right now.

"Wylde --"

"No! You'll do what I tell you, prospect. If Sting gives the OK, fine. But you will check with him before you come back inside this building." I was hoping that would give the police time to get here and the matter would be taken out of Deacon's hands, but he didn't need to know that.

Without waiting for him to acknowledge me, I continued on, making sure everyone we came to got out safely. We were getting closer and closer to the gunfire. It happened in sporadic bursts. Every time the big Magnum went off, I grew more and more angry.

"This fucker is rapidly losing any sympathy I had for him."

"Don't think about it," Cyrus cautioned. "I'm not." The other man had changed somewhat since finding Odette. I was happy for him. Of all the men in Iron Tzars, Cyrus probably understood me best.

We continued on. The area we were currently in had mostly evacuated, but now the gunfire was getting closer. I glanced at Cyrus as we approached a corner. He nodded back to me. I pulled out my phone and turned on the video recorder then carefully moved it around the corner to get an idea of what I was dealing with. I gave it a few seconds before easing it back and taking a look at the video.

Sure enough, the gunman was there. His back was to us, and he appeared to be walking away from us. There was a long expanse of hall ahead of him and he appeared in no hurry. I tucked my phone back in my pocket and caught Blaze's gaze. He shook his head, indicating I needed to back off. Like that was going to happen. I'd been told to find Lemon and get her out, but if I took out the gunman before I found Lemon, the problem would take care of itself. The bloodcurdling battle cry wasn't something I was expecting.

"Bloody hell," Blaze muttered.

"Fuck me." Cyrus's eyes widened, an uncharacteristic show of emotion on his part. Well, other than irritation. He was good at irritation.

I sighed, fear threatening to take over. "That's Lemon."

All three of us dashed around the corner, guns drawn, charging full speed. I yelled just as the gunmen raised that fucking Magnum in Lemon's direction.

"Move!" I yelled, trying to get the gunman to turn to me. I had no intention of letting him hurt Lemon, and I didn't mind shooting him if I had to, but I had no desire to shoot a man in the back.

Just as I hoped, the guy turned to look over his shoulder. Sure enough, Leo Winston looked back at me. His features were more scared than angry, as if he were doing something he wasn't sure he was fully committed to, yet couldn't seem to stop himself. Until he saw me. Then unadulterated rage filled his expression.

"Fucker!" he yelled. "This is all your fault! Why couldn't you just leave her alone!"

I figured he was talking about Dani, but I wasn't sure and didn't much care. His attention was on me and not on the small figure of Lemon… charging him from the back?

"What the fuck?"

"Lemon!"

"Don't!"

All of us spoke over top of each other. For all the good it did.

Lemon charged a man, armed to the teeth, with a bigass trophy from one of the cases along the front of the school. Instead of a repeat of the battle cry she'd given earlier, she charged him silently until she was close enough to swing. She hit him with the marble base in the back of the head with all her might. He fell, but Lemon wasn't done. She took one more swing, this time yelling at the top of her lungs, and hit him again in the back of the head. This time, the base broke and clattered to the floor, leaving Lemon standing over her prey like an Amazon warrior.

"Fucker," she muttered before throwing the remainder of the trophy to the ground. She kicked the gun that had fallen from his hand across the hall before bending to pick up the rifle in his other hand. She raised her head and met my gaze as I neared. The girl was as calm as any seasoned warrior, but angry as fuck. Glancing back down at Leo, she spat before stepping over him and marching toward us. Shoving the rifle at me, she stared me down.

"Get her out of here," Blaze ordered. "I'll deal with the cops."

"They just pulled up outside." Cyrus looked out the window. "There anyone else, Lemon?"

"Yeah. That fucking Jordan bitch. But she didn't stay long. She dropped off this fucker before she left."

"How do you know that?" I tilted my head as I looked at her. This girl was a fucking handful and then some.

She rolled her eyes. "Why the fuck do you think I was out of class in the first Goddamned place? I saw her. I saw Leo. Neither of them are supposed to be here, so," she shrugged, "I went to investigate." She sobered. "I thought I saw Deacon carrying Apple out. I tried to keep this guy's attention focused on me at this end of the school so she had time to get out, but I didn't know if she'd be able to leave. The lockdown…"

"Yeah, Lemon. She's safe."

When I first met Lemon, I knew she was tough as nails. The girl was gonna make one hell of an old lady to some poor bastard. But now, right before my eyes, she seemed to… crack. Her breathing sped up, then she heaved, vomiting violently. I knelt beside her, holding her hair out of her face, which seemed to piss her off even more. Or maybe it was her defense mechanism, because she was trembling almost violently.

"Get off me, Wylde!"

"Hey. I'm just tryin' to help, honey. You know I'm not gonna hurt you."

"Don't need help." She spat again, then wiped her mouth with her arm.

"Everyone needs help, Lemon." Blaze knelt beside her and handed her a bottle of water. "Even tough chicks like you."

Lemon took a pull of the water, swished her mouth out, then spat again. Then she took several gulps before wiping her mouth again with her arm.

"Fuck you, Blaze."

Blaze smirked. "You ain't old enough, sweetheart."

Lemon bared her teeth and threw the bottle at him. Blaze caught it with one hand before standing and reaching out a hand to her. Lemon ignored him and stood to stride to the closed door. She didn't look back.

"Yeah. Good luck with that one, Wylde."

"Leavin' her up to her sister. I just work here."

Despite everything that had just happened, I wanted to smile. But I couldn't. There was still the matter of Jordan to resolve.

"Let's get out of here. We need to find Jordan." As much as I wanted to, I knew I couldn't let the woman go. I wanted to turn it over to the cops and take my girls home, but the woman was too dangerous to leave out there to her own devices.

As we approached the entrance the police entered the building. I recognized one of the men from Danica's house. The one Lemon had given hell when I'd arrived at their house. The one who'd shot Dani. He nodded as he approached me. I wanted to shoot him in the face.

"What happened to him?" He nodded to Leo lying on the floor of the hall, blood steadily oozing from the wound on his head. Other officers filed past us, hunting for more threats.

"He turned his back on Lemon, thinking we were the real threat."

Surprisingly, the guy snorted. "Yeah. Big mistake. Anyone hurt besides him?"

"Don't know. Possibly. The school resource officers and the ROTC teachers would have been the main responders in the school. One of the first teachers we came to was worried they might be injured. Or worse. There's another woman you need to find." I pulled my phone out and pulled up Jordan's picture. "Lemon said she dropped this guy off. I've got proof she'd been baiting this guy for months."

"It possible she's still here?"

I shrugged. "Don't know."

"Was it you three who got the students and teachers out?"

"We cleared the hall and sent them in the direction we'd come from. Or out the windows. But we did our best."

"We're glad someone got here in time to help. We were caught blind, deaf, and flat-footed." The guy looked equal parts angry and anguished. "This happened at the worst possible time."

"Looks like it's all clear," one of the other officers said over the radio. "Got three male adults with injuries, one severe. Other than that, lots of scared people."

"Make one more check. I want every single closet and cubby double-checked before we release the lockdown. Looking for a female in her twenties. Blonde. Slender." He looked back at me. "I've got to go meet with the principal for the walk-through. I'll make sure everyone on each team knows to be on the lookout for this woman." He stuck out his hand to me. "Thanks for keeping the kids safe."

I took his hand, my opinion of the guy going up several notches. Didn't mean I still didn't want to at least maim him for shooting Danica.

"Glad we were able to help. I'm sending you another file. The one that shows the trail between Leo and Jordan. And how she pushed him into this on the same day and time your communications were taken offline for an update."

"Wait." His eyes narrowed. "Leo… Winston?"

"Yeah. He's the former mayor's nephew or some shit."

"And Jordan?"

I shrugged. "Besides a sociopath? I have no idea. I think she liked to play with people. Leo was a convenient target for her to use to get back at Danica."

"Trust me when I tell you we will find her. I have no desire to be the cause of someone's death, and I very well could have been because of that bitch."

"All I can say is that you better find her before I do."

He raised his hands. "I don't want to hear it, man. I do and she turns up dead, I still have a duty to investigate you."

"I kill her, there won't be anything for you to find." I smiled to take the sting out of my words, but it probably looked as evil as I felt at the moment.

"Come on, Wylde," Blaze took my upper arm and tugged me toward the exit. "Let's get the fuck outta here and back to the clubhouse."

# Chapter Eleven

**Danica**

"I'm going to be gray headed before this is all over."

They arrived back at the clubhouse to the whole of the Iron Tzars manning the fence around the compound. Armed men looking outside, watching everyone who approached gave the place a feel of being in the middle of a war zone. I wasn't so sure that wasn't an apt description given when we'd just been through.

There were only five of the club members who'd gone to the school while everyone else, including myself, had locked down the compound tighter than a snare. Once the others passed through the gate, Roman met them just outside the club house. I had to watch from a window because the bastard wouldn't let anyone out until he'd confirmed with Sting all was clear on their end.

"They got her," Roman said without preamble. "They've arrested Jordan. Not only did what you send the police help, Wylde, but it led them to the proof she was behind the cell outage. I didn't understand it all, but she's got more skill than we gave her credit for as a hacker. The resource officers and the ROTC teacher who were hit are in the hospital. One of them is fine, minor injuries, but two of them are in surgery now. Both are expected to be fine. This is from Stitches, so no one else is in the know yet." Roman continued. "Leo is at the hospital too. He has severe head trauma, but he's alive."

"Of *course*, he is," Lemon muttered. "I've got to start lifting weights to build more muscle. If I could've hit him harder, the fucker'd be dead. Though brain damage might be just as good."

"Lemon," I scolded. "Don't say things like that." I pulled her into my arms for a fierce hug. Surprisingly, she not only let me, but she hugged me back just as tightly.

"Don't worry, honey. There's a possibility he's going to have permanent brain damage. Anything legal they try to throw at you will be dealt with by Raven, though he doesn't anticipate anything," said Roman.

"Tell me you don't want him dead too and I'll take it back." The girl was going to be the death of me.

"Can't say that, but I can say that I don't want it to be you who kills him." I pulled back to look at her. "I'm so glad you're safe, Lemon. When neither Apple nor I could get a hold of you..." A strangled sob escaped before I could stop it. Lemon might show some normal emotions like fear or grief in private, but she absolutely wouldn't out in the open where everyone could see. It was just the way she was wired. Always the protector. The tough one.

"Pull yourself together, Dani," she hissed. "I'm fine."

I barked out a laugh. "I'll get right on that. This is twice in as many weeks. I'm not going to be able to pull myself together for a long fucking time."

Lemon grinned. "Nice f-bomb, Dani."

"Brat," I grumbled with no real heat.

"This could have ended so much worse." Apple wrapped her arms around me and leaned her head on my shoulder. "We could have all been killed."

"But we weren't." Lemon looked and sounded fierce. "We weren't, and you're not even going to think about it."

"Kinda hard not to. I was so scared he'd shot

you, Lemon. We could hear him shooting. How did he not kill anyone?"

"'Cause he's a fucking horrible shot. He even missed me with that bigass .357."

"Wait." Wylde wrapped his arms around both me and Apple as he confronted Lemon. "What do you mean he missed you?"

"I told you. I saw him and that bitch, Jordan, together outside the school, so I went to investigate. When he pulled a gun, I had to do something. I taunted him. Tried to get him to come after me and leave everyone else alone. It worked. Mostly. He got a couple of the resource officers and one of the ROTC guys. Good thing I lured him in that way instead of through the front door like he'd been going for."

"I think I'm gonna puke," I whimpered.

Sure enough...

When I finished, Lemon and Apple were on either side of me as I sat back on my ass and cried, the stress of the day finally crashing down around me. Wylde held my hair out of the way until the girls surrounded me with hugs. Apple cried quietly and Lemon... tried not to. I felt moisture on my shoulder where she tried to bury her face for a moment, but when she pulled back, she'd composed herself.

"I'm sorry, Dani," Lemon offered. "But I wasn't letting anything happen to Apple."

"I know, baby. And I'm proud of you. I really am. But you need to know you matter just as much as Apple. I love you both and don't want to lose either of you." I gave her a watery smile. "You're much stronger than I've ever been, honey, but you need to learn there are people all around you who can help you. You don't have to do it all yourself."

She shrugged. "I know." She glanced at Wylde

before looking away. "I just don't trust anyone to do as good a job as me. Except maybe I'll consider giving Wylde the benefit of the doubt. Unless he starts acting like a fucktard again."

I barked out a laugh. Wylde just sighed. "Appreciate that, sourpuss."

That got a scowl from Lemon, but I thought I saw a hint of relief also. Apple was quite possibly the only person she'd ever let see her feelings. Wylde seemed to recognize Lemon needed a way to regain her composure and had given it to her. It made me love him that much more.

"You sure Jordan's been taken care of, Wylde?" Apple looked up at him like he could fix anything.

"I am. The information I gave the police, combined with the security footage from the school, should be enough to put her away for a long time. Roman's right. She's a pretty good hacker. Good enough she hid from me. For a while at least. Raven said he's putting some bugs in important ears to make sure she gets held without bail, but given the results of her actions, I don't think that will be a problem."

Apple nodded her head slightly. "Good. That's good."

Lemon scowled. "How the fuck did she do all this anyway? Did she have anything to do with the cell towers fucking up?"

"Lemon…"

"She does it on purpose," Wylde said and chuckled. "I like her style." Lemon snorted. "But to answer your question, she was able to take down the cell towers briefly. Just long enough to allow Leo to get a head start on the police and to prevent information from getting to the right people. I haven't looked in to how she did that, but she has some skill with the computer." He shrugged. "Guess she really *was* after my Titan GT77. Don't really care at this point as long as the cops have her. School security camera caught her giving him a Magnum. Which was found on him. May be hard to prove it was that exact gun, but it's pretty compelling."

"Fuck." Lemon looked disgruntled. "Really wanted a shot at that bitch."

"All right, Lemon. That's enough. Take your sister and do whatever the two of you do when you need to destress."

"Can I hang out with Deacon?" Apple looked up at me. I could still see the terror in her eyes and knew she needed to feel safe. Deacon could give that to her. "I promise I won't do anything."

With a sigh, I nodded. "Yes, Apple. I think he's earned my trust. Just please respect my wishes in this?"

"I will. Thanks, Dani."

"I'll go with her." Lemon stood. "Make sure the lovebirds behave."

"Christ, Lemon." My lips wanted to curl despite everything that had just happened. "Can you try to not be so abrasive?"

"Works for him." She nodded at Wylde. "I reckon it'll work for me too. To be honest, I don't really care. See me, love me, motherfucker."

That got a bark of laughter from both Wylde and Blaze. Neither man bothered to hide their mirth.

"Don't encourage her. She's bad enough as it is."

"Why would I *not* encourage her?" Wylde chuckled. "She's me."

"Don't know about that," Lemon said. "But I know I'm either a pleasant surprise, or I make everything incredibly fucking uncomfortable and awkward. Like a finger in the asshole."

That was all Blaze could take. He doubled over with laughter. Wylde too. Both men had tears streaming down their cheeks. I'd be lying if I said I didn't too.

I pointed at Lemon. "Go pester someone else." She just shrugged and left, taking her sister with her.

"Got a guy I want Sting to look into, Blaze. Kid from the school. Not sure what he's got planned later, but he'd make a damned fine prospect. Maybe not now, but when he's ready. Big kid. Looked like a linebacker."

"Oh?" Blaze raised an eyebrow.

"Yeah. Was a really good help when we got to the first class. Even kept the teacher focused. Seems to have a good head on his shoulders. Obadiah Mason. Goes by Obie."

"In high school? You sure that's a good idea?"

"I'm just saying it might be a good idea for the officers to look into him. Maybe keep an eye on him while he's in town. I'm gonna be watchin' him. Just for shits and giggles."

Blaze nodded once. "I'll let Sting know. He'll likely get with you later." He gave me a wink. "Sure now's not the time. Go comfort your woman. That shit can wait."

Once everyone was gone but me and Wylde, he lifted me into his arms and left. I was glad because sitting so close to my own puke was a bit disconcerting. I probably should have protested, but it felt good to be in his embrace. So I just circled his neck with my arms and buried my face in his chest and let the tears come.

I don't really remember getting to the room we shared, but the next thing I knew Wylde stood me in front of the bathroom sink and opened a new toothbrush for me, fixing it so I could brush my teeth and rinse my mouth out. Not long after that I found myself sitting on the bed with Wylde holding me as tightly as I held him. He'd turned me so I was straddling his lap with my head resting on his shoulder.

"I've got you, baby. Everything's OK." He rubbed my back over and over, soothing me in a way no one in my life had ever been able to. Maybe it was because even before our mother had died, I'd felt responsible for the twins. Or maybe I just never trusted anyone enough to let them in.

"I only pretended not to want them, you know." I spoke softly, not really sure why I was telling Wylde this, but needing to get it out. "Lemon and Apple. I gave them those ridiculous names out of spite, but Mom just gave me a little knowing smile. I think she knew I'd end up being the one to raise them. It's why she wanted me to bond with them."

"You did, baby. You did exactly that." Wylde rocked me in his arms, all the while clinging to me as hard as I clung to him. "You love them like they were your own. Everyone can see that, including them."

We sat like that for a long while before I framed his face in my hands and kissed him with all the fear and desperation inside me. It seemed like we were always needing to comfort each other, but I was fine with it. It felt like... home. A family.

I surrendered to Wylde, letting him lead us because I knew he needed me as much as I needed him. As always, when he made love to me, my body sang in his embrace. Wylde took me to heights of wonder I'd only ever read about. Always, before he came, he saw to my pleasure. Several times. Now was no exception.

When we were spent, lying in the bed with Wylde draped over me, his head between my breasts, he lapped lazily at my nipple. I tunneled my fingers through his hair and massaged his scalp for the sheer luxury of it.

"I've set Ace up to get your tat tomorrow," Wylde murmured lazily to me. It sounded like he was half asleep already.

"You mean the one like the other women have? The property tattoo?"

"Yeah. Tomorrow." His words were slurred. The man had to be exhausted. I know I was. "Got a problem with that?"

"So defensive. You'd think you set it up without consulting me or something."

"Told you. I take the path of least resistance. You might have said no, and I'd still have set it up. Do you know what it means?"

"Yeah. You can thank Iris. She explained it all to me. I had a few questions and she answered everything. You gonna make me regret doing this for us?"

I could feel him smile around my nipple before he gave it another lick. "I'll do everything in my power to always keep you safe and happy, Danica. You and the girls."

We were silent for a long while after that. I think I dozed on and off in peaceful relaxation.

"You know I love you, right?" Wylde always sounded so vulnerable when he confessed his love. Or any emotions, really. He hid his feelings behind his quirky, snarky, prickly personality. I knew it was a self-defense mechanism, one I was glad he'd stopped using with me.

"I do, Wylde. You know I love you too. Right?"

"I certainly hope so. I'm not sure I could survive if you didn't."

I pushed him gently so he rolled off me. In the process I draped myself over him. "I love the feel of your hair-roughened skin sliding against mine. I love how protective you are of me and the girls. I love how you make love to me with both ferocity and tenderness." I leaned in and gave his lips a lingering, gentle kiss. "But most of all, I love how you love me, Wylde. You're everything I could have ever hoped for in a man."

"I'll always take care of you, you know. Even if you decide I'm too much for you to handle."

"You know, for anyone other than me you would be too much to handle. Me? I'm up to the task."

Then I proceeded to show him how much I loved him. And continued to show him the rest of the day. And into the night. Tomorrow, we'd make it official. Before we left this bed, though, I wanted Wylde to understand that I was never letting him go. He was my heart. My soul.

My... everything.

# Mars (Iron Tzars MC 10)
## *A Bones MC Romance*
### Marteeka Karland

Scarlet -- The day Hammer took me from Grim Road, my father's club, was the day my life went to hell. I've always considered myself a strong person, but I'm eighteen, still in high school, and living with a monster who brutalizes me at every turn. He's using my sisters as leverage to control me. I've got to find a way out, even if that means sacrificing myself to save them. Then Mars finds me. He's everything I've ever wanted. He makes me feel safe. But he has his own demons... and I'm not sure which of us needs saving most.

Mars -- Scarlet needs a hero. She's not asked for my help, but I can't leave well enough alone. Not when I can see she's hurting. I have demons of my own I can't escape, but when I see Smoke terrorizing the young woman he claims is his, I know I can't stand by and watch. I know I'm not what she needs, but when her daddy's club comes in hell bent on taking her home, I know I can't let her go. She's mine to protect. Mine to hold. And maybe, just maybe, she's the one to save me from myself.

# Chapter One

**Scarlet**

"We can show you around school if you like." The girl from my home room, Apple, was quite possibly the sweetest person I'd ever met. Her sister, Lemon, on the other hand... Yeah. Tart didn't even *begin* to cover it. But I really liked both of them.

"Thanks." I smiled at both girls. "I appreciate it."

"Seems like a strange move," Lemon commented, looking at me funny. Both twins were wicked smart, but Lemon really knew how to keep someone off balance. Like now.

"Strange move?" I smiled, probably looking like an idiot because I had no idea what she was talking about. What was strange?

"You know. The move. From Riviera Beach, Florida to Evansville, Indiana. Since you have no family here or anything. Seems like a strange move."

I shrugged. "My... uh... boyfriend. He wanted to move away until we got married." I gave them my brightest smile. "We have to wait until after I graduate, but he thought it would be best if we got away from my dad's, err... well, my family."

Lemon frowned. "I see."

Apple just shrugged it off. "I've got a boyfriend, too. We're waiting until I turn eighteen to actually date, but I'm betting my mom and dad will want me to wait until I graduate." Her smile was nearly as bright as mine but genuine. "His name's Deacon. He's --"

"Apple." Lemon nudged her sister. They gave each other a look. Apple ducked her head and her cheeks flushed.

"Sorry. It's kind of a long story."

"It's OK. My story is probably just as long." Or

longer. I felt my smile slip but tried to keep from looking at the door. School had let out ten minutes before. Everyone was leaving either on the buses, with their parents, or in their cars. I could drive, but Hammer made a point to always pick me up from school. In the beginning, it had been sweet, if unnecessary. Now... things had changed. He'd sold my car so I had nothing to drive. And I was more than a little frightened of Hammer. It wasn't anything overt, but I could sense something had changed. The feeling had been building since we'd moved to Evansville.

"We better go." Lemon took her sister by the upper arm. "See you tomorrow, Scarlet."

"Bye." Apple waved, still giving me that cheery smile of hers.

"Take care, guys." I waved as I hurried out to the parking lot where Hammer was waiting on his big Harley.

Hammer revved the engine as he saw me approaching. My heart rate increased, but not for the reasons it should. The sound the Harley made when he used it to get my attention never failed to make me nervous because that meant Hammer was getting impatient. I plastered a smile on my face and climbed onto the back of the bike, wrapping my arms tightly around his waist. He smelled of cigarette smoke and whiskey, a combination that made me faintly nauseated.

"Everything OK?" I asked hesitantly.

His eyes flicked toward me before quickly averting away. "Yeah, 'course. Should somethin' be wrong? You done somethin' you know's gonna piss me off?"

I swallowed hard, trying to push down the fear that was suddenly threatening to consume me. "No, of course not."

"Good." He let out a heavy breath like he was supremely disappointed in me, then peeled out of the parking lot. The wind whipping against my face prevented any further conversation, thank God.

As we made our way home, I knew I trembled against him. I also knew he loved to keep me on edge. The more frightened of him I was, the better he seemed to like it.

Hammer pulled the bike into our driveway and turned the engine off. I dismounted, stumbling to regain my balance. He watched me, a sneer flickering across his face before disappearing just as quickly.

"Go inside," he ordered, jerking his head toward the front door. "I'll be in in a bit. Got shit to do." He pointed a finger at me. "You better fuckin' be here when I get back."

I nodded numbly, feeling like a puppet whose strings were being pulled by a cruel master. Since my dad had decided I was going to be Hammer's woman, Hammer had been very possessive, but once we moved to Evansville he had become even more controlling. I didn't think my dad would approve of the way he treated me, but when Hammer requested to move us to Evansville until I'd graduated, my dad hadn't told him no.

Now, every day was a nightmare for me. The only solace I got was when I went to school and even that was a trial. Hammer had uprooted me in the middle of the school year, telling my dad I needed time away from the club so we could get to know each other better. Dad hadn't really seemed to like it, but when I hadn't protested he'd let us go. Probably because I was already old enough to be Hammer's old lady, but I'd wanted to finish high school before settling into that role.

As I made my way inside the house, I knew that things were about to get even worse. Hammer had been getting more and more violent lately, lashing out at me for the smallest things. The bruises on my arms and legs were proof of that. But I didn't dare tell my dad. He was too caught up in something Grim Road was working on and, given the secrecy with which the club operated, it was doubtful I could even reach him. I think it was the main reason my father agreed to Hammer taking me away from the club. So I'd be away from them if shit went sideways.

Unfortunately, he didn't take into account how sideways things could go for me once I was away from his protection. I was also hesitant to say anything to Apple and Lemon because, if Dad had sent us to Evansville intentionally, then their club, Iron Tzars MC, knew we were here. I knew nothing about them but the possibility they'd take my side over one of Grim Road's members was slim.

I went to my room, taking a deep breath as I closed the door behind me. The white of the walls was stark against the gloom the shadows cast from the sun through the only window, creating an eerie effect to add to my disquiet.

My hands shook as I sat on the edge of the bed, my mind racing with what Hammer could be doing out there. I didn't know what "shit" he had to take care of, but I knew it wouldn't be good.

I tried to stay away from him as much as I could. So far, he'd left me alone except when I didn't do exactly as he told me. Then I'd get a beating. Several times I thought about telling my dad, but what good would it do? He'd let Hammer bring me here.

We were a good fifteen hours from anyone in

Grim Road. If I told Dad and Hammer found out, there was no way I'd survive. Not only that, but Hammer had assured me he had men in the compound he could count on to take care of my sisters if I contacted my dad without permission. I was under no illusion that "take care of" meant anything other than they'd be killed. The reason I didn't defy Hammer and call someone I trusted, or leave and run back home as fast as I could, was because of my sisters. Hammer might be bluffing when he said they'd be taken care of, but I didn't think so. Besides, I wasn't willing to risk my sisters to save my own hide.

I sat there, trying to drown out the fear and anxiety that clawed its way up my throat. The sounds of the house were still eerie and unfamiliar. The tick of the old grandfather clock in the hallway seemed to mock me, making me wonder how much time I had left until Hammer returned.

With a shudder, I stood and went to my desk. I had homework. That's what I needed to concentrate on. Homework I could do something about. Hammer, I couldn't.

It was hours later, after I'd showered and gone to bed, before Hammer returned. I could hear him thumping through the house. He swore viciously, smashing something against a wall.

I had to bite back a whimper, trying to keep quiet and off Hammer's radar. He often came home drunk. When he did, any little noise could set him off.

Then the door to my room burst open and I gasped, clutching the covers tightly to me.

"Fuckin' bitch." Hammer stood in the doorway, a bottle of liquor grasped by the neck in one meaty fist. "You're only good for one thing. Too fuckin' skinny to make a good fuck. Too fuckin' stupid to help me." He brought the bottle to his mouth and took a hefty pull. "Since you ain't good for shit, I'm just gonna have to take out my frustrations on you." His laugh was sinister, meant to terrify me. Even knowing he wanted a response from me, I couldn't hold back my whimper of fear. He just laughed. "That's right, bitch. It's time to play."

Then the beating began, and I no longer had to worry about holding on to my small whimpers of fear. I fucking screamed.

* * *

**Scarlet**
*Three weeks later...*

"That's it, Scarlet. You're coming with us." Lemon, God bless her whole entire soul, took one look at me the second I walked into the high school building and lost her ever-loving shit. I knew what I looked like, though I'd tried to hide the damage with makeup. One side of my face was swollen where I'd landed against the nightstand, which was bad enough, but I was also pretty sure my right shoulder was dislocated. "I'm surprised the son of a bitch let you come to school today." Lemon wasn't quiet about her accusations either. Several of the kids walking past did a double take, their eyes widening before they averted their gazes and walked on past. Just like everyone else. Even my teachers. To be fair, I used every trick I could think of to fly under the radar. The last thing I wanted was for someone to try to get involved.

"He was afraid the school would send the truant officer to the house." I had no idea how Lemon and Apple had garnered my trust -- I grew up in an MC where you kept things close to the vest -- but they knew more than was safe for them. It was probably the fact that their adopted dad, Wylde, was in an MC. I'd actually heard my dad mention the Iron Tzars on occasion. He always spoke of them with respect. Whether it was because they were good men or because they represented a significant threat I had no idea, and no way of asking. Hammer had taken my phone three weeks earlier.

Lemon snorted. "Well, that's what he gets for keeping you out of school so often. You know. After he beats the ever-living fuck out of you."

"Keep your voice down, Lemon." Apple, in a rare show of assertiveness against her sister, chastised Lemon. I was grateful because the last thing I needed was for someone at school to decide it was time to call in social services.

"It's not like anyone'll do anything," Lemon shrugged, not lowering her voice at all. "She's eighteen. Which means, though she's still in high school, she's an adult. Besides, I have an idea." The younger girl looked positively vicious. "I'm going to have Wylde extend an invite to Hammer. From what you've said, it's what he wants anyway. Iron Tzars will invite him to the club for a sit-down. Wylde'll suggest he bring you since we're such close friends and will phrase it in such a way that, if he doesn't bring you, he shouldn't bother coming at all."

"Oh, that's a brilliant idea!" Apple actually clapped her hands a couple of times in excitement.

"Guys, I can't go to your clubhouse looking like this. I appreciate you trying to take care of me, but this is my mess. I'll figure it out." Then a thought occurred to me. "You said Wylde was the intel guy for Iron Tzars?"

"Yep." Lemon gave me a smirk. "And, though I'd never tell him to his face, the man is a badass on the computer."

"Maybe he could reach out to Claw at Grim Road? I could give him Dad's number."

"Let me have it." Lemon didn't hesitate or think it over. Just took out her phone, ready as I rattled off the number. "I'll take care of this right now."

"We've got class in five minutes." I shook my head. "It's not like there's anything Hammer can do while I'm at school."

Lemon leveled a look at me, her usual cockiness gone. In its place was the hard expression I usually saw with members of Grim Road. "I'll take care of it right now." This girl -- no, woman. She was a grown-ass woman. She might be the only person I'd ever met who might be able to save me. But I wasn't getting my hopes up. I certainly wasn't depending on it. I'd either have to get myself out or hope Hammer did something stupid and brought the wrath of the Grim down on himself.

I didn't see Apple or Lemon the rest of the day. Which was odd. One or the other usually found me between each class and, most especially, after school before Hammer came for me. When Hammer arrived, bursting with energy, I knew why.

"Get on, bitch," he growled. "We've got shit to do tonight."

I struggled getting on the bike because he kept rolling it forward every time I'd try to get on, putting my leg dangerously close to the hot pipe. "I'm gonna burn myself." I tried not to whine, but, honestly, I wasn't sure how much more of the abuse he dished out I could take.

Hammer shrugged. "On a hill, bitch. Can't help it if she rolls a little." The evil smirk he gave me told me he absolutely could help it and chose not to, probably trying to burn me so he could blame my injuries on my own stupidity.

Sure enough, the second I committed to mounting the bike, he rolled it again. I hissed in a breath as my leg came in contact. I only had on leggings, which provided little protection. It felt like the hot metal seared me, branding me with Hammer's mark. It was hard to bite back the cry, but I was proud I didn't make a sound. The breath I sucked in was the only indication the bastard had accomplished his goal.

He glanced over his shoulder at me, probably to judge how much I was hurting. I kept a mild expression on my face and even managed a small smile, like I was settled and ready to go. Hammer just scowled before goosing the bike and nearly had me tumbling off the back. I knew better than to bunch his colors in my fists so I braced one hand behind me and the other on his shoulder. Given my right arm was next to useless it was almost too much for me to keep my seat. With him wearing his colors in public, I knew Lemon had made good on her promise to get him invited to the Tzars clubhouse. I just hoped this didn't backfire on me. If so, I could be in worse trouble than I was now.

# Chapter Two

**Mars**

"What the fuck is goin' on with Hammer's old lady?" I leaned against the bar with my finger curled around the neck of a bottle of Bud Light. "She's right-handed and hasn't used her right arm to do anything while she's been here. Almost looks like her shoulder's dislocated. Look at the set of her shoulders."

"Really, Mars? The woman's a knockout and you're paying attention to how much she uses her dominant arm?" Rage shook his head and chuckled before taking a pull from his own beer. For some reason, the man had been pushing me toward this girl since the second she walked into the compound. Despite her belonging to another man. Which wasn't like Rage. Or anyone in Iron Tzars. Poaching on another man's territory wasn't something we ever did. That being said, he was right. The woman was a fuckin' knockout. Long, chocolate brown hair laying down her back in springy waves, creamy skin. She had a waif-like build and looked like she needed a good cheeseburger, but I definitely saw her appeal. "Besides, how do you know she's right-handed?"

I shrugged. "When she reaches for something, she tries to use her right arm, then stops and uses her left." I watched as she crossed the common room. Her smile looked forced to me, and there was a set to her jaw and a stiffness in her gait that made me think she was in pain. But that couldn't be right. "Are you sure they're married? I mean, she ain't wearin' a property patch. She's supposed to be Claw's daughter. As the daughter of Grim Road's vice president, I'd have thought her daddy'd insist she wear her man's patch." A property patch was as much for protection for the woman as it was to prevent anyone from hitting on her. I couldn't imagine Claw would allow her to *not* wear her vest with the club colors on it and the rockers telling anyone who saw her who she belonged to. Not only was she Hammer's, but she belonged to Grim Road MC.

"Maybe she ain't his woman. Maybe they're just fuckin'." That came from Breaker. He was an easy-going member of the Tzars, but also one of the deadliest. He'd just earned his patch and we all knew he'd make a great addition. He'd had my back more times than I cared to think about.

"You honestly think Claw, badass that he's supposed to be, is gonna let his baby girl be a club slut or even a steady lay to one of his patched members? He'd kick the kid's ass and ask forgiveness from his daughter after the fact. Besides, she might be legal, but the girl's still in high school. I'm surprised he let her go this far away from Grim at all, let alone without the protection of her man's property patch."

I studied Scarlet intently as she spoke briefly with Winter. Roman's old lady had pulled her aside and was chatting with her. Scarlet looked like she wanted to be anywhere but where she was. Lemon and Apple had mostly stayed by her side the whole time she'd been here, but she seemed way too uncomfortable with the whole scene. I knew Grim Road was different and preferred not to cross family with club like some did. Hell, the Tzars hadn't either until a bunch of the members and officers had acquired old ladies who were determined to take their roles seriously and help their men in any way they could. But she still shouldn't look this uncomfortable. Not if she'd been raised anywhere near that MC. Scarlet kept glancing at the door like she expected trouble, which was one more thing odd about her.

Rage grunted. "Point taken. Which raises more than a few questions."

"And makes me wonder what the fuck is goin' on." That last comment had been more musing to myself than anything else. Again, Rage grunted, his eyes narrowing at the girl in question. Apparently, he had a few musings himself.

As if Scarlet had summoned him, Hammer walked in from where he'd no doubt been pestering Sting and Brick. Hammer had aspirations of joining Iron Tzars, though he'd yet to give anyone a good reason why, or at least none that Sting or Brick cared to share with anyone. In fact, I wasn't even sure Hammer knew Sting was aware of his ties with Grim Road until he'd spoken with Roman earlier today. It was why he and Scarlet had been invited over tonight, so Hammer could meet with our president and vice president. Sting and Brick would have Wylde thoroughly vet Hammer, as well as discuss it with Rocket and Claw, the president and vice president of Grim Road. He may or may not have told Hammer that, but it was standard practice. Which might have something to do with Hammer's bad mood.

"Come on, Scarlet," he snapped. "We're leaving." He glanced around the place like he was looking for someone in particular. Then he muttered seemingly to himself, but I was pretty sure he meant for me and Rage to hear. "Fuckin' bastard wouldn't know a good member if one nailed him in the ass."

Rage and I looked at each other. Apparently, Sting hadn't immediately taken him on. I could have told the asshole he wouldn't. Being a member of Iron Tzars wasn't a trivial thing. We had blood on our hands. Literally. And as long as there were people who needed killing, we were up for the task. Also, becoming a member was a "for life" deal. No one left the club. The only member I knew of who had was our former president. Warlock had been accepted into Black Reign MC at the requested demand of their president. No one said no to El Diablo if he really wanted something.

"I'm just about finished," Scarlet said softly.

"You're finished," Hammer snapped. "We're leaving." He took a hold of her right upper arm and yanked her after him. Scarlet winced and gasped in pain, but quickly covered it with a blank expression. Instantly, both me and Rage were on our feet moving in their direction. Breaker was hot on our heels.

"Take it easy there, hoss." Atlas beat us to him. He had a smile on his face, but I could see the anger inside Atlas simmering underneath the surface. Mainly because I felt much the same way. Only I didn't bother to hide behind a thin veneer of civility.

"You're hurting her." I couldn't stop the growl as we advanced.

Hammer stopped and glared at us but didn't let go of Scarlet's arm. He was an intimidating man, but from what I'd seen of him, he was more bluster than action. He might talk a big talk, but he wasn't going to be anxious to take on me, Rage, Breaker and Atlas all together. "She got a fuckin' flu shot today. If she'd take some acetaminophen and ibuprofen like I fuckin' told her to, she wouldn't be sore." He jerked Scarlet's arm again. This time, she schooled her features, not seeming to mind the way he manhandled her.

"Bye, Winter. It was so wonderful to meet you." Scarlet waved at Roman's woman with a smile.

"It was nice to meet you too, Scarlet. I hope you can join us this weekend for girls' night out."

Scarlet glanced up at that shit, Hammer, as if his decision dictated whether or not she could go with the other old ladies. Hammer gave her a hard look and a slight shake of his head and Scarlet's face fell.

"I'm afraid I'm not going to be able to make it. Please tell Lemon and Apple I'll see them at school." Hammer tugged her arm again and nearly pulled Scarlet off her feet. She winced slightly but held in her cries when I knew she was hurting. "Bye, guys."

Hammer didn't slow down or give her time to catch up. Scarlet stumbled after him, and more than once I was sure she'd fall on her face. Each time, Hammer held her up by that arm. Each time he did, she winced in pain. I could see her jaw clench. That bastard didn't acknowledge she might be hurt. Rather, he shoved her onto the back of his bike. Scarlet didn't look the least bit steady, or able to hold on to him. When he took off, she nearly tumbled off the back before gaining her balance. Judging by the way he smirked back at Scarlet, Hammer had done it on purpose.

"What the fuck was that all about?" I muttered my question, not really expecting an answer.

"Not sure, but I think someone needs to tell Claw about this." Rage had an expression on his face as hard as I knew my own expression was.

I snorted. "You gonna do it?" Yeah. I could imagine how that conversation would work. Given that Claw was the vice president of a club rumored to be full of black ops soldiers, his temper had the potential to get more than a few men killed. My guess was it probably wouldn't bode well for the messenger.

"I'm not telling Claw." Me and Rage still watched the bike speeding off into the night.

"You're afraid to tell Claw." The barb was

automatic when I wasn't in the teasing mood. Rage and I always threw shade at each other. It was just how we rolled.

"Damned right I'm afraid to tell Claw. If it were just a guy from his club mistreating a woman, I wouldn't give a shit. But I ain't too chickenshit to admit I'm being a coward. I tell the vice president of Grim Road I think the man who's fuckin' his daughter might be abusing her too? *And* we just let him roll right on out of this fucking compound with his daughter on the back of his fuckin' bike? Yeah. I'll be part of any group you want to take to go after this bastard, but no fuckin' thanks. Get Sting to tell him. Or Brick or Roman. Above my fuckin' paygrade."

"Point taken." I moved toward my bike, climbing on and readying to take off. "Go talk to Sting, so he can give Claw the heads-up."

"You goin' after her? I'll back you up and worry about the other later."

"I can't let this go on. We'll need more than two of us if he's not alone. I don't think I'll have a problem with him, but he's a big fucker. Get Roman to send me some more backup before you follow." I started my bike and rolled out.

It took a few minutes to catch up to the little fuck, but once I did, I stayed back, putting a couple of cars between us. Hammer didn't seem to pay me any attention as he zigzagged between cars headed from Evansville to a little place just outside the city. I kept pace, but kept my riding sane and within the law, but also made sure to keep traffic between us. I didn't much care if Hammer got caught for reckless driving. That would make this all a whole lot easier. I just didn't want him to get Scarlet killed in the process.

More than once, I saw Scarlet lose her grip on

him, and I thought she'd go flying. He seemed to be deliberately goosing the bike in an attempt to make her fall. I saw him laugh when the girl nearly tumbled to the pavement. He was terrorizing her, enjoying the power play. I could only imagine how this was gonna play out once Claw heard about this. The question was, could I keep tailing the bastard without him knowing?

# Chapter Three

## Scarlet

We hadn't been home too long when there was a knock at the door. Hammer had hit the bottle the second we walked in. Well, after he backhanded me, he hit the bottle.

"Get your ass in your Goddamned room and fuckin' stay there." Hammer gave me a threatening look. He needn't have bothered. I recognized that particular tone of voice as one I'd better not ignore. And I'd better obey immediately.

He waited until I fled into my bedroom off the tiny living room before he answered the door. There was a pause before Hammer greeted the visitor like an old friend.

"Hey, man! Mars, right? How you doin'?"

"Was just concerned about your girl. She seemed like she could use a doctor. You know, Iron Tzars has a club doc. Stitches could take a look at her if you like."

"Your doc's road name's Stitches?" Hammer barked out a laugh. "Ain't no way in hell I'm lettin' a doc named Stitches touch Scarlet."

"You wanted to be part of Iron Tzars. Right?"

"Don't mean I want no guy named Stitches patchin' me up. We're fine here."

"You sure? Because Iron Tzars believes in protecting women and children. If there's even the chance she needs medical attention, you should take my offer of help."

OK, Hammer wasn't going to like that. He never took criticism well. But there was no way he was going to let anyone look at any injuries I had. Especially not someone with real medical training.

"I told you. It was just a fuckin' flu shot. She'll be

fine tomorrow. So how about you mind your own fuckin' business, and I'll mind mine." I could almost see the congenial smile on Hammer's face when he was actually seething. He did that. Smiled to make any perceived disrespect seem less.

"Take it easy. I'm only concerned. If you're serious about being a member of Tzars, you have to know we look out for each other and our families."

"I can take care of one small woman. Her daddy gave her to me because he knew I could protect her." That nearly broke me down to tears. I couldn't imagine my father knew how Hammer treated me, but I was biding my time until I could be sure he couldn't harm my sisters. I heard more bikes approach and glanced out the window to see two more members of Iron Tzars MC roll up behind Mars's bike.

"Gonna need to see her to make sure she's good, man. Nothing personal. It's what my club does."

"Well, she's asleep. Took some fuckin pain pills and went to fuckin' bed. I ain't wakin' her up just 'cause you want to see her. You tryin' to bang my woman, motherfucker?" OK, that didn't sound like he cared if he disrespected the other man or not. Which told me Hammer thought this Mars was an actual threat. Hammer was a big, intimidating man. Solid, bulky muscle. I thought my dad was grooming him to be Grim Road's enforcer or sergeant at arms, but that was club business. And as far as I knew Hammer wasn't an actual patched member yet. It was a forgone conclusion he would be, though. Or Dad wouldn't have given me to him.

"All right, all right. She left with you willingly, so I'll let it go. But these are things Sting's gonna want to investigate."

"Do what you have to. Maybe I don't wanna be

part of your fuckin' club now. I mean, if you're gonna be all up in my business -- or tryin' to steal my woman."

"That's your choice. I suggest you talk to Brick. As vice president he'll tell you this is standard. One of our women is sick or hurting, we check on her."

"Well, good Goddamned thing she ain't one of your women, now, ain't it?"

I heard the door slam and I moved to the far side of the room away from the window. If he thought I was trying to slip out or spy on him he'd use that as his excuse to beat me. I'd learned to huddle in the farthest corner of the bedroom if I wanted to have a shot at an uneventful night.

Surprisingly, Hammer didn't immediately come after me. With any luck, he was too busy worrying about what Mars would do to bother with me. Or he'd start drinking. I really didn't want him to start drinking.

I'd never been lucky.

\* \* \*

**Scarlet**

School the next day was uncomfortable as shit. Hammer hadn't been drunk enough to make mistakes like he did the last time and mark my face. Oh, no. He knew better. Hammer might be many things, but stupid he wasn't. He learned from his mistakes. The first thing he'd done when he entered my bedroom last night was to put my shoulder back in place. It had hurt worse going back in than it had coming out.

I avoided Apple and Lemon. Neither girl could do anything to help and there was every possibility I'd only get them hurt. Or worse. Anything Hammer could use to keep me under his control, he would. If that meant killing an innocent, I had no doubt he would. My dad kept everything he could about Grim Road from me, but I knew they were all killers. Every single one of them. They were casual about it. Secrets floated around that compound like ghosts and I knew more than my fair share.

I was about to leave the building and head to where Hammer always picked me up. He got angry if I wasn't waiting on him, so I hurried as fast as I could. Which, given how sore I was and the fact that I was pretty sure I had a couple of broken ribs, wasn't very fast.

"Scarlet!" I cringed. I'd chew my own arm off if that wasn't Lemon. "Scarlet, wait!"

"I can't, Lemon." I glanced over my shoulder at her. The last thing I wanted was for Hammer to see me with Lemon again. I needed him to think I'd severed ties with her, or at least, for him to think we weren't close. Which, I guess we weren't. I hadn't known her and Apple long. "I have to go."

"We can help you, Scarlet." Lemon grabbed hold of my left hand. I hadn't missed that she was careful of my right arm. Had she known how badly I'd been hurt?

"No, Lemon. All you'll do is get hurt. I need to go."

"Stop." Lemon hissed her command and tightened her grip on my hand. "Just… *stop*."

I was getting desperate. I figured I only had a couple of minutes before Hammer pulled up at the school. I needed to get going. "I can't. I have to go. He'll get angry if…"

"I can't help you if you keep going back to him, Scarlet. Come with me and Apple. Stitches can take care of any injuries you have, and the guys will protect you."

It was almost more than I could take. One tear leaked from my eye, but I batted it away. "He'll hurt everyone he can that I love if I leave. Starting with my sisters back in Florida." Lemon sucked in a breath, her features hardening. She might be only seventeen, but Lemon was going to command all she surveyed. Soon. God help anyone who went against her when she grew into her attitude.

"The Tzars will protect your sisters. All you have to do is tell us where they are, and Wylde can make sure they're safe."

"Wylde isn't your president."

"No, but he's the motherfucking tech guy. He'll take out anyone in that fucking club of your father's he has to, to keep you and your sisters safe. So will Sting and the rest of the guys, but Wylde can do it digitally. Nothing can be traced back to the club or you."

I sighed, scrubbing a hand over my face. "It's not that simple."

"Sure it is," she persisted. "Come home with us. Let me and Apple take care of everything."

I should have known Apple wasn't far away from Lemon. As different as the twins' personalities were, they were inseparable. Apple put her hand gently on my shoulder before giving me a worried look. "Lemon's right, Scarlet. We can help you."

I gave her a grateful but wistful smile. "I know you think you can. But you can't. No one can. I can't risk my sisters. If he finds out about any of this, he'll do something horrible to them." I could see Lemon processing this, wanting to say something else, but I didn't have time for a conversation. I gently extracted myself from both of their grips. "I have to go." Then I hurried outside to meet Hammer.

He was waiting by the curb where he always picked me up. One look at his face and I wished I'd taken Lemon up on her offer to take me back to the Iron Tzars clubhouse. I whimpered and tried to back away, but he shook his head. A warning.

Trembling, terrified beyond belief, I climbed on behind him. When Hammer took off, I could almost hear my death knell. I had to hold on. For my sisters. I had to do what he wanted so I could protect them.

When we got back to the little house he'd rented, he got off the bike, then yanked my upper arm so he practically dragged me off and inside. Where no one could see us. The second he shut the door, he gripped my hair, and pulled me close so he could stare down into my face.

"What'd you tell those bitches at school? Huh? I know you told them something. They both gave me looks that shoulda sent me six feet under."

"I didn't tell them anything, Hammer. They ain't stupid. I didn't *have* to say anything."

He backhanded me then, sending me flying across the floor. "Stupid cunt! If you cost me my chance to get into the Tzars, I'll fucking gut your sisters while you watch. Then I'll skin them alive."

"I heard your conversation with that man from Iron Tzars." I was angry, bordering on reckless now. I had to be careful, but it was hard. I'd had to control my temper for so long I wasn't sure how much more I could manage. "If you don't get in, it's not because of me. It's because you refused to let them see me. Besides, if my dad knew what you were doing here with another club, *and* what you were doing to me he'd kill you!" I was hurt. Hurt and angry. I was so tired of being so fucking helpless! I'd never been in this situation in my life. My mother might have died when my sisters were born, but my dad had been there for us. Even when he couldn't be physically with me, he'd made sure I had someone watching over us. Taking care of me. He'd treated me like a princess.

Hammer just laughed, the sound sinister and foreboding. "Claw is the one who gave you to me, bitch. You honestly think he cares what I do with my own woman?"

"I'm not your woman," I spat out. "I'll never be your woman!"

He backhanded me again, harder this time. I tasted blood as the room spun and my vision blurred.

"You *are* my woman. Only reason I ain't fucked you is because you ain't worth fuckin'. At least, not yet." He gave me a maniacal smile, one that had me wishing I'd kept my mouth shut. "Once I've worked you over, though…" He shrugged. "Maybe I'll let the guys in Grim have a go at you first. Then I'll see if I want what's left. You know. After they break you in."

No matter how much I knew better, no matter how hard I tried not to show fear, I whimpered. The implication was clear. He'd beat me half to death. Then he'd do whatever he wanted with me.

I hated being this helpless. My daddy was the vice president of one of the most powerful motorcycle clubs in the country. Sure, they kept on the down low and never wore their colors outside the compound, but Claw was a powerful man. My dad loved me! All I had to do was tell him --

Hammer really did laugh then. Actually threw back his head and laughed. "Who do you think gave you to me? Huh? And your momma?" Hammer shook his head. "I wasn't there myself cause I ain't an old fart like your old man, but word is he's the one who killed her. Right after your sisters were born cause at least one of 'em wasn't a boy. He was so enraged he killed her before he realized what he was doin'."

I shook my head. "You're lying." The words came out a whisper. I didn't believe a word of this bullshit. But part of me wondered. My dad loved me. I knew this. He might be shifty in what he allowed me to know about Grim Road, but he'd never keep something like that from me. Right?

"Am I? You honestly think he doesn't lie to you all the fuckin' time? Why would he let me take you so far away from him if he cared what I did to you? No. He's just been waitin' to take his revenge on you for bein' born a girl. And your sisters? Yeah. They'll be next. Assumin' I don't just take them myself. Might give them the same as I'm gonna give you. And Claw won't give a good Goddamn." He held his hands out to his sides before dropping them. "Here I am. Claw's revenge. Prepare yourself, you little puke. Tonight, you're gettin' what you've deserved a long fuckin' time. Take it like a good girl, and I'll spare your sisters. Maybe."

Despite his words, Hammer didn't give me more than the two seconds it took him to cross the room to me. Then he gave me the beating of my life.

After he left me broken and bleeding in my room, I lay there for a long time. The sun was still up but setting fast. Shadows started lengthening against the walls and the light outside dimmed.

I couldn't call my dad. It was too late to be sensible and go to Lemon. I had no phone anyway. No car. No way to escape. After tonight, I had no doubt I'd never leave this house again. Not alive at any rate. There was nowhere to go.

No way out.

Except there was. I'd prepared weeks ago. I just

needed to get outside to the backyard without Hammer seeing me. I remember hearing his bike bellowing as he sped off after he'd finished beating me. Though I'd passed out, I didn't think he'd come back yet. It was still partially daylight, and he usually wouldn't come home until the wee hours of the morning. Then he'd be so drunk he'd be lucky to make it home at all.

It took a while, but I managed to crawl to the bedroom door. I rested before carefully opening it to peek out. The house was dark. Still. Lifeless.

A sob broke free. Instead of fear, though, all I felt was peace. This was happening. When I was done, Hammer wouldn't be able to hurt me anymore. The thought was enough to give me the courage to open the door farther and crawl out into the living room. Sure enough, Hammer was nowhere to be found. Thank God.

With a muffled groan, I managed to make it to my feet. Bracing myself against the wall, I took one careful, tentative step. Pain shot through my left hip where he'd kicked me several times. I thought it was just bruised, but there was a good possibility he'd dislocated or broken my hip. It held my weight but hurt like a mother. Still, I managed to make it to the kitchen and the back door.

Almost there. Just a little farther.

I wasn't sure what I should be feeling, but my mind was at peace. Nothing beyond putting one foot in front of the next passed through my brain. Blessed emptiness. Calm.

My sisters' faces came to me then. They were only ten but already giving everyone hell. Lemon reminded me a lot of Sunshine and Rainbow. They both thought they could fix the world. Because our father had told us we could. Grim Road could. That's what Grim did. They took care of the bad guys. Except it seemed like there were bad guys in their ranks they were unaware of.

Well. I couldn't get that information to my dad. Hammer had taken me away from home and confiscated any means I had of contacting anyone who might be willing to help in Grim. Even if he hadn't, I wasn't sure there was anyone there whom I could trust other than my sisters. If I told the wrong person I was in trouble, Sunshine and Rainbow might pay the price.

No. It was better like this.

With hands more steady than I'd have thought, I pulled a chair with me to a tree in the backyard. I positioned it at just the right angle before climbing up onto it and reaching above me to the limb almost out of reach. I checked to make sure everything was secure…

Then did the only thing I knew might set me free. I only hoped my sisters would forgive me. Just before blackness dotted the edges of my vision, I heard the roar of a motorcycle. I hoped this would be over before Hammer found me. God help me if it wasn't.

# Chapter Four

**Mars**

"I'm telling you we need to go *now*!" Lemon was nothing if not persistent when she wanted something, but this was a record even for her. She was all up in Wylde's business, raging and more insistent than I'd ever seen her, and that was saying something.

"Honey, we don't have any reason to go barging into that house." Danica looked sympathetic but also helpless. I got the feeling she believed her younger sister when she came running full speed into the clubhouse to Wylde's office, but wasn't sure how to go about fixing the problem.

"Dani, we followed her to the house. That son of a bitch is *beating* her! Right this second!"

"She's right." Breaker trotted into the room. Likely, Lemon had jumped off the bike before it had fully stopped and gotten a head start on Breaker who had to shut off and park his bike. "I didn't want to leave her, but I had Lemon..." Breaker looked like he'd been gutted. Torn between saving one young woman or putting the sister of Wylde's old lady in danger, he'd gone the conservative route. Which Lemon, no doubt, would give him hell about later. The fact that she wasn't now told me -- and everyone else -- how upset she really was.

"Why didn't you call us?" I snapped my question with a bit more force than I should, but I had a sick feeling in my gut. I was already on my feet and heading toward the door when Brick grabbed my arm and halted me. "We could have been on the way there already."

"You've been out there, Mars. There's no service. Once I started, I was just trying to get Lemon back to the clubhouse."

Brick picked up a radio and tossed it to me, barking out orders on the way out the door. "Mars, Breaker, Rage, and Stitches. I want the four of you on the way to that fucker's place double time. Clutch, need you in the Expedition with Stitches. You do not leave Scarlet there under any circumstances. If you see that little shit Hammer, end him."

Me and Breaker snagged earwigs and external mics for our radios from one of the shelves in Wylde's office. It would make it easier to communicate with the rest of the club as necessary. Then we hurried to our bikes. Rage met us in the garage and the three of us hurried off, not waiting on Clutch and Stitches in the cage.

I tried to concentrate on the road while anger and stress beat at me. I'd been on more missions like this than I could count. Not all of them had ended well. Images of broken and dead bodies of women and girls flashed through my head, and I needed to rage at the injustice. But I didn't have that luxury at the moment. I had to get to Scarlet.

She was a lovely young woman, and so fragile-looking. I'd kind of been infatuated with her since I'd first laid eyes on her but had tried not to think about it. I know Lemon and Apple adored her and, though I'd only seen her once, there was something about her that snagged my attention. I knew there was something going on with that son of a bitch Hammer, but how anyone could willingly hurt that young woman was beyond me.

"Fuck!" I screamed once as I sped down the twisting, winding road. The house Hammer had rented was only ten minutes from the clubhouse, but it seemed to take an eternity. More than once I thought I was going to lose traction. Had there been gravel or dirt from logging, I was sure I'd have laid the fucking bike down.

When I pulled up in front of the little house, I got the eeriest feeling. It was like *déjà vu*. Like I'd been here before…

I shivered. No. This would not be like before. Scarlet would be alive. Maybe beaten and broken, but alive.

I jumped from my bike, not bothering to make sure I got the kickstand secured. As I sprinted to the house, I heard it crash to the ground but couldn't make myself care. The only thing I had to do was get inside and get Scarlet out. She would be alive.

*She would be alive, Goddamnit!*

Kicking in the door, I was greeted with silence. It was the kind of silence that made the hair on the back of my neck stand at attention. There were a few pieces of furniture turned over, but I couldn't see much else in the dimly lit interior. Something was wrong. Very wrong.

I heard my brothers pull up in front of the house, the roar of the pipes on their bikes loud. The light was dimming in the evening. There was barely enough to see inside the house. It took precious seconds to search the interior. There had obviously been an altercation of some kind. There was blood in what I could only assume was Scarlet's room, judging by the underwear strewn over the floor. Not much, but splatters and a few drops here and there. Other than that, there was precious little in the room that said it was hers. No pictures. No trinkets. There didn't seem to be anything of Hammer either.

There were only a few articles of clothing in the closet. One pair of shoes. Her backpack. But Scarlet wasn't there.

By the time I exited her room, Breaker and Rage were searching the rest of the house. My heart pounded in my chest, making my ears roar. I shook my head, trying to rid myself of the panic threatening to push its way through to my mind. I broke out in a sweat, and it was hard to put one foot in front of another.

"She's not in here." Rage sounded calm, but I could hear the underlying tension in his voice. "Check out back."

Breaker was the first out the door. He moved a few steps into the yard, then stopped dead in his tracks. "Fucking hell…"

I pushed past him to see a sight I never wanted to see. Scarlet. Hanging from a tree in the corner of the yard. I knew it was her like I knew my own name.

"Get Stitches!" I yelled on the run, needing to get to her. *Please, don't let it be too late…*

I pulled out the knife at my hip with one hand while I wrapped my arms around her legs with the other, trying to lessen the tension on the rope in case there was still a chance she was alive. I stumbled against the chair lying on its side underneath her. There was little doubt she'd done this to herself. How much Hammer had been involved remained to be seen, but once I found him, I was going to make him pay. Slowly. Painfully. He might not have killed her, but this was his fault as sure as if he'd put a gun to her head and pulled the trigger. It was also my fault. Because I'd stood outside on that fucking porch and hadn't pushed my way inside to make sure Scarlet didn't need help the day I'd followed her and Hammer from the clubhouse.

Reaching the rope with my knife was going to be

hard while I had my arms around her. I needn't have worried, though. Rage was at my side, snagging the knife from my fist and cutting Scarlet down.

"Lay her on the ground." Stitches hurried to us, a jump kit slung over his shoulder as he entered the yard.

I did as he ordered, laying her carefully on the plush grass, I saw the bruising to her face and arms. The rope burns around her neck. I'm sure there were more injuries, but I couldn't seem to look away from her face. I willed her to open her eyes, but she didn't.

Then Stitches was pushing me out of the way while Rage started CPR. Stitches hooked up an AED to her as I watched. He was barking orders, but I couldn't understand what he was saying. It was like his voice came from a deep well. Distorted. Vague.

Stitches called out something and Rage stopped doing chest compressions. I tried to force my way to Scarlet, to continue to try to save her life when it felt like Rage was giving up. The other man held me back.

Her body twitched slightly before Stitches put his fingers at her throat. Checking for a pulse? When he didn't start CPR again immediately, I howled with rage. I would find Hammer and kill the motherfucker. Then I'd go after her father and Grim Road.

"Get him under control," someone snapped. I honestly couldn't tell who.

The next thing I knew, Rage and Breaker grabbed me and pulled me farther away from Scarlet. I fought, throwing fists and lashing out in a blind rage. I had to get back to her. To save her.

"Mars, stop!" Rage had his arms wrapped around my neck in a choke hold. He wasn't trying to cut off my air or the circulation to my brain so I passed out. He was merely trying to pull me out of the hell inside my mind I'd stumbled into. What he didn't realize, and what I had no way of explaining, was that this rage wasn't the result of my past. At least, not solely. Somehow, Scarlet had become my present nightmare. Her. Not the ghosts from my pasts. "This isn't helping her, brother."

Rage tightened his hold on me, making dark spots swim in my vision. Slowly, the fight seeped out of me until all I could do was breathe. The big man loosened his hold fractionally. Probably trying to see if I was going to lose my mind again. I could have told him I had very little left of my mind to lose. All I could see was Scarlet's lifeless body...

She sucked in a breath. Her eyes fluttered open. Then she whimpered and turned her head away from us.

"It's all right, honey." Stitches tried to soothe her, but he was distracted as he started an IV in the bend of her elbow. "We're gonna take care of you."

"Please," she pleaded weakly. "No more. Let me go."

"No one's gonna hurt you anymore, Scarlet. We're gonna take you back with us, and you'll be safe."

"Never... be safe... again." She let out a broken sob, her voice scratchy from the constriction of the noose.

"Once I get these fluids started, we'll move her to the Expedition. Take her to my clinic in the compound so I can assess what needs to happen next." He continued to work with the IV, taping it down before spiking a bag and connecting it to the port in her arm. "She's talking and seems aware of her surroundings. Must have found her seconds after this happened." He didn't specify that she'd hanged herself or what exactly the "this" was, but we all knew. My guess was that Stitches was trying to push all that aside and get us all to focus on the immediate problem: Scarlet's physical well-being. The mental damage we could worry about later. Right now, though, we needed to get her out of here.

"Honey, do you know where Hammer went?" Breaker knelt on the other side of her, stroking her hair back. I growled at him, heedless of Rage's hold on my neck or that I might terrify the young woman on the ground.

"Get away from her!" I yelled at the Breaker, trying to lunge out of Rage's hold but the other man held fast.

"Calm the fuck down, Mars." Rage was at my ear, not raising his voice. The logical part of my mind knew they were right. I needed to get a fucking grip. But I also needed to get to Scarlet. Only then would I be able to get control of my baser instincts. "You're gonna scare the bejesus outta her."

"I said get away from her!" I was beyond caring. I needed the other man away from Scarlet and I needed to be the man at her side. I'd already failed her by not pushing my way inside that fucking house when I'd followed them after that fucking party. I wasn't ever leaving her side again. Not as long as I was able.

Scarlet's head turned toward the sound of my voice and our eyes met. I felt my breath catch in my chest as I looked into her clear hazel eyes, so full of fear and pain. I knew that look well. I had seen it in the eyes of so many women before her. Women who had been beaten, abused, used and discarded by men who had no right to touch them. Men I'd happily killed with a fucking smile on my face. It was those women who haunted me. I knew in the pit of my soul, Scarlet would be imprinted on me more than any of the ones before her.

"Please," she whispered, her voice breaking. "Let… me…" She took a shuddering breath and a small sob broke free. "… die…"

"Like bloody hell!" I finally shrugged off Rage and moved to kneel beside Scarlet, stroking the hair off her forehead. "You're ain't fuckin' dyin'."

A tear streaked from her eye down her temple to her hairline. That one single tear felt like a dagger to my heart and I had to focus all my concentration on those glassy green and gold eyes.

She took a shuddering breath, then a sob escaped. "I don't want to die." That little hopeless confession was all I could take.

I pulled Scarlet into my arms and held her tightly against me. "You ain't gonna die. I won't let you. Never let you die. You're safe. I've got you." My words all ran together.

"Please don't make me go back to him. I can't. Can't keep going…" Her voice was so thin and full of pain I clutched her to me and threw my head back and roared. She was weak and had to be in pain, but she bunched her fists in my colors and hung on like her life depended on it.

"Let me have her, Mars." Stitches tried to pull her from me, but Scarlet whimpered and pulled herself closer, burying her face in my chest and clinging tightly.

"Get your Goddamned hands off her!" In my mind, Scarlet was Scarlet but… not. She was one of dozens of women I'd come across over the years and couldn't save. Only this one wasn't dead. Almost, but we'd saved her.

"Please… no…" Scarlet whimpered and drew in

another shuddering breath.

"Is he with us?" That was Rage. He, more than anyone, might know what I was going through. And I knew he wasn't talking to me. Even if he was, I wasn't sure I could answer him. I was caught between the present and past. I knew it, but couldn't seem to do anything about it.

"Maybe? I don't know. She wants him and he's protecting her, so I'm not sure how much it matters. But we gotta get her some medical care."

I shook my head, trying to clear it. I could feel sweat trickle down my face. The night breeze chilled my skin and I tucked Scarlet tighter against me, closing my arms around her as much as I could to protect her from the cold. She whimpered, but burrowed closer and clutched me even tighter.

"Fuck," I gasped, shaking my head again. I had to pull myself out of this if I was going to help Scarlet. She needed me back in the here and now. So did my brothers. "Fuck."

"Here we go." Rage moved in front of me, gripping my shoulder. "You back with us, buddy?"

I nodded though I wasn't altogether certain I'd shaken off the pain this panic attack had brought back. It had been a cross between the present and the past, and I still wasn't sure if I'd completely fought my way free.

"Good. Can you stand?" Stitches had a syringe in his hand he injected into the tubing of the IV he'd started.

"We need to get her to the hospital." Breaker stood above me and I tilted my face up to him.

"No hospital," she whimpered. "Please."

"But--"

"If we take her to a hospital, they're gonna ask

questions." Stitches finished and helped me to my feet. I was able to let him, though my instinct was screaming at me to make him leave us the fuck alone. "They'll want to put her on a psych ward if she's medically clear and I'm sure she doesn't want to have to explain anything. Let's get her back to the clubhouse and I'll check her over. I'm not going to let her *not* get the care she needs if she's physically injured beyond what I can take care of."

"Get her in the Expedition." Rage urged me back inside the house and through the front door. I carried Scarlet, not even considering giving her off to someone else. Breaker and took the lead, scanning the area before Rage stepped out the door ahead of me. I had no idea where Hammer was, but it was a good fucking thing he wasn't here. Because I needed to kill, and I didn't want to do it in front of Scarlet. It would only terrify her, and she absolutely could not be afraid of me.

"All clear." Rage hurried to the cage and opened the backdoor. He protected Scarlet's head as I climbed in with her still in my arms. My bike was upright in front of the SUV, but I barely noticed. Clutch must have righted it. In fact, he conferred with Stitches, then climbed on my bike and took off with Breaker and Rage. Stitches slid behind the wheel and turned to look at me.

"You guys OK?"

I grunted but didn't say anything else. I was still struggling but holding the moment. I rested my chin on top of Scarlet's head as Stitches nodded once, then started up the truck and took off. Back toward the Iron Tzars clubhouse and home.

"Everythin's gonna be all right, Scarlet," I murmured. "It's all gonna be fine."

"I don't want to go back to Hammer," she whispered. "I know it's what my father wanted, but I can't do this anymore."

"Don't give a fuck what your daddy wants," I snapped. "You're stayin' with me. I'm gonna protect you from now on. No matter what." I tried to keep my voice soft, for her ears alone. But I was all too aware of the other men in the truck. Didn't matter. They'd all find out soon enough anyway. Scarlet was staying with me.

She looked up at me and we locked gazes for a long time. Scarlet seemed to be looking for something I had no idea how to give her. There was no give in me right now, and I knew I'd do everything in my power to keep her with me. Once my rational brain kicked back in, maybe I could let her go her own way. But I didn't think so.

When we pulled into the compound gate, she finally gave me a slow nod. "All right. I'll stay with you."

I grunted. "Damned straight, honey. Damned straight."

# Chapter Five

**Scarlet**

The second I agreed to stay with Mars, an immense peace enveloped me. I'd only seen the guy a couple of times, but the way he held me, refused to let me go, it was comforting. It shouldn't be. I didn't know this guy, and hadn't I just tried to kill myself to get away from a man who refused to let me go? This felt... different.

Mars carried me into the clubhouse and through the common room. Surprisingly, there were only a few club members and no club whores. There was usually one or two hanging around, even when the place was filled with old ladies. I'd only ever seen the place jovial and welcoming. Now, everything was silent.

Sting, the president of Iron Tzars, approached me, his old lady, Iris, at his side. "I'm sorry, Scarlet." His voice was soft, but his face was blank.

Iris looked like she'd been gutted. She reached out and stroked the hair from my forehead. "I'm so sorry. We should have helped you before..." Her voice broke and she swallowed, shaking her head like she couldn't bear to voice what had happened.

"I've been trying to talk to Claw since Rage followed you home yesterday." Sting scrubbed a hand over his face. "The guy I spoke with, Wolf, said he was otherwise occupied. He was supposed to reach out to him in the field, but I got the impression his team was unreachable except at certain intervals."

"Don't think it matters much." I hadn't really meant to say that out loud, but it was a bitter, sore spot. I still hoped Hammer was messing with me, but considering I hadn't spoken to my dad since we'd left, I was afraid he wasn't.

"If that's the case, we want to know that too." Sting shook his head a couple of times, like he wasn't sure what to say or do. "I'm sorry we let you down, Scarlet."

"It wasn't your fault." I still clung to Mars, but I managed to look at Sting and Iris. Tears flowed down Iris's face freely while Sting looked hard as nails.

Sting turned his head. Brick was standing next to him, a hard, angry expression on his face. To be fair, the few times I'd seen Brick, I'd never seen him anything other than very intense unless he was looking at his woman, Serelda. Then Sting seemed to come to a decision. "I'm done being nice. We talk to the highest-ranking person currently present at Grim Road. Now. I don't care if it's a fuckin' prospect." Sting's voice was low and menacing, his anger coming through in spades.

"Give me ten minutes." Wylde spoke softly. "I'll get someone on the phone." I'd met Wylde the one time I was at the Tzars clubhouse and laughed when Apple told me tales of him being a snarky, sarcastic riot of fun. Now he was very subdued. He looked as intense and angry as the rest of them.

"What if he says he doesn't care? What if he says I'm supposed to be with Hammer? It could cause you guys more trouble than I'm worth."

Mars growled and squeezed me tighter. God, I could barely breathe! It also hurt my bruised chest. But, Goddamned if it didn't keep me from shattering. Just like before.

"I don't give a good Goddamn what he wants, Scarlet," Mars growled. "If he's that kind of man, if Grim Road is the kind of club to condone the abuse of a woman until she felt like she had no way out, then they all need to fuckin' die."

I whimpered again, shaking my head. "No. That's my family."

"A family who pushed you into the arms of a fuckin' monster." Mars sounded livid, but his arms were still tight around me, like I was as much his lifeline as he was mine.

"Everybody just calm down a minute." Blaze was obviously trying to infuse some calm into the situation because it seemed like everyone was about to lose their shit. "We need to talk with someone at Grim Road before we assume their vice president is allowing his daughter to be abused. Eagle. You know Rocket. Do you know Claw?"

"Yeah." Eagle was leaned against the edge of the bar. His woman, Nyla, stood next to him, her arms wrapped around his middle as she watched everything going on in silence. "This isn't something I'd have thought he'd condone. Either Hammer brought her here to isolate her from the rest of Grim, or Rocket and Claw aren't the men I thought they were."

Blaze gave a slow nod. "Rocket's daughter is with Doc at Salvation's Bane MC in Palm Beach, Florida. I'll have Stitches reach out to him and see what he can tell us about Grim Road. Get it from the perspective of a man who took the Grim Road president's daughter for his old lady."

"Good." Sting looked like he felt better about the whole situation but still had lines of anger clearly visible on his face.

"I hope this is all just one big Goddamned misunderstanding," Blaze muttered.

"We'll know soon enough. Once Wylde gets them on the fuckin' phone."

It took eight minutes for Wylde to deliver, though it wasn't Claw he got ahold of but Dom. The sergeant at arms for Grim Road.

"What do you mean Hammer is abusing Scarlet? That can't be right." Dom didn't sound angry, but I knew better. His calm was always icy. Steady. I'd grown up around the man and knew he was positively livid.

"You callin' her a liar? The vice president's daughter?" Wylde did the talking while the rest of the Iron Tzars, including Sting, were silent in the background, listening intently. Sting and Brick were shoulder to shoulder standing over the phone Wylde had on speaker.

"I ain't callin' her nothin' cause I got no idea what the fuck's goin' on. I know Claw let Hammer take her north to get her away from Grim Road. For a while."

"I get he wanted to keep her out of danger, but why did he send her with someone who'd hurt her?" Wylde was still trying to play diplomat when I knew his personality was anything but diplomatic. I hated that I'd caused these people so much trouble. Especially when a club like Grim Road was involved. Some of the Tzars might know men from Grim, but they had no idea what they were really dealing with, and I couldn't tell them because I didn't really know anything concrete.

"Fuck that," Brick growled, interrupting Wylde. "If Grim Road allows this kind of treatment to its women, we may need to clean fuckin' house."

"You don't get to threaten us, Brick. Not unless you want a war."

"And you don't get to mistreat women in your care!" Brick looked and sounded ready to explode. "Christ, Dom! She's barely eighteen! Stitches says she's been beaten repeatedly over a long time. There are bruises in various stages of healing. He's also pretty sure she's got a dislocated shoulder. Maybe broken ribs. She says this was Hammer's doing, though we haven't had a chance to get the whole story."

"Scarlet knew all she had to do was call the club if she was in danger."

"He took my phone," I said faintly. "I couldn't call."

There was a pause. "Scarlet? You good?"

I looked up at Mars and he raised his chin in approval. I guess he liked that I was checking in with him before I answered. And, really, I had no idea why I had. "Be honest with him, honey," he murmured. "We've got your back." He shook his head like that wasn't exactly what he wanted to say. He looked like he was fighting off demons in his mind. It made sense. Things that happened before we left the house I shared with Hammer were a little fuzzy, but I thought I remembered Mars having some kind of breakdown. It seemed like my situation had triggered him. Seemed like I wasn't the only one fighting demons. "I've got your back."

"Yes, Dom. I'm all right now."

"Crow and Rocket are deep in something they can't get out of, Scarlet. But I will absolutely send a team for you if you need me to."

"It's OK, Dom. I'm good."

There was a heavy sigh on the other end of the phone. "Do you need me to send Angela?"

Calling and asking for Angela meant I was in trouble. It was a safeguard Grim Road had set up for the very few women and children in their care. Most of the time we stayed in our own compound, separate from the main part of the club. Angela was like a safe word. Asking for Angela meant I was in deep trouble and needed help immediately.

"No. I don't need Angela."

Mars looked down at me with a raised eyebrow. I shook my head at him, then lay back against his chest and closed my eyes.

"Good. I'll get in touch with Claw, but it could be several days before they're in a place where they can call you."

"I'm safe, Dom." I didn't move my head or open my eyes so my voice was a little muffled, but I thought I got the point across.

"Where's Hammer?" Dom asked.

At the mention of Hammer's name, I whimpered and turned my face more fully into Mars's chest. I didn't want to talk about the other man. And, honestly, I had no idea if I could trust Dom or not. I didn't want him knowing any of this in case what Hammer had told me was the truth and he could get to my sisters through someone at the compound. What if my dad really was good with Hammer treating me like this?

"That's not important at the moment," Sting interrupted. "You get word to Rocket. Tell him I want to talk with him. Scarlet is safe with us until I do. Even if Hammer comes for her, we're not letting her go with him."

"You will if she wants to go." Dom's tone of voice said he expected them all to abide by my wishes. I could have told him I had no desire to leave, but I wasn't sure what the right move was in this situation.

"Not happenin'," Mars bit out. Sting gave him an exasperated look but didn't contradict Mars.

"She's staying with us, in our compound, until Claw comes for her himself. Not before." Sting crossed his arms over his chest, looking and sounding every inch the Iron Tzars MC president.

"You'd hold her against her will?"

"We will if we believe her will has been compromised. She doesn't want to go back with Hammer. Nothing she can say at this point will convince me she wants to go back with him. And I have a feeling there's a reason she hasn't already run from Hammer before now. So, no. She's not leaving, even if she tells me she wants to go with him. He's got a hold on her, and I'm taking that decision out of her hands until I know what the fuck's goin' on." Sting didn't hesitate in answering.

No one had told Dom exactly what had happened, how they'd found me tonight. I really hoped they'd hold themselves to the promise they'd not let me leave with Hammer because, if he even hinted he'd hurt my sisters, I knew I'd go with him willingly. Eagerly. I'd do anything to protect my sisters. No matter the cost to me.

"I'll relay your message." Dom didn't sound at all happy. I figured he also knew he didn't have any choice. "I hope to God you know what you're doing, Sting. Claw ain't gonna be happy about this."

"About what? The fact that we're holding Scarlet in our compound where we can be sure she's safe? Or the fact that he sent his daughter away from the protection of his club with a man who beat the living shit out of her?"

There was silence for so long I thought Dom might have ended the call. When he spoke, there was a hardness in his voice I'd never heard. This was the side of club life my dad had always tried to shield his daughters from. Sunshine and Rainbow had met the officers in Grim Road, but as far as I knew, had never actually spoken with anyone other than Rocket. I knew there were men from the club watching out for their families but as a rule, we never saw them.

"That's a helleva accusation. You better sure you've got the facts before you push that narrative."

"Oh, I'm pretty fuckin' sure, you son of a bitch," Sting bit out. "And if I find Claw knew what was happening and sent her with Hammer anyway, I'll be comin' for him."

"I'll relay your... message."

Sting nodded at Wylde who ended the call. Sting then turned his gaze to me. I retreated into Mars's chest like a coward, but I wasn't ready for this. My throat hurt and the adrenaline leaving my body had left me strung out. Not to mention my chest hurt like a son of a bitch. I imagine it was where they'd given me CPR or something. I'd really done it. I just hadn't been good enough at killing myself for it to stick.

"You're safe here, Scarlet. And I meant every fuckin' word I said. I will bury any motherfucker who had a hand in what you went through. From this point forward, you're one of us. We protect our own. To the death."

# Chapter Six

Scarlet was passive in my arms while I carried her to Stitches's clinic. She was beaten down and at her end. Hell, she'd meant for it to be the end. "If we'd gotten there even a minute later…"

"I'm sorry." Her voice was small. Weak. Husky from her near strangulation.

"You got nothin' to be sorry for," I said in a gruff, tight tone. "We shoulda listened better to Lemon and Apple. They knew there was somethin' not right.

"You came," she said. "To the house. I heard you talking with Hammer."

"I didn't push to get in. I should have."

"You didn't know."

"But Lemon did." I shook my head, settling her closer to me as we walked down the hall. Once inside, I set her on the table but didn't let go of her. Her hand was firmly in mine and I wasn't letting go. Maybe not ever.

Stitches followed us in, moving to the corner to get some instruments and such. Didn't ask. Didn't care. All I was concerned with was Scarlet.

"I'd like to look you over, Scarlet. I won't do anything you don't want me to do or that you're uncomfortable with. But considering everything that happened, I'd like to do some lab work and check your neck and spine for problems."

"I'm really sorry." She gave a little broken sob. "So sorry."

Stitches shot me a quick look, his eyes saying 'stay put, don't move.' I nodded, my hand still holding Scarlet's, my gaze not leaving hers. She was broken. I could see it in her eyes, in the way her shoulders sagged, in the way her voice cracked.

"You have nothing to apologize for, honey." Stitches rested a hand on her shoulder and squeezed gently. "Let's just focus on getting you the care you need."

I could tell she was hesitant, but after a moment, she nodded her head slowly. Stitches took that as a sign to begin.

The exam was pretty straightforward. He checked the bruising around her neck, touching her gently. "How bad does your throat hurt?"

She shrugged. "Not bad."

"You've got bruises on your arms and legs. Can I look at your belly and back? See if I need to take some X-rays?"

She hesitated for a moment. Then she looked up at me like she didn't know what to do. I could tell she didn't want to bare herself and I'd never let her be completely naked in front of another man, but this was for her health and safety.

"It's all right, honey. Just lift your shirt over your belly. You don't have to completely undress."

She nodded and I saw what was happening. She needed me to take over but was probably uncomfortable asking since she didn't know me that well.

Once her shirt was out of the way, Stitches looked her over with an assessing eye. His expression hardened and I finally took my focus off of Scarlet's face and let my gaze shift to her torso…

And wished I hadn't.

Her skin was mottled with bruises along her belly, sides, and back. I could see reddish-blue areas snaking from her side down her hip to disappear into her pants which meant her hips and thighs were probably the same way.

"That motherfuckin' bastard..." My growled response got a look from Stitches but he didn't say anything. Scarlet didn't say a word. Only ducked her head like she was ashamed. Which wouldn't do at all. "Hey." I lifted her chin with my fingers gently. "Look at me, beautiful girl." When her eyes met mine, I held her gaze for a couple of seconds before I continued. "You don't duck your head to no one. Not about this. You survived. Hammer's a big bastard and you're just a tiny little thing. The fact you're still alive is more about your strength than his."

Her brows knit in confusion. "But... I tried to..."

Without thinking I moved in to press my lips to hers. It was only meant to stop her from voicing what she'd done but the second my lips met hers, I knew I was in huge fucking trouble.

Scarlet sucked in a breath but, instead of pushing me away as she should have, instead of being angry I was in her personal space and basically assaulting her, she let out a little sigh and melted into me.

I was all too aware of Stitches being in the room, especially when he put a hand on my shoulder and exerted pressure to pull me back. Normally, I'd have said fuck it and done as I pleased, but I knew Stitches was right. I was way the fuck outta line.

I pulled back but rested my forehead against hers lightly for a moment, trying to get my wits back about me. Unable to help myself, I gave her one more soft, lingering kiss. Then I stepped back and cleared my throat. I held her gaze, though. I wanted to see every expression that crossed her lovely face. If I saw fear, I might kick my own ass. I didn't. Only a wide-eyed innocence stunned at the intimate contact. She touched her lips lightly with trembling fingers before giving me a tentative smile.

"We know what almost happened," Stitches said softly. "But it didn't." He gave her a tight smile. "Now, let's finish this so you can rest."

Stitches probed a couple of the worst bruises with gentle fingers. Scarlet still winced and every time she did, I growled at Stitches.

After the fifth time, he stopped and turned to me, hands on his hips. "Would you shut up? I'm not touchin' you, you big pussy."

"No. You're touchin' her. And you're hurting her. Surely to God there's something else you can do besides poke and prod at every fucking bruise on her body."

"It's all right." Scarlet spoke softly, interrupting our little tiff. "It's not that bad. I know you're trying to help." She looked from Stitches to me and gave me a small, shy smile.

Stitches raised an eyebrow at me. "See? She's good."

"Fine," I grumbled, stepping back and crossing my arms over my chest, watching every move Stitches made. I was in protector mode and couldn't seem to pull myself out. The last thing I needed to do was have this girl imprinted on me. She didn't need my overbearing interference, and I didn't need a woman glued to my side. Because, if Scarlet was the woman, she would definitely be glued to my side. No way I could let her go her own way without my protection.

Not ten seconds later, Stitches used his fingers to touch an area on her lower back and Scarlet sucked in a breath. I growled again. Then to my complete and utter shock, Scarlet giggled. Just once, but it was there. She had her gaze fixed on me before turning back to Stitches, her expression innocent.

Stitches barked out a laugh. "You think he's funny." It wasn't a question.

Instead of verbalizing her answer, Scarlet shook her head before lowering her gaze to her lap. A smile tugged at the corner of her lips before she curled them inward.

I narrowed my gaze at her. "Did she... Did she just... bait me?"

"I think she likes your growly bear side. God only knows why." Stitches took out his stethoscope, warming the bell between his hands before putting the earpieces in his ears and placing the bell on Scarlet's chest. "Gotta admit, though. You are rather amusing." He nodded at Scarlet. "Deep breath in, honey."

Stitches repeated his instructions several times all the while moving the stethoscope around to different parts of Scarlet's chest and back. She stiffened a couple of times and once she grunted but immediately looked up at me and shook her head.

When Stitches was done he stood back and looked at her intently. "I think you've got a couple broken ribs on that left side, honey. I'd like to do an X-ray just to make sure you don't have a punctured lung."

"She ain't your honey, Stitches. And if we take her to the hospital, they'll want to know what happened. If we tell them, they bring the cops. If they do that, we can't kill that son of a bitch Hammer."

"Regardless of what you think of me, Mars, I'm not a complete dumbass." Stitches gave me a cheerful smile even when I knew he was aggravated with me. And probably more than a little insulted. "I can get her some images off the books at a friend's clinic. Broken ribs I can't do much for other than tell her to rest and give her pain medicine, but if she's got a pneumothorax, I won't have a choice but to get her to a hospital."

"Fuck," I muttered as I turned away, scrubbing a hand through my beard. "Just... *fuck*!"

"It's OK." Scarlet wrapped her arms around herself. When I sat beside her in a chair next to the exam table, she reached out and put her hand over mine. Immediately, I turned mine over to lace my fingers with hers. When I did, my mind settled and the pressure building inside my chest eased. "I've got a fake ID I can use if necessary. I'm sure if you can get hold of my dad. He can help with the money."

"Honey, we ain't worried about the money. Iron Tzars can take care of any hospital bill you rack up. If you've got a fake ID we'll get it to Wylde and let him tighten it up. That way it can hold up to scrutiny if necessary. We don't want the cops being able to find you after the fact."

"They won't." She sounded sure of herself. "Crush is the best at what he does."

"Crush?" I squeezed her hand, bringing her attention back to me.

"Yeah. He's... Uh..." She cleared her throat and color rose to her cheeks. "Nothing."

"If you're afraid of giving out information you shouldn't, don't be. Wylde is on it now. He'll know everything there is to know about Grim Road before he's done."

She nodded and sighed. "Maybe. Crush is the computer person for Grim Road. Dad kept me away from men in Grim Road and I never knew more than their road names, but I met Crush a few times." She lowered her gaze and looked away. "Right before Dad gave me to Hammer and we ended up here."

I looked up at Stitches, whose expression had

hardened. It was sounding more and more like Claw had sold out his daughter. I knew I was supposed to reserve judgment until Wylde gave us as many facts as he could, but this whole situation was fucking jacked up to shit and back.

"How about we take it one step at a time. All right?" Stitches gave her a reassuring smile, but I still bristled. Once again, I couldn't stop the growl that emerged from my throat.

Scarlet's smile was quickly smothered, but not before I noticed. "You think this is funny?" I wasn't certain I kept from scowling at the poor girl, but she didn't seem to mind. Instead, she gave me a full-on smile, one she gave up fighting.

"Maybe a little." Her voice, though soft and a little tentative, wrapped around my heart and squeezed. "But I promise I'll be scared if it will save your reputation."

Stitches outright guffawed at that. I ignored him and gave her a crisp nod. "See that you do. My brothers'll never let me live it down if they knew you laughed at me."

"Well, if you promise not to leave me alone, your secret's safe with me." She still smiled, but now her lips quivered slightly as if she were trying to fight off tears.

"Baby." I brushed my finger along her cheek, catching one tear that fell from her eye. "I'm with you as long as you need me to be."

Without another word, Scarlet reached for me. I gladly pulled her into my arms and held her while Stitches met my gaze and nodded.

"I'll tell Sting. If you need me, you know where to find me. I'll set up the X-ray for later tonight. In the meantime, see she drinks plenty of water and gets some rest."

"Tell the old ladies she'll need some shit." I stood with Scarlet's arms wrapped tightly around me. I couldn't say I didn't cling to her, though I tried to be mindful of her bruised and battered body.

"I will. I'll have them leave everything outside your door. That way she won't be disturbed."

"Text me when you're ready to go for the X-ray."

"Will do."

As I took her to my room in the clubhouse, I murmured to her, rubbing her back with one hand as we went. "I promise I'll be with you, Scarlet. I won't let you out of my sight for any reason."

She didn't answer and I could feel her body trembling. Dampness bled through my shirt and I knew she was crying.

So help me God, if it was the last thing I did, I was gonna murder that fucking fuck stick, Hammer. In unspeakable ways.

"Baby, I swear to you, Hammer's gonna endure every single thing he ever did to you. That's how he's gonna die. What he did to you will be done to him three times over because he's three times your size."

"You don't --"

"Hush, baby. I know I don't have to. But I'm gonna. He's gonna bleed. Then he's gonna die. Hard."

She didn't say anything else until we stepped inside my room and I shut the door. Then she pulled back slightly to look at me.

"All right."

"All right?"

"Make him die hard, Mars. Hard as you can."

"I promise. I'll do it with my bare hands."

# Chapter Seven

## Scarlet

Sting didn't hear back from my father. Not in the week I'd been with Mars in the Iron Tzars compound. It was surprising, as well as painful as hell. The longer things went on, the more I was convinced Claw had known exactly what was happening and didn't care. I was starting to question my whole life to this point. Thank God, the X-ray Stitches had taken didn't show any broken ribs or a punctured lung. It was one of the few things that had gone right, it seemed.

The only thing holding me together was Mars. The man hadn't left my side and I was growing entirely too dependent on him. And I wouldn't have it any other way. At first, he'd treated me like he was afraid I'd break at the drop of a hat. But as the days went by, my injuries healed and I grew more comfortable around everyone in the compound. Lemon and Apple were also not far from me most of the time. Only when they had to go to school, and they always made a point to come find me when they got home. Sting had decided it best I stay at the compound until they found Hammer and took care of him, and I agreed. After experiencing what it was like to truly be cared for by a man, I knew I'd die if Hammer took me back. Literally.

"How you doin', honey?"

Mars came up behind me where I stood at the bar in the clubhouse. He dropped a kiss on my neck, which made me shiver. He'd been doing things like that a lot this past week. It was driving me crazy but in a very good way.

"Better now that you're here distracting me." I looked up at him and smiled. "Pretty sure I'm not old enough to be here, though."

He chuckled warmly. "You ain't drinkin'. Besides, this is private property. You're eighteen and under my protection. I say you can do whatever the fuck you want. Given everything you've been through, no one is gonna give a fuck if you want a drink."

I grinned, grateful for Mars' protectiveness. "I don't want a drink," I said. "I just want to be close to you."

"Close to me, huh?" he said, smirking. "I can do that."

He wrapped his arms around me from behind and pulled me against him, and I sighed happily. I clung to the arm wrapped over my chest. "Thank you for staying with me. I know I'm probably cramping your style, but I want you to know how comforting it is to know you're looking out for me."

"Glad to do it. Besides, ain't no one around here smells as good as you." As if to emphasize his point, Mars buried his nose in my neck and inhaled. "Delicious…"

I giggled. Which made him root closer. Which tickled like a mother. It wasn't long before I was howling with laughter and trying to get away from the way he tickled my neck with his beard.

"If you two want to play grab-ass, I suggest you get a room."

I jumped and tried to push Mars away, but he held firm, not taking his face from my neck. "Go to hell, Wylde. Ain't doin' nothin' you and Danica don't do."

"Never said you were." Wylde had a big grin on his face, but it didn't seem to quite reach his eyes like normal. Wylde was the quirkiest guy I'd ever met. He was so much like Lemon it was a wonder Apple and their older sister, Danica, hadn't killed him yet. I absolutely loved him. "Lemon was lookin' for you, darlin'." He nodded at me. "Said she needed help with…" He shrugged, still grinning like he couldn't be bothered to know what Lemon really wanted. "Somethin'. She's upstairs in the media room. Maybe it was a movie or something. Ain't *Fortnite*. She's not allowed to play." Wylde was definitely up to something. And he wasn't trying all that hard to hide it.

"Why is she not allowed to play?" I couldn't help myself.

He scowled. A genuine reaction. "'Cause she beat me. I sweet-talked Dani into revoking her privileges."

I chuckled. "You know the only reason she worked so hard to beat you was to keep you from crowing about how good you were at the game. Right?"

Wylde narrowed his eyes. "That little hellion…"

"Go on, honey," Mars gave me one more squeeze before he let me go. "I'll come join you in a bit, and we'll all watch a movie together."

I looked up at Mars. Like Wylde, though he smiled, it didn't reach his eyes. "You guys are trying to manage me." My voice was soft, almost a whisper. I knew then something had happened with my dad. "What is it you don't want to tell me?"

Mars and Wylde exchanged a look before Wylde grinned. "Nothin's happened. Far as I know, he's fine. Still ain't talked to him."

I cocked my head to the side, narrowing my gaze at him. My heart sank and I could feel panic building though I tried to fight it off. "You're lying, Wylde. Why are you lying?"

Instantly, both men's demeanor changed. "No, honey," Wylde said, his normally cocky and somewhat juvenile personality all too serious now. "I'm not lying. We haven't spoken to your father, but he's not hurt. That much I know."

"Then what is it?"

Mars reached out and cupped the side of my face in his big hand. "Let me go deal with this, and I'll come back and fill you in. Will you trust me that much?"

"Mars, more than anyone in my life right now, I trust you. I think you know that. But this is my family. I need to know."

"I'll talk to Sting," Wylde offered. "She probably needs to be there."

"No." Mars said, not taking his gaze from mine. "Let me do this. Then I'll come for you and tell you everything."

"You want to filter it. In case there's something you think I can't handle."

Mars brushed a lock of hair out of my face. "You're my girl and I want to protect you, sugar. That's all. After everything you've gone through, the last thing I want for you is to bring you more pain. So I'm askin' you, real sweet like, let me go find out what's goin' on. Then I'll tell you everything. Just in my own way."

"Feels like I'm hiding." I met his gaze boldly. "I might be a victim, but I'm not a coward, Mars. I can handle whatever's going on."

He gave me a shake of his head, his brows knitting together. He framed my face in his hands and lowered his head to mine. My heart pounded in my chest and I knew I whimpered a little when his lips met mine.

The world seemed to fall away. All that existed

was Mars and me. My hands went to his chest and I clutched at his shirt. It was no more than a gentle pressing of his lips to mine. He'd done it a few times since that first kiss in Stitches's office. It was never more than a chaste kiss, but it never failed to thrill me. I was growing to expect it more and more, and Mars always seemed to know when I needed it. Like now.

"Honey. No one thinks you're a coward. You're not a victim either. You're a survivor."

"It doesn't feel like it sometimes." I didn't speak loud, all too aware of Wylde close to us. Surprisingly, he'd turned his back and stepped a few steps away, giving us a little bit of privacy to have this conversation. "I still feel broken."

"You leave that to me, too. You're healing every single fuckin' day, Scarlet. I see it in your beautiful smile." He kissed me once more before letting me go. "Now, please. Just this once. Trust me to take care of whatever's going on. I need to protect you. As many demons as you have, I have more. This is one of them."

I stared at him for several moments. Mars didn't rush me or try to tell me how this was for my own good or some other bullshit. He let me take my time. Think it over before giving him an answer.

"Okay, but you have to tell me everything when you're done. No sugarcoating it."

Mars leaned down and pressed a soft kiss to my lips once again. It was almost like he couldn't help himself. I know I was grateful for it because I was growing addicted to those kisses. "I promise."

"OK, then." I smiled up at him. It was still hard to believe I was in the care of a man who treated me the way Mars did. The first couple of days I'd been here, he hadn't let me walk anywhere. He'd either brought me anything I needed or carried me wherever

I needed to go. That had stopped. Mostly. But he never left my side for long if he could help it. When he did, he made sure someone else was with me.

Before leaving to go with Wylde, Mars took me to the media room where Apple and Lemon were waiting. Apple greeted me with a big smile and a hug while Lemon lounged in a chair with her leg hooked over the arm. She was blowing bubbles and twirling her hair, but looked bored as all get out. Except her gaze fixed on Mars was keen and all too knowing. The girl might be a year or so younger than me, but she wasn't a kid. She was a force to be reckoned with.

"I'll be back as soon as I can. Don't leave here unless you have one of the brothers with you." He hiked a thumb over his shoulder. "Breaker and Deacon are outside the door. You need something they can't get for you, you take one of them with you."

"I will." When I smiled up at him, Mars kissed me one more time before leaving, closing the door behind him.

# Chapter Eight

**Mars**

As I followed Wylde to his office, every protective instinct I had was screaming at me that this was gonna be bad. When we entered the office, Sting, Brick, and Roman were right behind us.

"You said it was urgent, Wylde." Sting didn't sit, but shut the door before leaning against it. "What's up?"

"I just got a call from Ripper at Salvation's Bane. We've got trouble headed our way."

Sting glanced at me. "This has something to do with Scarlet." It wasn't a question.

Wylde nodded, the normally snarky, fun-loving man as serious as I'd ever seen him. "This is all through back channels. Ripper's been keeping an eye on Grim Road ever since Doc took Rocket's daughter as his woman. He passed this on to me same time as he did Thorn. Seems like Hammer turned up back at the Grim compound in Florida the day after you contacted them."

There was a knock at the door and Sting moved before opening it. Stitches was there. Another grim-faced member of Tzars. "Finally heard back from Doc at Bane."

"We were just discussing him," Sting said. "What'd you find out?"

"That Rocket is pissed as fuck. He's coming here intent on wipin' this place of the fuckin' map."

"He say why?"

"That would be why I called this meeting," Wylde interrupted. "Hammer got to Claw before I could. I'm sorry, Sting. Mars."

Sting grunted. "Not your fault. Hammer's with

Grim Road. He's gonna have access to the officers easier than us. What happened?"

"Claw and Rocket believe Scarlet's being held here against her will. That we're the ones hurting her."

That was all I could take. I sprang to my feet, crossed the room and punched the wall with all my might. "Fuckin' Goddamn motherfucker! When I get my fuckin' hands on him, I'm gonna peel the fuckin' skin from his fuckin' body!"

"We're all gonna have a go," Sting said softly. "Can you track them, Wylde?"

"Can I track them, he asks. Of course, I can fuckin' track them." It was the first sign of Wylde's personality when he'd been subdued and very serious until now. "That's the other reason I called you guys. They took their time, getting everyone together. Whatever they were doing -- and I gotta say, it was buried so fuckin' deep I haven't figured out what it was yet -- they pulled the fuck out. I can tell you it was important enough they've got Bane watchin' their territory. Took every single member they could spare and fuckin' left Dodge a few months ago when Doc got together with his woman, Talia. They headed this way from their compound this morning. It's a fifteen-hour drive, so they're gonna be here in three hours."

"Hammer with them?"

"Oh, yeah." The grin Wylde gave me was positively evil. "He's the one I'm tracking. Started looking for him the second you brought Scarlet to us. His phone has some serious encryption. Took some doin' but I got the bastard. His kung-fu is not as strong as he thought." As always, Wylde looked smug as shit when delivering that news. "Tracking everyone else's phone too just to shove a leash up their asses, but Hammer was the most important." He leaned back in his chair. "Been listening in on their conversations. Claw insisted Hammer come with them. Said he wanted Hammer to point out who Scarlet had interactions with. The ones most likely to have snatched her. But he and Rocket have doubts about Hammer. Yes. They're coming to level this place and wipe out the Tzars in Evansville. But they're also not cashin' in all their chips." He nodded at Sting. "They'll listen to you. Most importantly, they'll listen to Scarlet."

"So they're coming with an open mind?" Sting didn't look convinced, but was apparently willing to continue listening.

"Eh, somewhat." Wylde made a gesture, rocking his opened hand back-and-forth. "Claw's out for blood. Rocket isn't far behind. They trust Hammer so it's going to take Scarlet to convince them what really happened but make no mistake. Grim Road is coming, and they're out for blood. If they don't find Scarlet immediately, they'll do their best to take this place apart."

"They can try." Sting's mien hardened. "Wylde, get all hands on deck. Lock down the women and children. Mars." My president gave me a look, pointing his finger at me. "Lock down your woman. I'll let Ace know to expect a call. It'll take him time to do a tattoo, so you don't have much time to convince her."

"I don't know if she's ready for that, Sting. I'm not letting her go, but she's still healing. Inside and out. It's only been a week since…"

"I know, brother. She's out of time. She has to make a decision. We won't allow a woman to be terrorized, but she can't stay here unless she's claimed."

"Sting…"

"I'm sorry, Mars. We'll protect her, but she has to be all in with you."

"I know the rules, Sting. Until this moment, I've never questioned them. She's not ready to commit to us, but she needs our protection."

"Are you sure she's not ready? Really sure? Because she's been raised in a hardass MC. Her father gave her to a monster. You think she won't welcome the protection of a strong man who's taken such good care of her? I see the way she looks at you, Mars. Give her some credit."

"You know," Wylde tapped a finger on his desk as if weighing what he was about to say and trying to decide if he wanted to voice it or not. "Lemon told me Scarlet is worried Hammer will hurt her sisters. She thinks the reason Scarlet hurt herself was to keep Hammer from being able to use her sisters against her. Probably thought that if she was gone, they'd be safe." He shook his head as if the very thought hurt him. His features were hard and dangerous. "She's a loyal, self-sacrificing woman. She ain't afraid of you or anyone else. Even Hammer. She fought back the only way she could."

Wylde was right. If she did what she did to protect her sisters, then I wasn't going to scare her. I just had to work through my issues and be really sure I could control myself. Otherwise, I'd be no better than that bastard, Hammer.

Sting gave me a hard look. "Go lock her down, Mars. Like I said."

I wanted to howl in frustration. Claiming Scarlet was the one thing I wanted with all my heart. I wanted the right to protect her from now until the day I died. Then I wanted her to have the protection of my club if my protection wasn't enough. Which meant she had to accept me. Whether or not she was ready.

"This isn't fair to her."

Sting raised an eyebrow. "Just talk to her. You might be surprised by what she wants."

As I left Wylde's office, I scrubbed a hand over my face. Though I wanted Scarlet with everything inside me, I didn't think she was ready. Sure, she let me kiss her -- I'd made sure to do it often until she was tilting her head up at me in anticipation. But she was still so fragile. The trauma of what she had been through was still fresh in her mind. And I didn't want to push her into anything she wasn't ready for.

As I made my way through the clubhouse, I couldn't help but wonder what she was doing right at that moment. Was she thinking about me or was she deep into something with Apple and Lemon? Likely the latter.

And why the fuck was I even contemplating this? This whole romantic thing with a woman fifteen years my junior? Sure, she liked my kisses, but tying herself to a biker of questionable morals who was so much older than her probably wasn't something she was considering. Or would ever consider. She had her whole life ahead of her and was so fucking beautiful and courageous she could have any man she wanted. In this club or any other club.

Yeah. That wasn't happening. As I got to the rec room, I noticed Breaker and Deacon outside the door. Both sat in chairs, chatting lightly. Breaker had a ball he bounced off the opposite wall before catching it and throwing it again. I opened my mouth to greet the two when a loud screech from inside the door interrupted me.

"Would you fuckin' stop that fuckin' racket before I come out there and rip off your nuts and throw them against that fuckin' wall, Breaker!" Lemon.

"Sorry, sunshine. My bad." Breaker grinned at me... before throwing the ball against the wall again.

"You must like living dangerously, man." Deacon chuckled and shook his head.

"Nope. It's just that she's so fun to bait. Gonna miss the little shit when some brother snatches her up. Hopefully from another club. On the other side of the country."

"I heard that."

Breaker winced even as he smiled. "Ouch."

Despite my misgivings about what I needed to propose to Scarlet, I found myself smiling. "Better watch Wylde doesn't hear you say that."

Breaker snorted. "Wylde would agree with me. It's Dani I'd be worried about overhearing."

"Better be worried about Apple overhearing," Deacon said softly. "You upset Apple, you get to answer to me."

"Dude! Bros before --"

"You finish that sentence, you won't finish a sentence ever again." Deacon didn't look like he was kidding. Breaker still smiled.

"I was gonna say foes, Deacon. Honest to God, man. I was sayin' foes." Breaker raised his hands in surrender and backed up a step even as he chuckled.

Deacon snorted but didn't look like he was buying it.

With a roll of my eyes, I opened the door and stepped inside. The second I did, Scarlet jumped up from her seat on the couch and threw herself into my arms. Her slight body trembled, and I kissed the side of her head through her hair.

"What's wrong, baby?"

"Nothing," she whispered. "Nothing at all now."

I loved the way she clung to me, but worried about why.

"Honey, you're trembling. Tell me why." I tried not to make it come out an order, but it was hard. I couldn't slay the dragon if I didn't know where it was. And when the fuck did I start thinking in princess metaphors? Just… *fuck*!

"She's been afraid Sting'll send her back with Hammer to keep the club out of a confrontation," Apple offered softly.

Lemon snorted. "That ain't it, Apple, and you Goddamned know it. She's been afraid you wouldn't come back, Mars."

"Lemon, shut up," Apple hissed before coming to Scarlet and rubbing her shoulder even though I still held her in my arms. "She's a dork. Don't mind her." Apple laughed nervously and looked up at me, a pleading look in her eyes.

My eyes narrowed in confusion and I pulled back to look down at Scarlet's lovely face. "Honey. Scarlet." I put my hands on her shoulders and leaned down so she was looking directly into my gaze. "I. Will. *Always* come for you. Fuckin' always. You're my girl. Remember?"

"You said that," Scarlet sniffled as she continued to look at me. Her eyes were glassy with unshed tears and her lips trembled. "But I don't… I don't know what that means. Exactly."

I smiled down at her before meeting her for a soft, lingering kiss. Then I pressed my forehead to hers. "That's what we're going back to our room to talk about. You ready?"

"Yes, Mars." She cupped my face in her, going up on her tiptoes to kiss me. I wanted to howl in relief. This was going to happen. At least, she was going to agree to be mine. I might not actually be able to take things physical, but she was going to wear my ink and my patch. It would be my right to protect her and to ask for the protection of the club. The rest would come with time. When she was ready. I could see that in her eyes. Taste it in her kiss. Feel it as she pressed her body against mine.

"Come on, baby." I snagged her hand and led her to our room.

Once inside, she threw herself back into my arms, wrapping her arms and legs around me tightly. I let her cling. Hell, I clung to her just as tightly, savoring the feel of her and craving more. I wanted to take her to bed. To spend the rest of the day and the entire night just holding her. Help her realize she was safe with me. Always. Instead, I walked to the couch and sat with her straddling my lap.

"Mars?"

"Yeah, baby."

"Thank you."

"For what?"

"For taking care of me. For staying by my side. I know I'm cramping your style. I see how the club girls watch you. I know they're just waiting for the chance for you to be alone."

"Honey, I've not touched a club girl in over two years. Hell, I've not been with any woman."

She pulled back then, giving me a disbelieving, hurt look. "Don't lie to me," she whispered. "Please, Mars. Not even to try to make me more comfortable."

"Ain't lyin', Scarlet." I sighed, scrubbing a hand over my face, but not letting her go. My arm was solidly around her, even when she tried to push back. It was a half-hearted attempt at best. "I have... issues." My confession was gruff and uncomfortable. "You know. With sex."

"Oh. OK." She looked away, her cheeks reddening. "I'm sorry."

"Don't be sorry. And don't look away from me." I gently tilted her chin upward so she had to look at me. I had one arm securely around her so she couldn't try to bolt on me. Not like this. "I have issues, Scarlet. I've seen and done things that should terrify you. They probably won't because you've lived them when I only witnessed them. I avoid sex because sometimes it can trigger a flashback."

"Oh, God. Mars, I'm so sorry. I--"

I leaned in and kissed her. It was my favorite way to silence her when she was fretting about things she had no need to fret over. "There's no reason for you to be sorry. And I'm telling you right now, I will work through those issues. Because I need to be with you, Scarlet. In every way possible."

As I looked into her eyes, she gasped and her whole body shivered. Her fingers curled into my shoulders as she clung. "But you said --"

"I did, sweetheart. Look. We don't have a lot of time so let me just say that you're not the first woman I've seen driven to the brink. But you're the one who snagged my heart." She sucked in a breath, tears forming in her lovely green and gold eyes. "And before you go thinkin' it's because I feel sorry for you, it's not. Not even close."

"I wasn't, you know, trying to escape for myself. If it were just me, I'd have left the second I realized there was an MC in the area willing to protect me."

I nodded. "Wylde said he was pretty sure you were protecting your sisters."

She nodded. "I was. Hammer said if I tried to tell Claw, Dad would just give him one of my sisters. Or both of them. He said if Claw didn't, he had plenty of men in Grim Road who'd take care of Sunshine and Rainbow. If I ran from him, I knew it would be the same. It wasn't something sexual, Mars. He never touched me, and I have no idea why. He was punishing me. He wanted to hurt me but seemed to think I was… I don't know. Dirty? Not someone he wanted to touch? He never said, really. He threatened to let his brothers in Grim have me if I tried to run, but he never touched me. Sexually, that is." She winced, tears spilling from her eyes now. "I thought that, if I… well, if I killed myself, I could get away from him and my sisters would still be safe."

"That bastard is gonna get everything he deserves when I get my hands on him. I promised you I'd make him suffer and that's a promise I intend to keep."

"I wish I could tell you I didn't want you to. I can see that it might take a piece of your soul when you do it. But I'm just selfish enough to let you do it anyway. But my promise to you is that I'll find a way to put your soul back together."

I couldn't help but smile at her. "Baby, I think you already have."

She leaned in to kiss me and this time, I took that kiss where I really wanted to go. I swept my tongue across the seam of her lips and she opened willingly, meeting my tongue with a tentative stroke of her own. She shivered again, letting go of a small whimper. When she continued lapping at the inside of my mouth with an experimental stroke, I knew she wasn't afraid. Still, I needed to make sure.

"I don't want to frighten or hurt you, Scarlet."

"You won't," she breathed. "You're not."

"Tell me what you want from me, honey. I have

to hear the words."

"I want you to make me yours. All the way, Mars. It's selfish, I know. But it's what I want."

"So I can keep you safe from Hammer."

"No." She smiled at me. A beautiful, tender smile. "Because you're the man who gave me hope. I'd never expect you to do something you didn't want, but I'm telling you right now, I never want to be with another man. *Could* never be with another man. Not in any sense of the word. I'd always compare him to you and that's not fair to anyone."

"Fuck. Me." It was my prayer. The only thing I could think of. "I'll be good to you, honey. I'll protect you with my life and I'll never cheat."

"I'll be your partner and always have your back. I'll be whatever you need."

"Together." I put my forehead against hers once again.

"Yes, Mars. Together."

I kissed her again because I had to. Unexpectedly, she tugged at my shirt until I moved my arms to let her pull it free from my body. She leaned in to nuzzle the notch in my chest just below my throat, then she licked up my neck and nipped my chin. My fucking cock shot rock-fucking-hard. I tried to shift away from her, but she just followed me with her hips. There was no doubt what she wanted. She wasn't being shy or even the least bit hesitant. No. She took this biker and brought it to him.

"I know you think I'm fragile, Mars. I promise you I'm not. I've been beaten down, and yes, I hurt myself, but not because I didn't want to live. Never that. But I'd do anything to protect the people I love. Anything."

"Never again, Scarlet," I whispered harshly. At

the thought, my heart pounded and I broke out in a sweat. "Christ! I never want to see you like that again!" I pulled her to me again, holding her tight. It was all I ever seemed to do. "I'm afraid I'm gonna squeeze you too hard."

"You could never be too hard, Mars. Your fierceness is what I need. Your tight hold on me kept me from flying apart. I was scared and broken. Still am in some ways. But you held me together. You still do."

"Takin' you to bed. I want to hold you. You don't have to do anything else, but I need the closeness." I stood, Scarlet still in my arms.

"Take me wherever you want. And I have a feeling that I'll love anything else you want to do with me." She smiled up at me as I carried her to the bedroom and sat with her on the bed. I scooted around until my back was against the headboard. Scarlet still straddled my lap. "You know, I never wanted to leave you that night Stitches had to look me over. You were so possessive, but in a protective way. I loved it when you growled at him." The smile she gave me then was glorious. I could tell she really had enjoyed that side of me. "I loved the sound and the threat that growl implied if he hurt me again."

"Bloodthirsty little thing."

"I'm the daughter of the vice president of Grim Road MC. I was born bloodthirsty."

That got a laugh from me. "You're like a honey badger, ain't you? I'm guessing Hammer didn't sleep much, or he'd be dead right now."

"No. He was usually up drinking. Must have gone somewhere else to sleep, because I'd've loved to have caught him passed out. But then, none of this would have happened and I'd never have met you."

"Honey, if I could have spared you any of that,

I'd have done it. Then *I'd* have found *you*. In a way, I think I've been looking for you all my life. It's why I put myself in situations where I saw so many abused women."

"I want to hear about that. I need to know what happened."

"I go with Rocket sometimes when he's on the trail of traffickers. I do it because my younger sister was taken when she was barely a teenager."

"Oh, no." She gasped and smuggled closer to me as she gazed up into my face with sorrow. "I'm so sorry, Mars."

"She was a beautiful girl. A mini version of our mother." I smiled at the memory of my family. "I lost both of them in one night, Scarlet. It's when I met your father. Rocket caught me hunting those bastards and let me come with him and Grim Road if I promised to always come when he called me. I did and he took me with him. I wasn't much more than a kid. I'd have done everything I had to to save my sister, but the reality was that I'd probably have died if I'd tried to get her myself.

"Rocket took me with him and trained me in the years afterward. Now, I'm one of the best hunters the club has. It's also why Rocket made me promise to help him. He saw that talent in me and intended to hone it to a fine point."

I took a breath, remembering even though I'd tried so hard to bury the pain deep. I didn't want to keep anything from Scarlet. Never. If it meant I was a little uncomfortable, I could deal. "When we finally got inside the warehouse, I was determined to kill every one of those bastards."

"As you should. Did you get them all?" Her voice was soft and soothing, somehow making the telling a little easier.

"Oh, yeah. Blood flowed like a fuckin' river in that place. What we did to those guys... They died in unspeakable ways. This is something I doubt Rocket would want you to know. I think I killed more than every man in Grim Road combined. It was a huge fuckin' ring. Dozens of men holding even more dozens of young women and a few boys and girls. But it didn't start immediately."

"What do you mean?"

"We were keeping it quiet. Only killing when we had to in order to keep the element of surprise until we could free all the kids. The plan was to go on a killing spree once the kids were safe." I swallowed. "Until I found my sister."

"I take it she was hurt."

"Yeah, honey. Found her hanging in the room where they'd kept her. So when I saw you... In that tree..." I cleared my throat.

"It reminded you of that night." She kissed my jaw. My neck.

"I got her down and we tried to resuscitate her. Thought we had her too, but she found my gaze. She clung to me like I was her lifeline. Then she whispered that she was sorry she doubted me. That's when I knew she'd done that herself. Because she didn't think I could find her and take her away."

"How horrible. I'm so sorry, Mars. So very sorry."

"The reason that warehouse was such a bloody mess was because of me. I... lost my mind, I guess. I remember... castrating a man. Maybe more than one. But it was like I was in a first-person video game or something. Like it wasn't really me doing all those things. Blood was everywhere. I felt like I'd bathed in it."

"They deserved everything you did to them and more."

"I know. I don't regret doing any of it. I only regret that I can't fuckin' remember it all. We…" I cleared my throat. This was the hard part. "We caught more than one of them raping one of the kids. The young women. Some of the shit those men did… It was sickening. The most revolting things you could possibly imagine.

"Grim Road believes in an eye for an eye. So we did to those men *every single fuckin' thing* they'd done to the kids. Every fuckin' thing, Scarlet. And it was the dirtiest I'd ever felt in my life. Not because of what I'd done to the men. But because of what I'd seen the men doing to the kids. Sometimes during sex, if I get triggered, I think I'm back in that fuckin' warehouse. Only I'm the one doing those things to kids. Like in the video game I described earlier. When that happens, I fight. I've accidentally hurt a couple of the club whores here in the past. Never too bad, but bad enough. So I stopped having sex."

"If sex isn't something you want to do, we can figure something out. I don't ever want to give you bad memories."

"Oh, honey, there's nothing about you that could give me anything but good memories. But I will never hurt you. And You have absolutely no idea how much I want sex to be a huge part what we do together. I'm considering lettin' you tie me up so there's no way I could hurt you and you could just have your wicked way with me."

That got a laugh out of Scarlet. "I could, huh?"

"Oh, yeah." My smile faded. "When I brought my sister's body home, my mother insisted on seeing her. My dad tried to keep her away, but Mom insisted. She held my sister's lifeless body for a good hour before me and Dad pulled her away and took her home. Dad put her to bed and came downstairs to get double-check the security system had been armed. That's when she shot herself." I had to stop and push through those memories. It had been the worst day of my life, and more than my dad could take.

"Dad didn't last long after that. The docs said he had Broken Heart Syndrome. After losing his daughter and his wife of more than half his life, I could see that being exactly what happened. So, I've lost my entire family. I absolutely will not lose you, Scarlet. Not for any reason. Certainly not because I had a flashback and hurt you."

"How do you feel now, Mars? Talking about all that. Reliving it."

I thought about that for a moment. "Surprisingly, it's not as traumatic as I thought it would be. But it's not me. It's you. Scarlet, you ground me somehow."

"We'll do whatever is comfortable for you, but I have to warn you. I fully intend to get you to try. At least once." The impish look on her face lightened my heart more than I realized I'd needed. This wouldn't be the only time we had this conversation and I thought I might be OK with it. I found it felt good to confide in someone. To tell someone else how I'd felt that night.

"How about this?" I brushed my fingers lightly over her cheek, letting my thumb play along her bottom lip. "We'll work through it together. Both of us got issues. And I'm not going to give up before we even try. I want you like I've never wanted another woman in my life."

"I bet, if we took it slow and just explored each other, we could control things a little better. If we wait until we're both so desperate things get out of hand, it might be worse. For both of us."

I felt my lips curl. "I think you're wantin' to play. Is that what you want?"

She shrugged. "I wouldn't object."

I leaned up and pulled her down for a kiss. I'd gotten so used to it, I knew exactly where to put my lips so they fit perfectly against hers. She sighed and opened her mouth, letting me sweep my tongue inside her before melting against me.

"Gonna take my time with you, honey. Before this is over, I'm gonna know every square inch of your flesh. Then I'm gonna find out exactly what drives you crazy."

Her smile was worth admitting any shortcomings or weaknesses on my part. Because I knew she felt the same way with me. She had things she perceived as weaknesses, too. "Good. Because I want to do the same with you."

For the first time since my sister and mother had died, the first time since my father had died and taken my last immediate family to the Hereafter, I felt... hope. Peace. So I smiled back at her, hoping to convey all the joy she'd given me in this moment.

"Then, let's begin."

# Chapter Nine

**Scarlet**

This was happening. This was really happening! I was going to be with Mars however I could. If that meant sex, I'd welcome it with open arms and eagerness in my heart. If not, I'd still welcome it because Mars was nothing like Hammer. Or any man I'd ever been around, really. Sure, my dad was protective and good to me -- until he gave me to Hammer -- but it wasn't the same. No one had treated me the way Mars had since the first time I'd really met him.

Now, as we lay back on the bed, I met his kisses eagerly and welcomed the weight of his body on top of mine. His grunts and growls as he kissed me belied the tenderness and gentleness he showed me. I felt cherished. Almost… loved.

But no. I wasn't going there. Not yet. I had no doubt it would come if he meant what he said and was serious about keeping me with him, but I absolutely would not try to rush this any more than I already was.

Mars slid his hand under my shirt to find my breast. Though covered by a bra, he still kneaded and squeezed my eager flesh. He took his time, not shoving my clothing out of the way or pushing hard to find skin even though that's exactly what I wanted him to do. No. Mars did exactly what he said. He took his time learning every hollow and hill of my body. I arched to his touch with more and more eagerness until I felt like I was a writhing mass of nerves.

"How many lovers you had, Scarlet?"

I stiffened. "Does it matter?"

He grinned down at me. "Of course, it matters. But only because I don't want to hurt you."

I sighed in relief. That was the answer I was hoping for. Mars was different. "Just one. When I was sixteen. It was a guy I was dating back in Florida. It was the first time for both of us. Neither of us had any finesse, but we did have a good time."

Mars chuckled at that, and I loved the sound. Loved the look too. When he smiled, he made my heart melt. And he was devastating to look at.

I reached up to stroke his face through his beard. "You're so beautiful…" I know I sounded a little star-struck, but that's kind of how I felt.

"Not me, honey. That's all you."

"You should smile more often." I grinned up at him. Then that smile died as I had another thought. "Unless you're around club girls. Or any other unattached woman. Or even attached women." I huffed out a breath. "You know what? Don't smile unless we're alone together."

As I hoped, Mars threw back his head and laughed, rolling to his back on the bed. That's when I noticed his hard cock pressing against his jeans. I took the opportunity to roll on top of him, straddling his hips and pressing myself down to rub my pussy against his dick.

He still chuckled even though he thrust his hips at me. "We're gonna have a helluva good time together, woman."

"I plan to make sure of that." I grinned as I stripped off my shirt and bra. I knew the bruises were still stark on my skin, but they were fading to a greenish yellow mostly. My ribs were a little sore, but not as bad as they were.

The second he had an unimpeded view of my tits, Mars growled, his hands going straight to cup the small mounds. "You're beautiful, Scarlet. And you're all mine."

"You promise you're mine too?"

His gaze shot to mine instantly. "I do. I'm yours and your mine. I won't let anything change that."

We kissed again and I let myself melt against him. He let me carry on for a moment before rolling us so he was once again on top. His cock pressed against me insistently and he rocked his hips up and down, creating a delicious friction.

"I'm going to make love to my beautiful Scarlet," he murmured against my lips, and I let myself forget the world. I just let myself feel him and love him. I knew I was safe here, and nothing else mattered.

I gasped, digging my fingers into his back. He held my gaze as he thrust against me. His movements became more urgent and desperate as the pleasure built between, and we were both pushed closer to the edge. All this and I was the only one missing any clothes.

I pushed against his shoulders and Mars immediately pushed himself up on stiffened arms. "You good, baby?"

"Not really." When he frowned, I grinned. "I'd be much better if you'd get us naked."

Again, Mars barked out a laugh. "I can see you're gonna be a handful."

"Problem?"

"Not in the least. Keeps me on my toes. Besides, I like your sass. Makes me hard as a motherfucker."

It was my turn to chuckle. But Mars sat up and whipped off his shirt and it didn't really matter much anymore.

Mars was muscled and inked. Just like most bikers I'd seen. Though my father kept me and my sisters away from most of the men in Grim Road, living in a secure area inside the main compound, there was no way we could miss the abundance of men in the area. They guarded us. Protected us from the outside world. As good as some of those men were to look at, I'd never seen any of them who could compare to Mars. His body was absolutely magnificent. Smooth, tanned skin beckoned me to touch. To taste. And I vowed right then I'd do both to my heart's content before we left this bed.

I reached for his pants, unfastening the button at the waist. He chuckled and dropped his hands to his side, letting me undo his fly…

I looked up at him, raising an eyebrow. "Commando? Really, Mars?"

He shrugged. "I gotta be free."

It was my turn to laugh, but that laughter died on my lips as I freed his magnificent cock. It was long, thick, and abundantly veined. As beautiful as the rest of him. I took him in my hand and gave him a tentative stroke. His cock pulsed in my hand and a glistening, pearly drop of precum beaded on the top.

"You keep that up, and you're gonna get more than you bargained for, darlin'." Despite everything he'd told me before about his issues with sex, Mars looked relaxed. He was playing with me in an erotic way I loved.

"Maybe I want more than I bargained for?" I bit my lip nervously, but still did my best to slide him a cheeky grin.

"Mmm…" He snagged my jeans and tugged them off along with my panties. I gasped and tucked my legs up instinctively, but he merely raised an eyebrow. "I can't do all the wicked things I want to do to you if you don't let me see you, darlin'."

"Sorry. I'm just a bit nervous."

"Me too, baby. But I think we can muddle through this together."

I slid my palms up his chest, enjoying the hair roughened texture. Muscles played under his skin in an erotic dance. "Yeah. I think we can."

With a cocky smirk, Mars lowered his head to my breast and took one nipple into his mouth. My whole world lit up. I was sure I saw fairy lights behind my eyes as I sighed. Pleasure shot straight through my body to my clit, and I squealed in excitement at the unexpected sensation.

Mars looked up at me and grinned before giving the other breast the same treatment. This time, I bucked against him, unable to help myself.

"You like that?" His expression was positively wicked.

"You know I do."

"Good. Because it's only going to get better."

He trailed his beard down my body until he reached my mound. I trembled as he parted my legs and kissed the skin of each inner thigh. It tickled in the most erotic way, and I cried out as I watched his face descend toward my pussy. When he took one long, slow lick with his tongue, I gave up trying to act dignified and screamed.

"That's it, honey. Let me hear how much you enjoy this."

He slid two fingers into me and pumped them slowly as his tongue lapped at my clit. I tightened around him, wanting more. He obliged, pressing a third finger in and curling it just right so I writhed against the bed in pleasure.

"Oh, God... Mars, please don't stop!"

He sucked, licked, and nibbled every inch of my sensitive flesh, and by the time he lay on the bed, urging my legs over his shoulders and flicked his tongue directly against my clit, I simply couldn't take anymore. I came explosively, each wave of pleasure sending me higher and higher until I thought I might pass out. My vision blurred as one wave after another rolled through me.

I was lost in the pleasure he created, never wanting it to end. I'm not sure exactly when he moved, but the next thing I knew, Mars had rolled on a condom and positioned himself over me, his body between my legs, his cock poking at my entrance.

"Are you ready for me?"

"Yes," I breathed, too stunned to say more. This was pleasure unlike any I'd ever experienced. Sure, the one time I'd had sex had been fun and I'd made myself come plenty of times since, but this was on a whole other level.

He entered me slowly, inch by inch, stretching me as he went until his hips were pressed against my inner thighs. I wrapped my legs around him and let out a little whimper as I adjusted to his size.

"So Goddamned tight," he bit out. Sweat erupted over his skin. I think I'd been sweating since he made me come before, but I honestly wasn't sure. I knew cool air kissed us both, and I shivered even as goose flesh broke out over my skin. My nipples tightened and my pussy clamped around his dick in a tight embrace.

I gasped as he pushed himself in, feeling myself stretch around him. His thickness filled me completely, and as he began to move, I clung to his back, my nails digging into his skin and my moans echoing off the walls.

He moved slowly at first, rocking back-and-forth in shallow thrusts that sent tingles of pleasure through me. I bit my lip, not wanting to let go or give in too soon before the pleasure consumed me once again.

Mars seemed to read my thoughts because he quickened his pace, moving faster. With each thrust, Mars went deeper, hitting places I didn't even know existed. The pleasure was so intense I could hardly bear it. I felt my orgasm building and I threw my head back, screaming with pleasure and begging for more as wave after wave crashed over me.

Finally, with one last thrust, Mars exploded with a brutal shout. The feel of his cock pulsing inside me triggered my own orgasm and I screamed along with him, clinging as tightly as I could.

I couldn't catch my breath. I was so sensitive and overstimulated, every movement seemed to pulse through me straight to my clit. I whimpered, trying to hold him tighter when I already had a stranglehold on him.

Mars was breathing as hard as I was. When he pulled back slightly to look at me, he had an adorably bemused look on his face.

He shook his head like he had no idea what to think. "I didn't have to fight for control even once." I was pretty sure he hadn't meant to voice that thought out loud, and if he did that it was more to himself than to me. Then his eyes widened and he pushed off me slightly, bracing his weight on one arm. "I didn't hurt you, did I?"

"No, Mars." I smiled up at him, pulling him down for a soft kiss. "It was absolutely wonderful."

With a sigh, he lowered himself back on top of me and continued to kiss me as if simply enjoying the feel of our lips brushing together. Our tongues twining together in a sensual dance.

All too soon, he groaned and pushed off me.

"Don't move, baby. I'll be right back."

He went to the bathroom. I heard water running and when he returned, it was with a warm, wet washcloth. Mars gently cleaned me before tossing the cloth back toward the bathroom and lying back down beside me, pulling me into his arms. I rested my head on his chest and purred like a contented kitten.

"I could listen to that sound every day for the rest of my life. You promise I didn't hurt you?"

"You didn't. Mars... that was the best experience of my life. I never knew sex could be so wonderful."

"Baby, I didn't either." He chuckled and ran his hand up and down my arm. "Much as I'd love to stay here, we can't. Your father is on the way here with his club. And Hammer."

I stiffened. "Oh, no."

"Don't worry. Everything will be fine. I'm not letting anyone hurt you or take you from me."

"But your club --"

"Will protect you the same as they'd protect me. Did you mean it when you said you wanted to stay with me? Really mean it, Scarlet?" He looked down at me, his expression serious.

"I did. I've heard rumors that joining the Iron Tzars is a for-life thing. Even for your club girls and prospects. Old ladies too."

"It is. We'll have to get you a tattoo along with my property patch."

"It's pretty quick to make that kind of decision, but honestly, I could wait five years from now and my answer would still be the same. You've proven yourself. You'd never hurt me, and you'll protect me."

"With my life, honey. Always."

"Then I'm all in. Whatever it takes."

"Whatever it takes."

# Chapter Ten

**Mars**

Ace didn't have time to do the entire tattoo, but he helped Scarlet pick out one that suited her and laid out the prep work. She chose a bracelet of delicate, scarlet-colored chain links accented in gold. My property declaration was woven into a ribbon surrounding the links. Once completed, I had no doubt it would be lovely. Ace didn't have time to work on my tatt, but he would create a matching tattoo for my left ring finger. Just like the other attached men in Iron Tzars had opted to do. Her property cut was ready in record time, and I was sure I owed someone big-time for that.

Later. I'd figure it out and thank someone later. Right now, we had guests approaching in force. Rage like I'd never known before threatened to drag me under, but I held on to Scarlet's hand firmly. The touch of her skin seemed to calm me when nothing else possibly could. It wasn't that I was no longer feeling anger. No. My feelings were worse than I'd ever experienced. But, thanks to her nearness and soothing touch I was able to keep all that rage tightly leashed.

For now.

"What's happening?" I approached Sting with Scarlet in tow. The president was leaning against the door to Wylde's office while our tech guy studied various monitors and listened to something on his headphones.

"They'll be here in ten minutes. I've got a contingent to greet them at the gate and bring them to the field outside the barn. If there's a fight, I want it contained. No matter what, there's gonna be killin'. So?" Sting shrugged. "The barn."

"Have you spoken to Claw or Rocket?"

"Nothing besides for them to let me know they were coming. You know. Fifteen minutes before they were due to be here."

"They're expecting a war," Scarlet said softly. "Testing your readiness."

Sting raised an eyebrow at me. I just grinned. "My girl knows."

"She'll make you a fine old lady, Mars."

I looked down at Scarlet. She ducked her head and hid her face in my arm. No doubt she hadn't meant to speak out loud, but I was glad she did. She fully understood what Grim Road was doing and what would happen once we had them in our compound. "She already does, Sting. She already does."

As I'd hoped, Scarlet looked up to meet my gaze. I winked at her, and she blushed before moving to wrap her arms around my middle and bury her face in my chest without a word.

As if on cue, I heard the roar of motorcycles approaching. Grim Road was now in our territory. In our compound. Our home.

Scarlet took a breath before straightening and putting her hand back in mine. She pushed her shoulders back and donned a hard expression. I had no doubt she'd learned that particular look from her father.

"Let's do this," she said. There was a brave fierceness to her voice that made me proud. I squeezed her hand and gave her a nod before turning to Sting.

"I think we're ready."

The other man grinned. "Yeah. I think you are."

"This is going to be all right." She spoke softly, obviously a mantra to herself. I nodded, a silent agreement that no matter what we would all survive this day. Hammer, on the other hand…

Yeah. I was looking forward to this. As if she could read my mind, Scarlet said, "I'm not leaving here with Hammer, Sting. I'm staying with Mars. If my dad threatens a war I'll defer to Mars, but I'm not going anywhere with Hammer."

Sting gave me a hard look. "Didn't Mars explain to you how Iron Tzars works?"

"He did. But I don't expect you guys to go to war for me. You've got your own women to think about."

"And the kids. There are children here too." Iris approached us and took her place at Sting's side. Behind her and with their men were Winter and Serelda.

Scarlet stiffened and I could see the shock on her face. If she thought the women were turning against her, she had a surprise coming.

"What kind of club would we be if we didn't show our children how hard we'd fight for one of our own?" Serelda walked up to Scarlet and squeezed her shoulder. "Fuck Grim Road. If they want a war because they're trying to take you away from us, we'll all fucking fight for you."

"Fuckin' A!" I turned to see Lemon approaching Wylde's office, Danica hot on her heels.

"Lemon, go back upstairs. Please?"

"I will not, Dani. Scarlet's my friend. I'm fighting with her."

"No one said anyone was fighting." Sting chuckled. He scrubbed his hand over the back of his neck before meeting Brick's gaze. "We had no idea what we were gettin' into when we all took fierce old ladies."

Brick shrugged. "They are who they are. I wouldn't have mine any other way. That vicious streak she shows sometimes gives me a hard-on."

That got a bark of laughter from Scarlet and a frown from Serelda.

"Once this is over, I'll show you vicious, Brick. Good luck getting through it with your balls intact."

Brick just smirked. "You love my balls too much to permanently remove them, and I already survived a kick to them once from you. It'll hurt like a bitch, but I'll survive. Then we'll see what happens next."

His woman tilted her chin and raised an eyebrow. "Challenge accepted, big guy."

"If the two of you are done playing a verbal game of grab ass, we got company," Roman groused as he came into the common room from outside. "The boys are takin' them to the barn field." Roman nodded at Sting. "We're ready."

"Then let's show these motherfuckers what happens when they treat women like shit."

"Are we really takin' the women with us?" Shooter checked his weapon and tossed a spare clip to Roman as he walked into the room. "I'm not sure that's a good idea."

"The better question would be" -- Atlas's old lady gave Shooter a hard look I'd never seen before from Bellarose --"how do you think you're gonna stop us from going?"

Shooter winced, looking at a point over Bellarose's shoulder where Atlas stood at his wife's side. "Sorry, man. I just don't like the idea of the women being anywhere near a group of men if there's a possibility there might be fighting." He shook his head. "I meant no disrespect."

"We fight for our families," Bellarose said. "To the death." No one argued with the woman. She'd lost her unborn child when we'd been attacked several months back. Eagle's woman, Nyla, had men after her. They'd attacked the compound with drones carrying explosives. Bellarose had been injured and lost her baby during the attack. If she wanted to fight for those she considered family, no one was going to stop her.

"With that settled, let's ride." Sting led the rest of us to the yard where our bikes were ready. We'd be behind the Grim Road procession, putting us between them and escape. No one was leaving this compound until we'd extracted our pound of flesh for Hammer's treatment of Scarlet.

I mounted and started my bike, Scarlet securely behind me. She wrapped her arms around my waist and I took off. Ten minutes later, we pulled up to the barn. It was a structure in the middle of a field lined with thick woods on all sides. Only a dirt road was cut through the trees to allow us to bring vehicles through to the secluded field. This was where we brought someone we intended to take apart. I hoped Hammer was the only one we had to take care of, but I knew the Iron Tzars were ready and able to take care of more if it was necessary.

When we all parked, lined up in a solid row blocking the entrance to the road from the field, Sting led us toward the barn. The Grim Road members stood shoulder to shoulder in a show of force even in unfamiliar territory.

"I gotta give it to 'em," Roman said softly, never taking his eyes off the group of fourteen men we approached. "They got balls the size of Texas."

Sting grunted but said nothing.

As we drew closer, I could feel the tension in the air, like a hot, electric charge that had everyone on edge. The sun was setting behind us, casting long shadows across the field and painting the sky in deep oranges and purples. It was a beautiful scene, but also gave a portent of the violence that was about to take place.

Scarlet's body tensed behind me. She was always brave, but I knew she was scared. Most women would be in her place. Then I glanced down at her and I'll be Goddamned if my cock didn't get hard as fucking diamond. No. If Scarlet was scared, she didn't show it. She looked fucking furious.

"Woman, you better put that face away."

She jerked her head in my direction, meeting my gaze with that lingering fierceness still firmly planted on her features. It was muted now in her surprise at my comment, but still there nonetheless. "What?"

"Your face. You look like you're about to carve someone's liver out. Makes me hard and now ain't the time."

Now she looked annoyed. "Well, it's the only face I got so deal with it."

It took all my control not to bark out a laugh. Last thing I wanted to do was set someone off. But it was hard.

"Don't think I don't know this is your killin' field, Sting. Got a similar place of my own." Rocket, a man I'd considered a comrade in arms, went toe to toe with my president. "You think you can take us all?"

"Scarlet, come here." Claw bit out his command and I felt Scarlet move beside me, like she was going to obey his command without question. Instead, she stopped and took a tight grip on my arm. It didn't escape my notice that she'd left my hand free, making it easy for me to snag a weapon if necessary. Girl knew what she was about.

"I'm sorry, Claw." She used her father's road name instead of addressing him in a more familiar manner. "I'm not going back with Grim Road. Or Hammer."

Claw narrowed his eyes, then glanced at Hammer before settling on Scarlet once more but said nothing. Sting nodded at Hammer.

"Don't know if we can take you all." Sting continued the narrative he and Rocket had going on, not acknowledging Scarlet or Claw at all. She shrugged. "I'm willing to bet we could give it a good show, though. Besides, we're only interested in takin' out one of your people." He pointed to Hammer. "Leave him here and you can go your way. Or you can fight for him. Makes no Goddamn difference to me. But that man don't leave this compound alive."

"You know that's not happening, Sting. He's Grim Road. We don't give up one of our own." I knew from my experience with Rocket he had as little give to him as Sting did. Which was to say, none.

"Are you fully aware of the situation, Rocket? Do you know what's going on?"

Rocket shrugged. "I got one side of it. That's the reason we're here talking instead of us wiping your entire club off the map."

Sting gave the man a humorless bark of laughter. "That sure of yourselves? I get it. And yeah. I know at least some of what your club is. Not all, but enough to know you're true badasses. So, yeah. You might be able to take us all. But you'd betray every fuckin' thing you stood for and that's not the Grim Road I've been told about."

Rocket grinned. "Guess we need to hear the other side then, huh? That why you let your women tag along? Or you plannin' on hiding behind them?"

Surprisingly, Iris was the one who spoke up. She stood at Sting's side, though the president put himself slightly in front of her in a protective stance. "Their women are here to support Scarlet." She spoke in as hard a voice as Sting could. She might be young, but Iris was definitely an MC president's old lady. "She's one of us and we'll lay down our lives to protect her. Same as the rest of the club will. You were quick to declare Hammer one of you. Of your family. One would think you'd give your vice president's daughter the same fucking respect."

"And no one let us do anything." The voice came from behind me. "We do what we want and we choose to stand with Scarlet, you bitchass motherfucker." I thought I heard Wylde groan behind me. Probably because the woman who spoke now was Lemon. Who most decidedly shouldn't be here.

"Bloody hell," Wylde muttered. "The day's goin' to shit now."

Rocket and Claw's attention both swung to the girl in question. Rocket looked amused. Claw, annoyed.

"You lettin' kids dictate the way Iron Tzars does things, Sting?" Rocket delivered the words like a rebuke, but Sting just shrugged it off.

"I know my people, Rocket. No one corrals Lemon if she doesn't want to be corralled. By the way, Claw, you owe Scarlet's life to that little spitfire. If it hadn't been for her, Scarlet would be dead."

That got more than one of the Grim Road men shifting uneasily. It didn't escape my notice that more than one of them looked Hammer's way.

"How's that?" Claw snapped. "She pull your man off her?" He indicated me. "Seems like a little thing to be doin' something like that."

"Fuuuuuck…" Wylde groaned and dropped his head. "You done it now, hoss."

He had barely started speaking when Lemon broke ranks and marched straight up to Claw. He gave her an amused smirk as she approached.

"Motherfucker." Lemon delivered a kick to Claw's balls that had him giving a startled yelp before clutching his privates and sinking to his knees. Which gave Lemon the opening she was looking for, apparently, because she snapped out a folding baton and got in three good licks to Hammer -- who stood beside Claw -- before Deacon and Wylde were able to pull her off the man. Rocket snagged the baton from her hand but didn't otherwise touch her. He did eye her with new respect, though.

"Stand down, Lemon!" Brick snarled. Lemon just hissed at him.

"Why? They're the ones who put her in Hammer's tender care!" She put as much contempt into her voice as anyone I'd ever heard. "They're the ones who abandoned her!"

"Those are some serious accusations, girl." Rocket gave Lemon his full attention. "You got proof to back it up?"

"I know she's his daughter," Lemon pointed to Claw. "And I know Scarlet said he gave her to Hammer, then gave his approval for him to take her away from the safety of her club. And before you say she's not a member of Grim Road, that don't matter. I'm not a 'member'" -- she made air quotes --"of Iron Tzars. But it's still my club. They have my back and I have theirs. We're a family! You should be a fuckin' family!"

The more she spoke, the louder Lemon got. It was clear to everyone she was more than just blustering or being a brat. Lemon was ready to go on a killing rampage and damn the consequences. All for

Scarlet.

"We *are* a family, girl." Rocket said softly. He looked down at Claw who was trying to catch his breath. He was still down on one knee, but trying to push up. Just didn't look like he could quite manage it yet. "Claw did what he did to keep Scarlet safe. He put her in the hands of a trusted member and sent them out of our territory for her safety."

A couple of things registered. First, Rocket didn't talk down to Lemon, or scoff at her concern. He spoke to her as an equal who had a right to know Claw's reasoning. Second, Hammer had either fooled the entire club, or he had an ax to grind specifically with Scarlet. Either way, I doubted Grim Road would give us any trouble when we took Hammer apart.

"What's your real name, girl? I know it ain't Lemon. Though, I gotta say, it kinda suits you."

Lemon gave him a disgusted look. "I could give two shits what you think about my name, you bastard. You're an asshole in the extreme and I hope you rot in hell."

Rocket made eye contact with Sting. Our president just shrugged. "Gotta have a strong personality to hang with this group. In Lemon's case, we try to keep up with her."

That got the first genuine reaction from Rocket since I'd seen him inside our compound. He chuckled, his gaze going back to Lemon. "Yeah. I can see that."

"How about we go inside the barn and fill you in on what's been going on since Lemon met Scarlet. Because that's all we can attest to. Scarlet can tell you the rest." Sting tilted his head. "I'm assuming you'll believe your own daughter, Claw?"

"Bastard," Claw muttered in a painful grimace. "Of course, I'll believe Scarlet. All she had to do was call if she was in trouble."

Lemon, who'd been let go because it seemed like she'd calmed down, lunged for Claw again with a battle cry that would do any Viking proud. She kicked him in the face, since he was still on his knees. This time it was Rocket who pulled her off his vice president.

"Girl, you need to learn when you're outmatched."

Rocket had circled her with his muscular arms, pinning hers to her body so she was helpless to strike out at him. He lifted her slight frame off the ground which... was his second mistake. His first was underestimating Lemon enough to get that close to her. Instead of kicking and thrashing as Rocket probably expected, Lemon simply snapped her head back and into Rocket's nose. Blood squirted from both sides of his face and he gave a sharp grunt, but didn't drop Lemon. So she did it again. Then one more time for good measure.

"Goddamnit, Lemon," Wylde sounded weary instead of angry, like this was a scene he'd witnessed repeatedly while he had all but given up trying to tame the feral little hellcat. "What have I told you about bashing the badass MC president of another club? Leave him alone. Bad Lemon!"

Claw looked up at his president. "That one's rabid." His voice still sounded strained, but he'd finally managed to get to his feet. He was still bent at the waist and still guarding his nuts.

"Bloody hell," Rocket muttered, spitting blood from his mouth onto the ground. He pulled a rag from his back pocket and scrubbed over his nose to keep the blood from dripping. I think what surprised me the most was how none of Grim Road retaliated. They'd let us pull Lemon off one of their own the first time and left Rocket to his own this time. It was clear they weren't into hurting women. Especially if they didn't deserve it. Didn't absolve them of what had happened to Scarlet. Just meant they might get to live. Well, except for Hammer. His hours were numbered.

# Chapter Eleven

**Scarlet**

The second everyone headed inside the barn, I let go of Mars to make my way to Lemon. I threw my arms around her and hugged her fiercely. "I can't thank you enough, Lemon." I was right at her ear. I knew she'd push me away soon, but I had to let her know how deeply grateful I was for her coming to my defense. "You're the bravest, most vicious person I've ever met and I love you so much!"

Lemon grumbled something but didn't push me away. She even gave me a hug back, if a bit awkwardly.

When we parted she scowled in the direction of the Grim Road men. "You make sure you tell everyone you come across what a badass I am. It'll save me the trouble of teaching them."

I grinned. "You got it."

"Come on. I don't want to miss a second of the fun."

"You'll stay out of the fun," Wylde admonished, giving Lemon a stern look. "No fun." Then his lips twitched.

"One would almost think you're doing it on purpose, Wylde," Lemon said in a singsong voice. "In fact, I'm pretty sure that was the go ahead to do whatever the fuck I want."

When Sting gave Wylde a look, the other man just shrugged. "Hey. I never said she could do what she wanted."

"You didn't have to. You tell Lemon not to do something, the probability is better than good she's gonna do it just for spite."

"Really?" Wylde gave Sting a wide-eyed look of

innocence. Like the man hadn't realized what he'd just done when everyone in the area knew he'd done it on purpose. I knew Lemon realized what he did and took it for what it was. A token gesture that, hey, he'd "tried to contain the damage, but the girl just goes her own way." Yeah. No one was buying that.

More than once, I saw Rocket looking over his shoulder as he tried to clean up his bleeding nose. His gaze always narrowed on Lemon.

"You may have bitten off more than you can chew this time, Lemon." I kept my voice low, but my gaze was firmly on the president of Grim Road.

She merely shrugged. "He's an asshole who deserved what I dished out."

"He's the president of Grim Road. You don't want his attention on you and you've snagged it in spades."

"Good. Maybe he'll realize I mean business. No one messes with my family, Scarlet. No one. He should have had your back with Hammer and your father. Where was your mother when Claw gave you to that bastard?"

"My mother's dead. She was killed by one of Grim's enemies when I was ten. Her death's the reason they moved everyone to a separate compound within the main compound. Everyone not a patched member who is a part of Grim Road stays inside those walls."

"Then why didn't he protect you?"

"He thought he was, Lemon."

"Yeah? How many times did you talk to him after you left Riviera Beach?"

She had me there. "None, once Hammer took my phone. But I did talk to him before that."

"So what happened after?"

I didn't have an answer. Before this was over,

though, I'd get one.

We entered the barn behind all the men. Iris, Serelda, and Bellarose were all with us. Lemon led the way, but the older women all surrounded me. I'd never felt such a show of support in my life. I loved my father and the idea of the protection of Grim Road, but I'd never experienced it like this. The women had my back. The men had the women's back. And I had no doubt we all had the men's back. I know I certainly had Mars's.

"All right," Rocket said, crossing his arms over his chest. "What the fuck's goin' on?"

"I'll tell you what's goin' on," Hammer said, speaking up for the first time. "That bastard is holding Scarlet here. He's probably brainwashed her. Or groomed her or some shit."

"She's only been here a week, you motherfucker," Mars snapped, taking a step toward Hammer before Brick put a hand out to stay him.

"How about we hear from sourpuss over there," Rocket said, nodding to Lemon.

"You really are looking to get your balls handed to you, aren't you?" Lemon shook her head, chuckling. "Sourpuss?"

Rocket shrugged. "If it fits…"

"Fine. I'll tell you what happened. Your boy Hammer there beat the shit outta Scarlet. More than once."

"Again, that's a serious allegation. You got proof?" Though Rocket seemed belligerent toward Lemon, I could see he was deadly serious and taking in everything she said with an open mind. His entire being was focused on my friend and I wasn't sure I liked it.

"You mean besides Scarlet's word?"

Rocket narrowed his eyes at Lemon. "Scarlet is one of us. If she says that's what happened, I'll believe her."

"I told you, Rocket," Hammer jumped in, looking furious. "They've brainwashed her. You know I'd never hurt Scarlet. It's why Claw gave her to me. Because he knew I'd protect her with my life."

"You're such a Goddamned liar," Lemon muttered, raising an eyebrow to look straight at Hammer. "I saw it. Me. I saw you kicking her while she was on the floor. I saw you backhand her, though you mostly kicked and punched her torso. Probably to keep the obvious evidence of the abuse to a minimum. The only reason I didn't intervene is because Breaker over there" -- she hiked a thumb at the big biker in question --"thought he'd get his ass handed to him by Sting if we busted in, we couldn't stop you, and I got hurt. He opted to bring back backup and get me to safety." Lemon gave Breaker an annoyed look. "Which, I get it, Breaker. I really do. Under normal circumstances I'd have been mostly OK with it, but it nearly cost Scarlet her life."

"You sayin' I nearly beat her to death?" Hammer snorted out a laugh. "That's an outright lie."

Lemon shook her head and immediately continued. "Didn't say that, you bastard. What happened next isn't something I can tell. Ain't my story. But suffice it to say, Scarlet would do anything -- *anything* -- to keep her sisters safe."

That got Claw's attention good and proper. "What do her sisters got to do with this?"

"Everything," I said before I could stop myself. This was my moment. I'd always been in the background because I understood what Grim Road did. What it stood for. That meant they had to have all their concentration focused in the right area. But it was my sisters who were in danger. Lemon was right. I'd do what it took to make sure they never went through what I had. I pointed an accusing finger at Hammer. "If anyone manipulated anyone, it was Hammer. He threatened to hurt Sunshine and Rainbow if I didn't do what he said."

My dad shook his head. "He wouldn't do that."

I stuck up my chin. "You sayin' you don't believe me? That I'd lie to you?"

"Scarlet…"

"No, Claw." I shook my head almost violently, my temper finally redlining the way it should have with Hammer months ago. "There isn't any in-between. Either you believe me or you don't. If you don't, then I have no father anymore." The more I spoke, the angrier I got. I felt Mars land a gentle hand on my shoulder, but I shrugged him off. "That man, Hammer, the man you gave me to, terrorized me from the day we left Riviera Beach. He beat me. Dislocated my shoulder. Kept me isolated from my family. Did you even call to check on me after the first few weeks?"

"I did," Claw said, looking shocked. I wasn't sure if it was the info dump I was laying on him or the fact that I was asserting myself against him.

"You didn't think it odd that you never got to talk to me?"

"Scarlet, honey. We were in the middle of a really bad situation --"

"So bad you didn't care to make sure your daughter was safe? What about my sisters? You gonna do them the same way? Because, if you are, I'll come at Grim Road like a tidal wave and destroy everything I possibly can before you have to kill me."

My dad looked like I'd just gutted him. In fact, he

staggered backward before clutching his chest and falling to one knee. "I'd never hurt you, honey. Never in a million years."

"Yeah?" I stepped closer to him, giving Hammer a wide berth. I needn't have bothered because Mars was right at my shoulder between me and my own personal nightmare. "Then why didn't you insist on speaking to me? Directly to me." It was a demand more than a question and I knew I was skating on thin ice. At least, in any other situation I would be.

"I'm so sorry, honey." He reached for me, still on his knee. When I stepped back, not letting him touch me, he looked like he'd been gutted. "Scarlet…"

"Answer me!" I yelled at my father. Never in my life had I shown so much disrespect to him. Never wanted to. He was my father. Larger than life. Until the months Hammer had me, I'd never questioned the fact that he loved me.

"I'm sorry. I was so focused on --"

"Everything but my well-being? I get it." He shook his head, but I plowed on. "Was Hammer right? Were you so disappointed my mother didn't have boys that you killed her after the twins were born? Is that the reason you abandoned me to Hammer? Because I was of no use to you?" I didn't really believe what Hammer had told me, but this had to be done now. If for no other reason than to restore my faith in my father.

Claw threw back his head and roared his anger and rage. Hammer took a step sideways, but two members of Grim Road had already blocked his path should he decide to try a retreat.

"I'll fuckin' kill you, Hammer!" Claw got to his feet now, his hands balled into fists. He advanced on Hammer. To his credit, Hammer played the part well. I wanted to scratch his fucking eyes out.

"If you really think I'd say such a thing, then do your worst, Claw. I was good to Scarlet. She's just upset because you sent us away. She didn't want to leave home and took out her anger and frustration on me. Then along came these fuckers and she got strange ideas in her head." He waved his hand toward Mars. "I'm completely loyal to you and Grim Road."

Claw barely let Hammer finish before he punched him in the gut. Hammer doubled over, but stayed on his feet. Surprisingly, Claw didn't do anything else other than get up in Hammer's face nose to nose. "You're fixin' to fuckin' die, motherfucker. My advice is to make peace with whatever deity you worship. Because Sting's right. You ain't leavin' this compound alive."

"You're really takin' the word of a brainwashed kid over me? I realize she's your daughter, but I've always been loyal to Grim Road. To you and Rocket. I had one lapse in good sense, but I stayed true, even after Madina was dead." Hammer sounded so reasonable I'd have questioned my own judgment if I hadn't still had sore ribs to prove he was lying. I nearly missed the fact he'd used my mother's name, but figured it was because their enemies had gotten to her.

"I am." Claw didn't hesitate.

"Then at least take me back to my home territory to kill me." Hammer lifted his chin. Like he was being brave or something. But I noticed the sweat bead over his forehead. "I should have the right to die at home."

"And give you a chance to escape or call in reinforcements?" Lemon chuckled. "Not bloody likely. They don't do it, Iron Tzars will take all y'all out."

"That's enough, Lemon." Sting's voice was hard this time. There was no indulgence like there usually was. He was all the president of Iron Tzars now. "You don't make those decisions for the club, and you know it."

Lemon bared her teeth at Hammer. I could just imagine the thoughts running through her head. As if she'd read my mind, she amended her statement. "If Iron Tzars won't, I will. And before you doubt I have the ability, I'll remind you what happens when you underestimate me."

"Now's not the time, Lemon," Wylde said softly. "You'll get your turn."

"I fuckin' better." Lemon moved to stand directly at my side. She took my hand, but not before whipping out a wicked-looking serrated knife from a sheath at the small of her back. She didn't raise it in a threatening manner. Just let it rest at her side at the ready.

"Fuck." That came from Deacon of all people. I glanced at the other man and he just grinned. "Glad I picked the docile sister."

I thought his comment would break the tension, but it didn't. Rocket shook his head addressing me directly.

"What happened, Scarlet? How did Lemon save your life that night?"

This was so fucking hard. Harder than I thought it would be. Harder than standing up to my dad and being so angry with the one person in the world who I'd trusted to protect me before I'd met Mars. "He said if I tried to run or to contact Claw, that he had people inside Grim Road he'd order to hurt Sunshine and Rainbow. At first I thought I could last until we came back to Florida. But as the weeks and months went on, I doubted myself."

"What do you mean you doubted yourself?"

"That I could last that long." I took a breath, trying to get myself back under control. In a way, my temper redlining was good. I got rid of some toxic shit I hadn't realized I'd held inside. I felt like I could breathe easier. "Hammer never took it far enough that I was afraid for my life. He seemed to want to torture me, though I had no idea why. He beat me down both mentally and physically until I knew I had to escape. But I wasn't about to sacrifice my sisters for my own safety."

Rocket paled and his gaze snapped to Claw who looked even more upset than before. Claw shook his head while Rocket's jaw clenched, the sides bulging almost convulsively.

"No, Scarlet. Just... no!" Claw looked like he was on the verge of a breakdown. Sweat beaded his forehead and I could see the pulse beating like mad in his neck.

"Yes, *Dad*." I nearly spat the word. I loved my father, had thought he loved me, and I wasn't entirely convinced Claw didn't love me. "In order to save my sisters, I took the only way out I had available. I tried to kill myself. I'd been preparing for a couple of weeks but hadn't gotten to that point. I had the rope behind the house in the corner of the yard already tied to the perfect branch in a perfect fucking tree. The last time Hammer beat me was my tipping point. Was it a weak moment for me? Maybe. But I had Lemon and Apple wanting me to come to the Tzars compound with them and the thought was just too tempting. To be able to sleep at night and not worry about Hammer coming into my room in a drunken rage to hit me? To have people who cared about what happened to me and be willing to protect me? I knew I'd give in and when I did, I was thoroughly convinced I'd condemn

Sunshine and Rainbow to death. Or worse. To a life of what I'd been suffering."

Once I'd started, all I could do was continue. I laid it all out there with a starkness I hadn't really intended on relaying. But it was how I felt. If I were honest, I wanted to see Claw's reaction. I wanted to see if it would hurt him. Maybe that made me petty and a bad person, but I didn't care. If he'd tried to talk to me, even once, I'd have told him to come get me and I thought he would have. At least, I had thought so at the time. I guess I just needed to hear from him why he hadn't tried to force Hammer to let me speak with him.

Claw stumbled toward me. He tried to pull me into his arms, but I wasn't sure I was ready. Thankfully, Mars was right there. The second I took one step back he pushed his way in front of me to keep my father away from me. I wasn't ready to forgive him yet. Claw growled at Mars, and I thought my father was going to plow his way through him, but Mars stood his ground and shook his head.

"Not until she's ready, Claw."

"She's my daughter!"

"Shoulda thought about that before you threw yourself so far into your work you put her in the hands of a monster."

"I didn't do anything! Why won't you believe me!"

That was all I could take. With a battle yell, I snagged the baton Rocket had dropped and swung it at Hammer. Over and over. And over. No one had secured his hands so he blocked as many hits as I landed, but it felt good to finally be able to fight back.

"How does it feel, huh?" I screamed at him, raining blows down on him again and again. "How does it feel, you motherfucker!"

I kept hitting him. The more I hit him, the more I wanted to hit him. I wanted him to feel as hopeless and desperate as I had all those months. I was to the point I was about to wear myself out when Hammer finally broke.

With a roar, he lunged at me, snagging the baton before I could hit him with it again. He struck out, trying to backhand me. When I was pulled out of the way by someone, he yelled again, this time trying to swing at me with the baton.

"Fuckin' cunt! I'll fuckin' kill you!"

There was a deafening gunshot. I screamed and threw my hands over my ears. I thought Hammer would topple over or something and was surprised at the surge of disappointment I felt that he was dead already. Instead, he screamed before he fell to his side. Like someone had swept his leg from underneath him. When I finally got a closer look at Hammer, I saw his right leg from the knee down was lying beside him.

"Gag that motherfucker," Rocket ordered. "I'm tired of hearing his fuckin' whinin'." He didn't even acknowledge someone had shot Hammer's leg off. I didn't see a gun.

Hammer fought now. He lashed out as best he could from the sawdust floor of the barn. Even as hurt as he was, he was still a serious threat. His arms were seriously muscled. I remembered well how they could deliver his punishment with those arms and huge hands.

I looked around to see who had shot and was surprised to see it was Claw. My father. His face was a mask of rage and anguish. He found me in the chaos that was happening. OK, so chaos wasn't really the word. There were two members of Grim Road -- Dom and Ringo -- along with three members of Iron Tzars gagging and restraining Hammer. I thought they might chain him upright. Like hang him from the rafters or something. Instead, they tied him down to a steel table. It looked to have been made for restraining someone. It reminded me of images I'd seen on TV of a lethal injection table. Only there were clamps at the ankle and thigh instead of just the ankles. There were also clamps at the wrists and upper arms. Like they expected someone to be missing body parts. When Hammer continued to thrash, they slid a metal clamp around his neck.

The men from Grim Road stepped back until the Iron Tzars started cutting Hammer's clothes from his body. Then Grim helped until Hammer was naked and laid out on the table. The stump that was his leg bled, but not as much as I thought it would. Probably because the limb was completely severed. Roman still tied a tourniquet just over the stump until the bleeding completely stopped.

"Don't let him bleed out," Sting said. He looked for all the world like he could really give two shits about his leg, but was looking forward to whatever was about to happen next. "Mars. Wylde. Get the women out of here."

"Like hell," Lemon muttered.

"I'm not leaving, Mars." My voice was surprisingly steady and the moment I uttered the words, I knew they were true. It wasn't so much for myself, though I resented everything he'd put me through. I was the daughter of the vice president of Grim Road. I might be angry at my dad, I might not understand how he could not protect me, but I admired him for how he did his job for the club. I could honor him even if I wasn't certain I could ever trust him again.

"Honey, please." Mars gripped my shoulder. I knew he wanted to pull me into his arms, and I wanted that too. But there was another club of questionable integrity in very close proximity and I knew he needed his hands free. I might not know much about fighting, but I knew about safety and that these clubs might be loose allies, but given this situation they didn't trust each other. "I think it's best if we go."

"Not happening. Do I want to see this? Not really. But I owe it to my sisters to make sure it's done."

Mars shook his head but finally he leaned down and pressed his lips to mine before murmuring for my ears alone. "You're gonna be one fine old lady, Scarlet. And a fine mother. Plan on knockin' you up first chance I get."

That got a bark of laughter from me even though there was nothing about this entire situation fit to laugh at.

"Do you mean that, Mars?" Claw stepped to the side but backed up several steps instead of coming closer. "Really mean it. You'll make my daughter your old lady? You'll take care of her?" Apparently, Mars hadn't been quiet enough.

"It's already done, Claw. You know Iron Tzars is for life. She's wearin' my property patch and Ace has started her tattoo. She's mine and I'm hers."

"I know you have… issues. Can you fight your demons and not hurt Scarlet accidentally?"

"He already has fought those, Claw." I gave my father a frown. "Did you ask Hammer the same questions before you sent me off with a smile and a fucking princess wave?"

Claw winced. Surprisingly, he answered. "No, Scarlet. I didn't." His voice was barely audible. That's when I noticed he had a gun in his hand. It was a gun I'd seen him carry on multiple occasions. He'd once told me it was powerful enough that all you had to do was hit your target anywhere and it would incapacitate them. "I should have."

Something told me I needed to get any answers I wanted from my father now, so I blurted out the one question burning in my mind. "Did Mom really die giving birth to the twins?"

Claw winced and my heart sank. "I'm sorry, honey. No."

I couldn't breathe. My knees went weak and it took every ounce of will I had to lock them and stay upright. My ears roared and my vision wanted to close in. White dots danced on the periphery and I forced myself to suck in a breath before I passed out.

Then Mars asked the question I couldn't. "What happened to her? What happened to Scarlet's mother?"

"It was complicated," Claw said. "But the short of it is, she betrayed the club. That's really all that matters. Once she gave birth, I killed her."

"So, my whole life's been a lie?" My question was whispered. It was hard to speak. My throat wanted to close up, and I knew it was only a matter of time before I passed out. "How can I trust what you say ever again?"

"I can vouch for him on this, Scarlet." Rocket's voice was gentle. He glanced at his vice president. The look he gave Claw was one of deep disapproval. "He was supposed to tell you. When you were old enough. I was unaware he'd told you Madina had died in childbirth. And it was more that she betrayed you, Claw, not the club, and you damned well know it."

"How was I supposed to tell my daughter that I killed her mother, Rocket, huh? You tell me how I do that!"

"I could have helped you, Claw. Now, I have no idea what to do. Why did you send her away with Hammer?"

"You know why," Claw snarled. "We had terrorists breathing down our neck."

"We always have terrorists breathing down our neck," Rocket snarled. "Fuck! What the fuck did you do? You said she asked to go. That she begged you to let Hammer take her away from Grim."

"It was the right thing to do, Rocket! I had to send her away!"

"No. You didn't. Everyone was safe in Grim. You even left Sunshine and Rainbow in the compound. Scarlet could have stayed in Grim. And with someone other than Hammer. My God, man! You sent her into the fuckin' lion's den!"

"Wait." Lemon stepped forward to stand beside me. Now I was flanked by Mars and Lemon. I was glad because I needed their tough brand of support just now. "Are you telling me you didn't know Claw sent Scarlet with Hammer?"

Rocket didn't take his eyes off Claw. "I knew they'd left, but I was under the impression the trip was Scarlet's idea. That she and Hammer had something going on. I didn't think it was a good idea, but it wasn't really my business since Scarlet was eighteen."

"I had no choice, Rocket." Claw shook his head. "He was going to tell Scarlet."

"So? You knew the connection he had with Madina. With your wife. With the twins."

"What?" My voice was barely above a whisper. "What connection?"

Rocket adjusted his stance and glared at Claw. When Claw said nothing, Rocket shifted again, this time, bringing his boot down on the floor harder than strictly necessary to command Claw's obedience without words.

"I'm sorry, Scarlet." Claw shook his head. "So fuckin' sorry."

"Tell her, Claw. You owe her that much."

"Hammer had an affair with your mother. He's the father of Sunshine and Rainbow. She told me after she had them, and I just... lost my mind. I barely remember what I did, but I was covered in her blood when I finally came back to myself. He wanted you to get back at me for killing the woman he loved."

"Why didn't you kill this son of a bitch back then, Rocket?" Sting bit out. "Fuck. He'd rather keep his fuckin' secret than protect his daughter."

"Because it was done in the heat of the moment. And I wasn't ready to give up on him. I still needed him."

"Not good enough!" Sting snapped.

Rocket looked thunderous. "I had my reasons. While I didn't condone what he did, the fact remained that Madina broke her vow to Claw. Hammer was just as guilty because he knew she was Claw's woman. While neither of them deserved to die, it was done. I couldn't bring Madina back any more than I could take away the affair."

"And now? After this?"

Rocket sighed. "He's my friend. We all make mistakes."

"He killed his wife, Rocket! He sold out his daughter! If you don't end him, I'm going to."

"He has three daughters he's raised all on his own! You don't get to tell me what to do in my own club, Sting! What about Warlock? No one leaves the Tzars. Right?" That last was said with a mocking expression I was certain Sting didn't appreciate.

"They do when El Diablo demands to take them in."

"But you didn't want to kill him even though you should have."

Sting clenched his jaw but said nothing.

"Shoulda known this would happen." Rocket muttered, scrubbing a hand over his face. "Hammer didn't seem to want the girls, but this was about revenge for Claw killing Madina as much as Claw taking Hammer's girls as his own. All to keep a fuckin' secret."

Then, Claw did something I never expected. "I'm so sorry, Scarlet. But you should know, I'm so very, very proud of you. I love you." He stepped back another couple of steps, raised the .45 to his head, and pulled the trigger.

# Chapter Twelve

**Mars**

I wasn't sure what I expected after Claw offed himself. I thought maybe Scarlet would break down or grieve or... something. She didn't. She would later, I was sure, but right now, the woman was pissed to hell and back.

"Are you fucking kidding me right now?" She stared at the remains of her father. And really, there wasn't much left of his head. My instinct was to take her out of there. Now. Yesterday. But Scarlet was having none of it.

"Holy. Fuck." Lemon looked like this might be more than even she could take, but she held on to Scarlet's hand like both their lives depended on it.

"Christ." Rocket quickly stepped in front of the women to block their view of Claw. "Can't someone get the women the fuck out of here?"

"Why?" Shit and piss. And fuck it all to fucking hell. Bellarose spoke up, her gaze hard when I glanced over her. Atlas was by her side and looked like he'd been trying to take her out, but the woman was having none of it. Neither was Serelda. Winter averted her gaze but came up behind Scarlet and Lemon. She put her arms around both women and spoke softly to them. "You think just because we're women we can't handle the hard shit?" Bellarose had changed since she'd lost her baby. Atlas had too. He was more protective than ever of Bellarose, but also more indulgent with her. If she wanted to be here, by God, she'd be here. Atlas would also protect her with the viciousness of a rabid Doberman. "We're here to support Scarlet. She needs us here, so we're here. Seems like supporting each other is something Grim

Road has a fucking problem with."

Everyone stared at her, and I could see Lemon and Scarlet were both in shock. It was almost like they hadn't expected Bellarose to speak up and stand with Scarlet like she did. I hadn't either, but she really had changed. All our women had after that incident. It hadn't happened immediately, but over the last several months, it was like they'd banded together and decided they were in charge of keeping the kids and each other safe. A last line of defense as it were. It wasn't a bad thing. But I'm pretty sure none of us expected them to be part of something like this.

"Rose, honey," Atlas tried to plead with her gently. "Let's go. We can take Scarlet with us."

"Only if that's what Scarlet wants," Bellarose said. Her voice was strong and clear, her head held high. "If not, we stand by her."

As if Bellarose had given some kind of signal, all the women surrounded Scarlet. I was surprised Winter was still there. The woman hated blood in any form. I noticed she kept her gaze on anything but the gruesome scene before us -- Claw and Hammer were both a mess -- but stood firmly where she was.

Rocket took a breath, looked around, and found Sting. "Are all your women like this?"

Sting shrugged, looking for all the world like this happened every day. I wasn't sure if he was pissed and hiding it or just going with the flow. "They've been through a lot this past year. And they are part of Iron Tzars. No wimps here."

Rocket was silent but moved his gaze to fix on Scarlet. He just stared hard at her, as if he were sizing her up. For her part, Scarlet held his gaze with an equally hard one of her own.

"I'm sorry, Scarlet," Rocket said softly, never

looking away from her. "You didn't deserve any of this."

"I got it anyway. Are you saying this was all about Hammer getting revenge for Claw killing my mother?"

"Looks that way, kid."

"I'm many things, Rocket. But I'm not a kid. Not anymore."

"Point taken. I never thought Claw was capable of betraying you. Or killing himself. Not like this. Every member of Grim Road has secrets they don't want anyone to know and that was Claw's. I guess it's better this way. For what he did to keep his secret from you, I'd have had to kill him anyway." Rocket scrubbed a hand over his face. "No one inside Grim knew Claw had killed Madina but me. I honestly hadn't realized Hammer knew until now. Had I known, I'd have overridden his approval of you leaving with that bastard."

The bastard in question was hollering behind his gag. Didn't matter. The sound was muffled, and no one gave a shit about what he had to say anyway.

"It's done now. At least, Claw is done." Scarlet glanced over toward Hammer. "What's gonna happen to him?"

Roman had been at the table the whole time, laying out instruments until there was a veritable smorgasbord of blades, saws, and pincers. He was currently lowering a full-length mirror from the rafters and checking the angle. Looked like Hammer could watch whatever was about to happen and he wasn't too happy about it. Hell, it was almost enough to give me the heebie-jeebies. If he hadn't hurt Scarlet so much she'd thought the only way she had out was to kill herself... Nope. Fucker had it coming.

"Well." Sting let out a breath. "We can't torture him over several months like we should. This will likely only last a few hours. Six or eight tops." Hammer thrashed against his bonds but they held firm. "First thing we're gonna do is slice away his eyelids. Don't want him to miss a fuckin' thing."

"Good," Scarlet snapped. "What next?"

"Stitches is gonna start an IV and put heart monitors on him and all kinds of monitoring shit. 'Cause, you know…"

"You don't want him dying too fast." Scarlet's grin was positively evil. "This is a good plan. Stitches gonna make sure he stays alive as long as possible?"

"Oh, yeah. We're gonna take him apart one appendage at a time. Then cauterize the wound. Got O Neg blood standing by in case we hit a major artery too fast and have to take a break, but we'll stop the bleeding and give him more blood. When he passes out, we've got adrenaline to kickstart his heart and wake him up."

Scarlet moved to stand over Hammer. "Sounds like you're getting ready to have a fun time. Bet you wished you'd never fucked with me now, huh?" She spit in his face before grabbing a scalpel and slicing a bit of skin off of his chest. Not a big piece, but enough she made the man scream behind his gag.

"We should go, Scarlet." I wanted her out of here before she checked out. She was holding her own and I had no doubt she needed at least part of this, but I wasn't comfortable having her here any longer.

"I can see this through, Mars. He was my nightmare. I can watch his demise."

"I know you can, honey. But maybe I can't." I even managed to keep the wince off my face. I could absolutely watch every second of this and laugh every time the bastard squealed or woke up when Stitches hit him with a shot of Epi. But I knew Scarlet would have nightmares for the rest of her life if I let her stay here.

Her gaze met mine immediately, and she nodded once. "You're right." She looked back down at Hammer, still hesitant to leave.

"I'll stay in your place, Scarlet," Lemon volunteered. "I'll be your witness."

"Not on your life." Danica, Lemon's sister, spoke up for the first time. "You're coming back to the compound with me and Wylde. Right now."

Lemon rolled her eyes. "You forgot to add 'young lady' at the end."

Danica looked like she wanted to throttle Lemon. Wylde looked like he was ready to burst into laughter. Well, until Danica looked up at him. Then he schooled his features and looked appropriately concerned.

"I swear to God, Lemon." Danica gave an exasperated huff. "Can you, for once in your life, please do what I tell you?"

"If it were your best friend, Dani. If you were in the same position I'm in right now. Would you not see this through when your friend couldn't?" It wasn't a question. Lemon already knew the answer.

"Sting can do that for her. He'll see this through."

"But he's not her best friend." The stubborn look on Lemon's face told me everything I needed to know. "I am."

"Let her stay." Curiously, it was Rocket who spoke. His gaze was firmly fixed on Lemon, studying her as intently as he might a bug under a microscope. "I'll see to it she gets back to the clubhouse safely."

"Like hell," Wylde growled. "You couldn't keep one of your own women safe. You expect me to trust you with one of ours?"

"I'd never have permitted Scarlet to leave the safety of our territory if I'd known she didn't want to go. I know I have a lot to make up for because of Claw, but despite what it looks like, I take the safety of everyone in my club seriously. Especially our women and children."

"I'll keep an eye on them both, Wylde." Sting spoke softly, gripping Wylde's shoulder. "I'll bring her back. If she wants to stay, let her. Trust her to know where her limit is."

"Sting, I don't want her to do this." Danica was insistent, but I could see she was going to give in. "This is going to be brutal."

"I got this, Dani. Go on." Lemon actually reached out to her sister and squeezed her hand.

Surprisingly, it was Wylde who turned Danica, whispering softly to her and guiding her out of the barn. Lemon moved over to the table where Stitches had started a couple of IVs on Hammer. One in the bend of his left arm, the other in the right side of his neck.

"Looks like we're gonna be here a while, Hammer." Lemon grinned down at him. "I'm new to this whole death by torture bit, but I'm confident I can outlast you."

"Fuckin' hell." Rocket scrubbed a hand over his mouth. "This might not be such a great idea after all." He looked at Lemon with a strange expression on his face. It almost looked like… lust? But no. That couldn't be right. God help him if it was. I could almost feel sorry for the bastard because I was pretty sure Lemon could run circles around him. And he'd better not go to sleep in her presence. He'd be minus his balls if he did.

Scarlet stood beside Lemon. Hammer gave her a

look so filled with hate there was no way they could let the man live. He'd kill Scarlet the first chance he got.

"I'd say good luck, but I wouldn't mean it. Maybe I should pity you. You lost the woman you loved. Claw said she betrayed the club, but it seems to me like you both did. Or at least you betrayed the vice president. She didn't deserve to die and neither do you. At least not for that. But anyone who could do the things you did to me simply because you hated my dad? You'd do it again to someone just as innocent so I'm not going to lose a moment's sleep over you, you son of a bitch." She shook her head once. "I hope you rot in hell."

Then Scarlet took my hand, and I led her out of the barn and to my bike. She tilted her face up to the night sky and inhaled deeply. "Let's go home, Mars."

"With pleasure, honey. With pleasure."

## Chapter Thirteen

**Scarlet**

I don't remember much about the ride back to the clubhouse. The second we pulled into the parking lot, though, I hopped off the bike and pulled Mars along with me inside.

The second we went to our room, I was on him. I jumped into his arms and wrapped my legs around his waist. Mars didn't hesitate to give me what I needed. He met my kiss with a hard, hungry one of his own.

I tugged at his shirt, needing to get to his deliciously hair-roughened skin.

I groaned in pleasure when his hands roamed beneath my shirt and against my back.

Mars was gentle and rough all at once. He kissed me deeply, holding me close enough for me to feel the beat of his heart pounding against my chest. His arms trembled and I knew he was fighting hard to control himself. I trusted him completely, but he didn't trust himself not to get lost in a flashback.

Mars put us on the bed before whipping the shirt from my body. I got rid of my bra while he worked on my jeans and panties. The sensations of his warm lips, his strong hands, and his hard body all playing over my skin in an exotic slide brought all the pain of my earlier torment crashing down around me.

The betrayal of my father for nearly my entire life. His death right in front of me. The knowledge that Rocket had known but hadn't warned me… I knew that last wasn't really fair because I knew how Grim Road was about their secrets. Rocket was right. I was eighteen. He believed his vice president. But after seeing how Iron Tzars dealt with this situation, how they had my back through the whole thing and made sure I was good with everything they did, still made me a little bitter toward Rocket.

I cried out as much from pleasure as pain, clinging to Mars's back and shoulders as he moved down my body. When he reached my mound, he shoved my legs farther apart, and with a growl, fastened his mouth over my pussy.

My hips lifted off the bed as he scraped his teeth against my clit and then sucked hard. His tongue licked and swept down between my folds, tasting and teasing me until I was crying out, my hands splayed in the bed above my head. His beard created a perfect friction as he continued to devour me.

"Fuckin' sweet little cunt." His growl sent a vibration through my clit, setting me off in an explosive detonation.

I arched up hard and my back pressed into the bed, my pussy grinding against his face. I whimpered and pleaded, but Mars kept going, licking and sucking me until my orgasm started to build again. I came hard and fast, my body vibrating with pleasure as I clung to him and shouted his name over and over.

Mars waited until I'd settled before he stopped. Looking down at him, his head between my legs, his lips glistening with my cum, the fierce look on his face, even the harsh, bruising grip he had on my thighs was like a homecoming. I knew that very moment I was right where I was meant to be.

"I love you, Mars. With all my heart, I love you."

"Fuuuuuck…" He lowered his head to rest against my belly. "How the fuck do you do it?"

He crawled up my body and situated himself with his hips between my legs, his cock kissing the entrance to my wet pussy.

"Do what?"

"Calm my demons. I thought all the violence would push me over the edge. But all I feel is need. Desire. Lust. There's no violence or the need to punish. I'm not back in that time loop where it's me hurting those kids. All I see, all I taste or smell, is you, Scarlet. It's always you."

He sank inside deeply inside me, kissing me as he moved. His hips rocked against mine in the slow, steady rhythm I needed to adjust to his length and size. I loved the burn when he first filled me. The small bite of pain was a surprising aphrodisiac. I relished the sensation of his length as it filled me, and his warmth encircled my heart in a loving embrace.

Mars kissed his way up my neck and cupped my face in his calloused hands. "I love you, Scarlet. It happened quicker than I ever thought it could, but I know with every fiber of my being that I love you."

He surged forward, sinking his cock deep inside me, claiming me as his own. His steady rhythm increased, building us higher and higher until the pleasure was just shy of unbearable. His kiss became passionate and desperate, as if he needed to consume me in order to survive.

My whole body trembled with pleasure as Mars continued to push me toward the stars. I wanted to tell him I loved him too, but I couldn't form words. Any words. All I could do was whimper and moan in an incoherent mess.

With a loud shout, I was flying, dizzy with pleasure and my heart felt so full of love and gratitude for the man between my legs. The pressure inside increased until I could take no more and cried out as my orgasm rocked through me.

"Scarlet," he breathed, his voice shaking with emotion. "You are everything to me. Fucking everything!" Mars followed me over the edge, his voice filling the room as he too found his release. Deep inside my body.

Mars collapsed against me, groaning in pleasure, our bodies slick with sweat as we lay there in each other's arms.

"Thank you," he said finally, "for giving me a way to come back from the darkness."

I kissed his lips, sweet and soft, and smiled up at him. "I love you, Mars. With all my heart."

He smiled back. "I love you too, honey."

Mars cleaned us both up before collapsing back onto the bed with a groan. Then he pulled me against him so I rested with my head on his chest, his arms tightly around me. It felt good. Right. This was the way my life was supposed to be. At least, I hoped it was because I never wanted to let go of this life I'd found with Mars. I wanted the man and all he represented. Forever.

Then a question popped into my brain and, try as I might, I couldn't let it go.

"Mars?"

"Yeah, baby." His voice was sexy with sleep. It made my toes curl.

"Why do they call you Mars? How'd you get your road name?"

"It's my last name. Hard to improve on that."

I giggled. "Yeah. You have a point there." Again we were silent and I was near the point of drifting when I asked another question. "What's your first name?"

He stiffened beneath me and was silent so long I didn't think he was going to answer me. I pushed up to look down at him. The expression on his face was one of stubbornness. "What? What's wrong?"

"First name don't matter. It's Mars."

I raised an eyebrow. "You're telling me I'm going to be your old lady, the mother of your children, and you're not going to tell me your first name?"

Now he looked disgruntled. "Don't want to."

"Mars. What's this? You're not acting like the badass biker I know you to be."

"Don't wanna tell you my first name." He frowned, but I was pretty sure I saw his lips twitch.

"Fine. I'll make up one for you. I'll get Lemon to help. We'll start calling you by your new name, and I promise you, it will stick. Everyone will start calling you by your new name instead of Mars. You really willing to risk that?"

"Fine, you little hellion. It's Francis. My first name is Francis."

I had to purse my lips to keep from smiling, which I'm sure he wouldn't appreciate. Finally, unable to help myself, I stroked his beard with my hand and gave him a look of sympathy. "You poor thing…" Then I burst into giggles.

"That's it. Now you're gettin' it."

Mars tickled me until I was screaming for mercy, pressing my legs together so I didn't pee. When he finally let me up so I could relieve myself I realized I felt lighter in spirit. If not happier, at least better able to process everything that had happened.

He leaned against the bathroom door as I cleaned up. I looked at him in the mirror. "You're so good for me. I'm lucky to have met you."

"Same here, honey."

"I think I checked out when Claw… you know."

"Yeah. I know." He just gave me a steady look, not judging or forcing me to finish my sentence. It was just one more thing I was grateful to him for.

"You knew before I acknowledged it to myself."

"Baby, that was too much to ask of anyone to go through. You had what you saw a reason for what you did, though I still wish you'd have let Lemon bring you to us before it got that far. You didn't know us then, and there was no reason for you to think we'd help your sisters. I hope you realize now that there's nothing anyone in this club won't do to protect you and any you call yours."

"I do." I smiled up at him. "I'm sorry I put you through that. The memories it brought back to you…"

"Gave me the strength to control my demons and begin to heal. Ain't promisin' it'll always be perfect, but I know now that I can lose myself in you and it's like a natural balm for what ails my mind."

"I disagree," I said as I stepped to him and circled his neck with my arms. "I think it absolutely will always be perfect."

"As long as we're together. I can't do it without you."

"As long as I'm alive, Mars. You'll never have to."

He kissed me then, lifting into his arms and carrying me back to the bed. We made love again. It started out slow and tender but soon became more aggressive and so thrilling I never wanted the moment to end. Never once did Mars voice a fear he might hurt me. He even gave me a brilliant smile afterward, like a carefree kid who'd learned to ride a bicycle without his training wheels.

"God, I love you, Scarlet!" He rolled us over so I lay against him with his arms tightly around me.

"I'm gonna remember this moment for the rest of my life," I said, resting on his chest.

"Me too, honey." Mars tucked my head under

his chin with both arms securely around me, and I felt like I was finally home.

"One thing, though." I said as sleep threatened to take me.

"Yeah? What's that."

"How much trouble will I be in if I tell Lemon your first name's Francis?"

# Lifelines

If you or someone you know is experiencing domestic violence or thoughts of suicide, these hotlines can help:

- **National Domestic Abuse Hotline: 800-799-7233**
- **Suicide and Crisis Lifeline (formerly known as the National Suicide Prevention Lifeline): 988**

# Marteeka Karland

International bestselling author Marteeka Karland leads a double life as an action romance writer by evening and a semi-domesticated housewife by day. Known for her down-and-dirty MC romances, Marteeka takes pleasure in spinning tales of tenacious, protective heroes and spirited heroines. She staunchly advocates that every character deserves a blissful ending.

Marteeka finds joy in baking, and gardening with her husband. Make sure to visit her website to stay updated with her most recent projects. Don't forget to register for her newsletter which will pepper you with a potpourri of Teeka's beloved recipes, book suggestions, autograph events, and a plethora of interesting tidbits.

Marteeka at Changeling: changelingpress.com/marteeka-karland-a-39

Wanda Violet O. (Teeka's Dark Erotica side) changelingpress.com/wanda-violet-o-a-226

## Bones MC Multiverse

Bones MC
Shadow Demons
Salvation's Bane MC
Black Reign MC
Iron Tzars MC
Grim Road MC
Bones MC Print Duets
Bones MC Audio
Salvation's Bane MC Audio
Iron Tzars MC Audio
Grim Road MC Audio

## Changeling Press LLC

Contemporary Action Adventure, Sci-Fi, Steampunk, Dark Fantasy, Urban Fantasy, Paranormal, and BDSM Romance available in e-book, audio, and print format at ChangelingPress.com – MC Romance, Werewolves, Vampires, Dragons, Shapeshifters and Horror -- Tales from the edge of your imagination.

## Where can I get Changeling Press Books?

Changeling Press e-books are available at ChangelingPress.com, Amazon, Apple Books, Barnes & Noble, Kobo, Smashwords, and other online retailers, including Everand Subscription and Kobo Subscription Services. Print books are available at Amazon, Barnes and Noble, and by ISBN special order through your local bookstores.

**ChangelingPress.com**